From Somewhere in a Dream

by

H. B. Berlow

The Ark City Confidential Chronicles
Book 4

From Somewhere in a Dream

Cover Art by *Jennifer Greeff*

The Wild Rose Press, Inc.
PO Box 708
Adams Basin, NY 14410-0708
Visit us at www.thewildrosepress.com

Publishing History
First Rose Edition, 2021
Trade Paperback ISBN 978-1-5092-3431-8
Digital ISBN 978-1-5092-3432-5

The Ark City Confidential Chronicles, Book 4
Published in the United States of America

This was not one of those vague nightmares Dr. Brenz tried his best to help me shake. This was a wide-awake dream that brought up memories of my youth on the North Side of Chicago, schmoozing with Hickey before he earned his nickname, while a compassionate but sinister Dion O'Banion encouraged me to go off to war because he recognized I wasn't fit to be a gangster. Now, I would have thirty years of those memories stare me in the face every day just because a sweet, sad woman wanted to find her wayward son. I realized the only way to put those dreams to bed was to locate Jimmy O'Donnell, above or below ground.

Dedication

For Larry Hammer (1943-2020).
Thank you for telling me the stories
and allowing me to dream even bigger.

Part One:
A Mother's Anguish

How long will he vex my soul,
and break me in pieces with words?

~Job 19:2

Chapter One

I woke up one morning and I was fifty. At least that was the way it appeared to me. I looked back over my shoulder, saw a scrappy Irish kid grow up on Chicago's North Side who barely missed a possibly brief career as a gangster. This was largely because a big-time gangster suggested I become patriotic instead. I witnessed a scared, young man learn such concepts as Friendship and Life and Death in a war run by mad generals, where survival was often a worse horror than a bloody and painful demise. I squeezed into the body of a dead friend, took over his life, and became a beat cop in a small Kansas town, as much to run away from the possibility of disgrace as to honor him. I watched too many good and decent people die, unable to do much about it other than pick up the pieces at the end and try to figure out the meaning, while I somehow came through with barely a scratch and an unidentifiable mask for a face. And then I woke up one morning and I was fifty. That was it.

It was Thursday, April 1, 1948, my birthday. I knew a surprise celebration awaited me at the station, more than likely orchestrated by Dave Morton. The guys were always up for a festivity to break up the boredom of a cop's life in a burg of our size. However, this was unlike a similar gathering ten years earlier when my former landlady, the late Miss Banister, brought forth chocolate zucchini bread and lemon bars and other succulent delicacies. This time, the local bakery would have to suffice. I didn't figure anyone would complain too much.

Dave was settling in quite comfortably in his new position as desk sergeant spending more of his time with paperwork and saving the wear and tear on his feet. Unlike Clifford Smiley, Dave used this as a stepping-stone to something bigger. He had plans. Right now, however, this little shindig was just another excuse to eat cake. It lacked some of the camaraderie of the past on account of fewer old timers still on the force, but I appreciated the gesture, nonetheless.

I tried hard to enjoy myself and allow everyone to celebrate my "elder years." Marcus Hayes retired shortly after we captured the escaped German POW back in '43. He had enough adventure to last him the rest of his life and opted to move to New Orleans for some fun. They had no idea what they were in for in The Crescent City. Evan Cobb and his family moved to Boston when he got a job managing a brokerage house and made a darn sight better salary than walking a beat in Arkansas City, Kansas. I can only imagine his wife was happy about the greater income as well as his safety. I'm sure he also got to spend a lot more time with his family. Clyde B. King, the city manager appointed Walter Gray, the former night police captain, as chief of police in 1945 after Chief Richardson tendered his resignation. I missed Lester Richardson's stoic demeanor on the outside with an intelligent and thoughtful man underneath. Maybe Chief Gray had the same qualities but you would never know under the surface of a face with a perpetual scowl. I convinced myself that everyone had his or her own particular way and style that worked best.

I was just about the longest serving officer left on the force but it certainly wasn't my intention to break any records. I didn't have anything else to do and really nowhere to go. I never went through long sleepless nights concerned about my future. I figured it would get here soon enough.

Out of the corner of my eye, I saw Chief Gray watch the revelry from his office, with nothing approaching a smile alight on his face. I really couldn't tell if all the merry-making bothered him or if he didn't think it was very important. By the same token, I often wondered if I was a thorn in his side, a remnant from the past and someone who might possibly not change his ways. In his first year as chief, drunkenness was the leading cause for arrests. There were no big city gangsters, vicious killers, or escaped German POWs to deal with, just whatever demon the unfortunate and desperate found in a bottle. He didn't come across as the fire and brimstone type per se. To his way of thinking, "keeping the peace" was a real thing to him. He stood up and with a stern look on his face, beckoned me with a single index finger. I walked in, stood at attention, and then sat in the chair opposite his desk as he waved his arm.

"So, Witherspoon, what are your plans?" he asked succinctly. I found it hard to believe he would be concerned about how I planned to continue with my birthday celebration later in the evening.

"My plans, sir?" My face went slack with surprise, like a bloodhound that lost a scent. This was more than he had spoken to me in the past and lacked any clear meaning.

"In the department. A fifty-year-old officer walking a beat is somewhat out of the ordinary. Wouldn't you say?"

"Well, Cliff Smiley walked a beat for a long time."

"Yes, but Officer Smiley has a desk job now. Has had one since"—Gray referred to one of the two files on his desk. I assumed the other was mine—"Nineteen thirty six. You, however, continue your patrol work, seemingly without any consideration for doing anything else." Caught off guard, I wondered what Chief Gray had in mind. As there hadn't been many in-depth conversations between us, I doubted he was overly concerned about my well-being. I couldn't imagine he felt threatened by me in any sense as I did not seek a higher position and wasn't very comfortable with the politics of the department. He perused my file for a full minute before continuing. "I'd like you to have a full physical with Dr. Brenz as soon as you can. I want to ensure the officers we have on the street are one hundred percent fit for duty. Assuming that is your intention." He looked up at me with a face as immobile as a block of Kansas limestone.

There was no sense in arguing or getting defensive. Neither one would have made much of a difference. Walter Gray had a notion about my fitness, mental and physical, and was the kind who would gather all his ducks in a row in order to validate whatever decision he most likely already made. Clifford Smiley was a good ten years older than I was. Despite a constant a polite smile on his face, he always looked tired and worn down. Maybe he was better off at his desk job. However, I wasn't all that sure if it would work out for me. All I wanted was a fair shake, same as Chiefs Taylor and Richardson would have done. I was beginning to think the cards were on the table already.

My regular checkup was a month away but Doctie was able to get me in sooner, almost as though he expected me. I sat quietly while he did all the same things he had done for over twenty-five years. I was quiet and patient, not anticipating anything out of the ordinary.

"Your blood pressure is a little high," he said after removing the cuff from my arm.

"Well, I am fifty you know."

"Yes, but even for a fifty-year-old man, your blood pressure is a little high." My ear caught that like he read from a script, one written by a local policeman and not a Hollywood scribe. I smiled inside, half wondering what was going on and half knowing. It wasn't going to take a police report or a medical examiner to identify the death of a career.

He continued with all the typical tests: temperature, reflexes, glands, breathing. The bland wooden tongue depressor nearly made me gag. Other than that, I was fine most of the time, perhaps a little annoyed but overall in good shape. He finally got around to the examination of the scars on my face. He rubbed his thumbs along each one. I could feel the skin move independently, sliding against my skull. There was no pain to speak of, just an awkward feeling as though my flesh was melting slowly like the wax on a candle causing odd shapes to form. When I fell into barbed wire after a shell exploded behind me back in the first war in Europe, the surgical procedures were new and untested. I was fortunate to have a face all these years later, such as it was. Now it was unrecognizable even to me.

"What is this all about?" I finally asked, calmly and simply, trying to not sound annoyed.

"Isn't it time you thought about a desk job?"

"Is that your advice or what Chief Gray wants you to suggest? To have me sit behind a desk and file reports all day. Can't the man just come out and talk to me himself?"

"I think what he wants is to forget Jake Hickey and those horrible murders and the escaped German soldier and anything else that doesn't have to do with underage drinking and petty theft. Just remember—all those other events have only got one thing in common."

"Me." I didn't have to say it but doing so made the whole thing clear. I was involved in the worst circumstances that occurred in Ark City for the past fifteen years. That made me either a magnet or a bad luck charm.

"What do you do when you are not working, Baron?"

"Read the newspaper. Listen to the radio. Hang out at Junior's."

"Is that all?"

I nodded. I had come to a point in my life where everything from the past was a dream, filled with death and loss, and nothing about the future was clear, other than more of the same. Maybe I thought I could just walk a beat until I collapsed or died in the line of duty. Now, I was guided toward something safe and quiet and utterly boring, itself a living death.

He didn't offer up a "tsk, tsk" or commentary. But when you say something out loud, it becomes real enough. For a single instant, I wished that shell had hit me, and Baron Witherspoon, the real son of Kansas, made it home alive.

I went back to my room at the Elmo Hotel, changed into civilian clothes, and continued the celebration of fifty years on this planet at Junior's. You could no longer find the down-and-outs, old-timers, or good old boys. It was now a place for respectable gentlemen of means. They still welcomed me there for old time's sake. Nevertheless, it was rather quiet for a Thursday night, less than ten people in the place. I sat at a table with a bottle and shot glass filled with something that passed for corn mash. Like counting sheep, names passed through my head, some with images attached, mostly just echoes calling out to me. I didn't respond.

This wasn't what I was expecting. It had come out of the blue and made me a mix of angry and scared. The realization struck me you either make a choice or one is made for you. I had no problem with that. I just wasn't sure which one to make.

Chapter Two

Sandy Clevenger, the long-time secretary at the *Ark City Traveler* asked me to drop by the office specifically the Tuesday after my birthday at eleven in the morning. Her manner was casual but the exactness of the request had an ominous tone. She may have been gray haired and bespectacled but I couldn't put anything past her. As she provided me with a great deal of research assistance over the years, I was only too happy to oblige. It was my day off so I dragged myself away from a crossword puzzle and ambled on over. A deep yawn escaped my mouth as I entered.

"You look bored," she said as I walked in. Despite a few cups of coffee, I must have still had the sluggish look of a factory worker on a Saturday morning after payday on Friday afternoon.

"I am bored."

She smiled. "Mr. Stauffer wants to see you," she said matter-of-factly but just like a secretary for a chairman of the board at a big corporation in a big city. It had an air of importance to it.

Oscar S. Stauffer bought the *Traveler* back in 1924 along with a mess of other local newspapers, two in Independence and two in Pittsburg. He moved up to Topeka shortly before the war when he bought the *Topeka State Journal.* He was certainly the most important newspaperman in Kansas since the passing of

William Allen White and probably the highest respected in the Great Plains. All of that and he came on back to Arkansas City from his cozy digs in the state capitol just to see me. This was right up there with my first meeting with Eliot Ness. I wasn't sure whether to be honored or nervous. I settled for both.

Sandy indicated Mr. Stauffer was in the editor's office and motioned for me to go on back. I pinched my cheeks and rubbed my eyes so I wouldn't look quite so tired or bored. If I had known he was to be there, I would have put on my best Sunday shirt. Actually, it was my only Sunday shirt. He sat behind a simple desk reading today's copy and appeared quite relaxed as though he didn't have a care in the world. The man was clean-shaven with a high forehead and clear eyes that lacked any emotion. Not mean or dour, just waiting to respond to life as it unfolded. If it weren't for the impeccable suit he wore, I would have taken him to be a farmer or rancher. I reached across the desk to shake his hand. For a man in his late sixties, one who sat behind a desk for most of his days, his grip was strong and impressive.

"Officer Witherspoon, thank you for taking the time to visit with me." Between the two of us, he was the one with more irons in the fire. His graciousness caught me off guard even more than his presence.

"Well, it is certainly my pleasure, sir."

"You ever think about what you might do after you leave the police department?" In the past few days, this had become a common theme. I started to think mind readers infested the town. Everyone that is, except for me.

"Not really. I mean, on occasion but nothing with

9

any degree of seriousness." I didn't want it to sound like I didn't have the slightest notion about my future even though that was the case. At best, I tried not to stutter.

"Have you ever considered a career as a newspaper columnist?" The question threw me an even bigger curveball than the appearance of Jake Hickey. If I had given it half a thought, I might have seen myself as a bartender at Junior's.

"To be honest, I don't rightly know the first thing about it, Mr. Stauffer." It was all I could do to not bust out and laugh. I figured he wouldn't have come all this way to tell jokes. I was torn between flattery and total astonishment. I couldn't quite figure what this man saw in me to make these type of comments.

He leaned forward as if he was about to let me in on a big secret and encouraged me toward him as well. We were in the middle of a secret conference except no one was around to eavesdrop. However, as his invitee, it was my obligation to listen.

"Circulation of the paper has been down since the war. I need something to boost it. My thinking was if you write a weekly column about the life of a police officer, you know, some of the tales from your rather heroic life, it might make for a few extra copies sold. People know you, Baron. But this would be an opportunity for you to show them a different side of yourself."

That part didn't entice me a whole lot given the circumstances of how I got to Ark City. I still wondered whether Chief Richardson and Dr. Brenz had any inkling as to my true past. Further, while I appreciated his consideration, I knew I was no writer. I filled out police reports for nearly thirty years but they weren't worthy of a Pulitzer or any other prize for that matter. Most of the folks I knew were already familiar with Jake Hickey, the gruesome killings in '35, and the escaped German POW. What was the use of slinging old hash if all it would do was to make me sound like a blowhard and sell newspapers? I had the strange sensation my eyebrows squished together and before I knew it, my head shook slightly in the negative.

"Sir, I just don't—"

"As far as the writing goes, Charlie Gullickson, the English teacher at the high school, can guide you until you get on your feet. And of course, Miss Clevenger will be more than happy to oversee your work. She has a great deal of admiration and respect for you. I'm sure she would want to see you succeed as much as I do. Well, as much as we all do."

I looked at him square in the face in order to find a reason either to accept or decline. It is too hard at times to make a decision, but I knew well enough I had to make this one for myself. I couldn't help but think Chief Gray and Doctie were in on this somehow, especially given my recent conversations with both. As it turned out neither of them was aware of it. After a while, I figured I could go on day after day with the uncertainty of a life as a policeman or the insecurity of something brand new at my age. The difference, as it turned out, was writing a newspaper column wasn't going to get me killed. As long as I didn't get too political, make accusations, or disparage some guy's girlfriend or wife, I should wind up dying in bed. That was something I couldn't have considered thirty years ago.

The letter of resignation I handed to Chief Gray was the first thing I wrote on the typewriter at my new desk. Since it wasn't for publication, I didn't worry too much about grammatical errors. Nevertheless, it was as professional as I could make it. Gray was gracious and courteous yet lacked a certain empathy and humanity. He read it, understood it, and accepted it. That was it. His efforts were to get me to take a desk job. My departure was a bonus. It was the mission of Chief Walter Gray to form the department in his own image. It didn't include an old relic like me to show the new guys the ropes and die in an embarrassing fashion or draw attention to the force with national headlines. Dr. Brenz, on the other hand was entirely happy for me, knew I would do well, and wished me the best. He figured this alone would add years to my life. How good they might be was squarely on my shoulders.

Charlie Gullickson extensively reviewed the first few columns as he knew more about writing than I did. This was the most schooling I think I ever had in my life. After I corrected the same mistakes I made over and over again, he finally helped me find my "voice" even though I didn't know I had one. He was far more patient with me than he was most of his students. Once it became second nature to me, Sandy encouraged me to alternate between funny stories of the everyday life of a policeman with the serious and darker stories of crime in our fair city. In this way, she explained, newspaper subscribers would read more often to wait for the "juicy stuff" as she liked to call it. I got the feeling it was she who made the recommendation to Mr. Stauffer. It just might be we all have a guardian angel over our shoulder. Mine apparently was gray haired and bespectacled.

On occasion, I visited the station and caught wind of a local domestic disturbance, a minor theft, or public drunkenness. My contacts were former co-workers, young guys who saw me as an older brother. I would try to educate the readers on local city ordinances. However, the managing editor heavily censored my story about Article 6—Offenses Affecting Morals and Decency, particularly 9-612, Section 82 on Street Walking. It might be something I could put into a book at a later point in my developing career. For the decent people of Arkansas City, it was like taking cod liver oil.

Whenever I was at Daisy Mae's, someone would likely lift their paper and point out the column of mine they were reading. Bernard Welch's favorite comment was, "Well, you done it again." Twenty-eight years as a policeman made me recognizable around town. In a few short months, I now achieved a notoriety of a different sort. I was amazed to consider the many changes in my life, the various versions of myself I had been. Now, I was on a par with Walter Winchell or Ernie Pyle. A scribe, a guy named Scoop, hat pushed back from my head, pencil behind my ear, banging out a story you couldn't stop reading, on the verge of breaking The Big One and yelling "Stop the presses!", and rubbing elbows with butter and egg men and canaries.

It was as though I had been given a new life, or at the very least a new chance. I slept better, didn't have quite the tingling in my face, and many of the dreams vanished like a puff of smoke. It was as though the past became a distant memory.

Until the day I came face to face with it.

Chapter Three

She looked a lot older than the sixty-two years she said she was. Bloodshot eyes stood out in a face filled with deep etched lines of experience, pain, grief, and loss as though tears flowed like the Big Muddy. She appeared breathless and weary, the very act of wakefulness and sitting upright too much to bear. Life itself was a malady; the more days that passed, the sicker she grew and the heavier the burden. When I finally got in, I found her waiting patiently with hands crossed on her lap, Sandy told her earlier she didn't know when I would be back. The woman simply allowed time to pass without consideration guiding her every action. The clock was an enemy she constantly battled, like Satan himself, and the chair was no different from a pew in church.

We went into the same office I sat in with Mr. Stauffer only three and a half months prior. This time, I was the one who sat behind the desk but with no great air of authority. She announced her name as Regina O'Donnell, a declaration of person and character. An air of pride exhaled as if her name was the most valuable thing she owned. She indicated she lived in the unincorporated town of Hackney, which didn't mean anything to me until I realized it was where Strother Army Airfield had been. She worked as a clerk there after the army left and turned the base over to civilian control. She was a remnant of a past most chose to forget. It was something we both shared.

"I have nothing left to speak of anymore," she stated. "My husband died when my three boys were young. The two oldest died in the war."

"I'm sorry to hear that, ma'am."

She leaned forward, just as Mr. Stauffer, as though it were some kind of conspiracy. Tears appeared in her eyes, a glaze like the rains on a summer day to coat everything with a heavenly grace.

"My youngest, Jimmy"—she stopped from either fear or distress. Her own son's name caught in her throat as though it were cursed and too painful to recite—"I don't know where I went wrong. He got himself caught up with some bad men. I didn't mind none he had no hankering for schooling. At least he worked here and there, brought a little money into the house. He was always good to me, Mr. Witherspoon. Never raised a hand or his voice. But after a bit, he was off with fellers who only had a thought for stealing and robbing and goodness knows what else. He couldn't be bothered with me anymore after that."

"What became of him?" I asked quietly. It felt like it was my next line in this script. She shook her head.

"That's what I'm hoping you can find out."

I blinked suddenly and sat up straight, perhaps too fast as though a bolt of lightning had struck me. This was as surprising as Chief Gray's personal assessment of my abilities as a beat cop or Mr. Stauffer's job offer. These last months brought more surprises than the previous years, far more than I wanted to accept. I should have been used to them by now, but all I really wanted was to just fall into a meaningful life and not allow heavier considerations to bother me.

"Mrs. O'Donnell, I am not a police officer anymore. And I'm certainly no private detective of any sort, like in the movies. For something like this, it is still best to go to the police. They are far better equipped to handle issues like this."

"I did go."

"When?"

"Back in 1934."

My face must have looked the same as when I worked a crossword puzzle. My eyes grew thin and my eyebrows scrunched together in a sad version of contemplation if you could tell through all the scars. It would have been best if she had been a little clearer. It made no sense to revisit such a request fourteen years later.

"Ma'am, I guess I'm not following you. Your youngest son, Jimmy, was involved with some criminals back in 1934 and just up and disappeared. Is that correct?"

She nodded.

"And you haven't heard from him in fourteen years?"

She continued to nod.

My mind flung back just a few months prior to when I was a police officer. My thought was if she were to walk into the station now and file a report, there would be a few guys who would just shake their heads in amazement after she left. A missing person case from so far back, especially if he was involved with the criminals from those days, would likely not yield any positive results. There were a whole slew of things that probably happened to him, none of them good. Killed or incarcerated were my best guesses. On the other hand, the likelihood of him becoming a policeman or newspaperman was not something I would put money on. I reached out to touch her arm gently and tried to make her understand this was a pointless cause.

"Mrs. O'Donnell, there is just too much time that's passed for anyone, much less the police, to make any determination on where your son might be. Chances are he could be in prison or, sorry to say, killed somewhere. Anywhere from among half a dozen states or more. The gangsters back in the day roamed a good deal of the country. Far too many jurisdictions to try to track down. And of course, there are very few records to access. Outside of a couple of good old boys telling stories, there are hardly any facts to nail down."

"Isn't there anything you can do?"

"I honestly doubt it, I'm sorry to say. I mean, what crimes might he have been involved in? Were there any known associates? Did he?—"

"Jack Hale."

The name struck me like an unexpected knife in the back sending a cold tingle up and down my arms and legs. It was the alias used by Jake Hickey when he lived in Ark City. It was likely he had a gang and pulled jobs in the area. The underground tunnels were the gang's hideout. It might have been this kid Jimmy was involved. Too many ifs and maybes.

"And how do you know about this Jack Hale?" The name tasted like vinegar rolling off my tongue.

"Jimmy mentioned him. Said he was starting a business and Jimmy would be a big part of it. I could see right through those lies. I don't know who the man was but I doubt he had Jimmy's best interests in mind."

I figured this much was certain, knowing Jake Hickey.

"And you say you reported this to the police?"

"Well, actually, I had a visit with Councilman Hallett."

It was everything I could do to keep my face straight and not let on I understood.

It all made sense. Jake was involved with Hallett and Martin Childers, the late owner of the Kanotex refinery. I had always known the two of them were crooked as the day was long but were never at risk of capture because of their protection. It was just as likely they had a whole bunch of Chicago gangsters hidden in the area on their payroll. I could imagine "Crazy" Jake bored as an underling to a Kansas politician, and ran off to pull his own lucrative heists to put together enough of a bankroll to take over Ark City or some other burg in the area. After all, he was the trusted right-hand man to George "Bugs" Moran. He would want to be the big boss he always envisioned. Furthermore, I knew Hallett too well to think he would not have made an attempt to squash Hickey like a pesky insect. It was fortunate for him the Arkansas City Police Department got Hickey first.

I rubbed the side of my face to make sure it was still there then drew my hand across my mouth to keep from saying anything too soon. This was not one of those vague nightmares Dr. Brenz tried his best to help me shake. This was a wide-awake dream that brought up memories of my youth on the North Side of Chicago, schmoozing with Hickey before he earned his nickname, while a compassionate but sinister Dion O'Banion encouraged me to go off to war because he recognized I wasn't fit to be a gangster. Now, I would have thirty years of those memories stare me in the face every day just because a sweet, sad woman wanted to find her wayward son. I realized the only way to put those dreams to bed was to locate Jimmy O'Donnell, above or below ground.

"Please understand if I undertake this, it could lead anywhere. He might be alive, living under an assumed name, rehabilitated from all the bad things he's done. He could be in jail somewhere. Or, he could be…"

"Dead," she interrupted. "Yes, I know that."

We looked at each other for a spell, a silent understanding between us.

"I can't pay you much."

"Like I said, I'm not a detective. What I am is a newspaperman, and well, this just might make a heck of a story. I'm sure the *Traveler* will take care of any expenses I might have. You needn't worry about any of that." My big vaudeville smile was an effort at trying to provide her a little peace. I knew I wouldn't have any until I got to the end of this. Then again, it might haunt me for the rest of my life.

I needed to keep telling myself this was all going to make a great story. Otherwise, coming face to face with ghosts would tear me up inside to a point where I no longer knew who I was.

Chapter Four

A couple of years ago I saw *The Big Sleep* at the Burford Theater. Humphrey Bogart played Philip Marlowe, a private detective who was a fired investigator for the district attorney's office. Well, I had been a police officer and was encouraged to retire so that was pretty close. Outside of a few Boston Blackie movies and the adventures of Philo Vance on the radio, I had no idea what it took to be a private eye. I knew how to be a policeman, but I carried a gun and a badge with the backing of the legitimate and legal forces of law and order behind me. The problem I had was none of these movie and radio guys was like me. Marlowe was a decent guy in a world filled with rich men who had more power. A man filled to the brim with a confident determination while I always wondered when the next shoe would drop. Blackie was a former jewel thief turned detective. I didn't have the first clue about stealing anything valuable. Heck, I never even stole a kiss from Beth Handy. Vance was the kind of smoothie who could get any gal he wanted. I was severely limited in my social skills. On top of all that, I was no longer a policeman.

The only thing left in my bag of tricks was I could still think the way I used to, like I did back in '35 and '38 during the investigation of those gruesome murders, or back when an escaped German POW headed for Ark

City like a bullet to the head. I had to think that way still and unravel a fourteen-year-old riddle. I needed a place to start.

It was obvious my first stop would be to see Dave, now Sergeant Morton. It was a well-deserved promotion and one that would put him in line to be a detective inspector. I guessed that would be the next step in his career. He had the brains and experience to be both, but I knew he would have a lot to prove to Chief Gray who demanded results. Dave was more than up for the task. He had always been that way and was even more so now.

I laid everything out to Dave. We always shared our thoughts and ideas freely. Of course, the only thing I never told him was my background as Eric Kimble and my years-long masquerade as Baron Witherspoon. He might have known, and for that matter, might not really have cared. We had been through so much we defined our friendship by how we acted toward each other. Little things like personal truths didn't mean all that much in the long run.

We went to the file room in the basement and dug up all there was on Jake Hickey, his death at the hands of Officer Ray Vernon as Jake held Beth Handy and her dad hostage, and the tragic murder of Heather Devore, which we determined Hickey did not commit, especially since he had nothing to gain by it. Most of the files were merely observation reports, times when I or another officer encountered him in town and documented his activities. I realized we never got around to digging up anything specific on him before our attempt to transport him to the Cowley County Courthouse in Winfield, a task that resulted in the death of Officer George McAllister.

"Outside of Jake Hickey, we were never able to identify any of the men in the gang. And now with Childers dead, there's no one left from those days who might have the foggiest idea. That time is past and those men are long gone."

"Hallett's still alive."

Dave practically snorted.

"Good luck getting that hyena to give you anything, much less the time of day. His secrets are the only power he has left. And he'll take them all with him to his grave."

"Remember the guy in the flower shop?" A tall, bald, sinister man was traipsing around in Clark's Flower Shop, didn't respond to calls to come out with his hands up, fired at us, and we fired back and killed him. It was from there we discovered the underground tunnels that connected various businesses in the city Hickey and his men used as both a hideout and a place to store stolen loot. That's what finally revealed what "Crazy" Jake had been doing.

"We never figured out who he was. He had nothing on him as I recall, no driver's license, no ID to speak of. Hardly anyone remembered him from the hotels or restaurants. Childers made no identification on him as an employee. He'd have stayed mum even if he did know who the guy was. And after no one came to claim his body, he was buried in an unmarked grave in Parker Cemetery."

A big sigh came out of me before I realized it. My ears heard defeat, and I hadn't even given myself a chance to get started. If it weren't for the memories of all the other tough cases I had over the years, I might have gone back to Mrs. O'Donnell right then and there and told her this was a pipe dream. It was the last look on her face plus my own stubbornness that pushed me forward.

Dave indicated he would ask around but on the Q.T. as Chief Gray would probably not approve of dredging up the past. It wouldn't have made for good publicity. On top of that, I no longer had influence with the Arkansas City Police Department.

The only one left to talk with was Ray Vernon or "Big Ray" as we called him because of his height. He had the skills to play for Phog Allen at University of Kansas but chose to be a policeman instead. In spite of his constant fear of gangsters like Bonnie and Clyde and Charlie Floyd, it was Ray who shot "Crazy" Jake Hickey and ended a standoff in Handy's Millinery. However, he left the force and wound up as the basketball coach at Arkansas City High School before Art Kahler recommended him for the same position at Sterling College.

It took a while for Sandy to get a hold of Ray by phone. I would have gone to visit, for old time's sake, but I didn't own a car, and it would have been a good three hour drive one way just on a lark. Sandy figured this case would result in a whole series of articles so she was more than willing to help. When I finally did reach him, he sounded as enthusiastic and young as I last remembered him.

"Got my hands full with these young kids," he said right off, "but they sure are taking a shine to my coaching." To hear him talk about the youth he guided when I remembered him as a young man made me realize just how much time had passed.

"Are you guys winning?"

"Well, we've had winning records, just no championships."

I knew he was busy so I ran it down for him briefly in order to see if I could shake anything from the tree. A long pause lingered at the other end of the line. It got me worried a bit until he started to speak.

"Right before we came up against Hickey in Mr. Handy's place, there was a clerk over at"—I heard him snap his fingers a couple of times—"Ranney's Fifth Avenue Hotel who mentioned a guy from out of town. I believe he said the guy was from Chicago. What was his name? Wait! Paul, no, Pat. McArdle. That's it. Pat McArdle."

"You ever get a handle on this guy?"

"No. It wasn't too long after we shook down the punk at the Gladstone and tracked down Hickey."

At the very least, I had a name, a thread, the start of something. I could feel as though continuing would be possible as opposed to just walking off a cliff.

"I really appreciate this, Ray. It means an awful lot to me."

An awkward silence hung in the dead air. I wasn't sure if I embarrassed him.

"Baron?"

"Yeah?"

"I know about George." Officer George McAllister thought he would get a big payday from "Crazy" Jake Hickey for helping him escape. All he got for his trouble was a bullet to the head. It broke us all up real bad. I never let Ray know my suspicions back then. I obviously underestimated him.

"Lot of water under the bridge."

There was nothing more to say. Time passed, and we all moved on. And still there was a further road to travel.

Chapter Five

The clack and ping from my typewriter was less like the sweet melody of a classic piano and more like a ball peen hammer swung by a desperate man on a tin roof. Delicacy was not my strong suit. Sandy looked over the column I prepared for the Friday edition while I worked on Monday's offering. I had gotten into a routine in order to put out three interesting columns per week: Monday, Wednesday, and Friday. By maintaining a kind of regularity, there was talk of syndication. I got excited once I learned what that meant. With all the noise I made, I was surprised I was able to hear her chuckle over the story of chasing a stray pig running down Summit Ave. after it escaped from Marty Eckels' farm from well beyond the north end of town.

I didn't realize I was so engrossed in my work when I just about jumped out of my seat as she started to point out an error. Then it occurred to me it was not a deep focus on a newspaper column. I was lost in a world I had tried so hard to put behind me. The excessive writing was just a cover.

"I'm sorry. You were saying?"

She repeated herself but I didn't really hear a word she said. There were a few nods and grunts. It gave the impression I paid attention, but I still hadn't shaken off the clouds that smothered my mind. I agreed with her assessment, whatever it was, and then calmly advised I needed some fresh air and would be in tomorrow. At that point, I didn't know when tomorrow was.

My face made me recognizable anywhere I went, but without a uniform someone had to look in my direction to know it was me. From a distance, I was a regular Joe in a buttoned down shirt, pants, and shoes, and a hat that lay quietly on my head. I ambled in a meandering way and came across Handy's Millinery. Beth moved out of town with her husband, Frank Appleby, after the death of her cousin, Natalie Dixon, who I knew to be a killer seeking revenge. Perhaps Beth did as well but couldn't bring herself to admit it. She was never able to talk to me after that. Whether she thought I was responsible or not, I never knew. In the long rung it didn't really matter. Life with her new husband lay elsewhere. Mr. Handy, on the other hand, stayed and perhaps was not as swayed by the past. Rather he merely held on to whatever future there might be. I stared at the big windows on either side of the main door and remembered trying not to allow "Crazy" Jake Hickey to see me as he held poor Beth hostage. I would have let him kill me to save her if that's what it took. I hoped she realized that back then. I could never figure out his rage against me. After so many years passed it just didn't seem to make any sense. Maybe it was because I found something worthwhile in life, and he would never be more than a gangster on the run without any place he could call a home. Whatever it was, the truth, or something like it, died with him.

It wasn't typical for me to look at the Elmo from the opposite side of the street. Most days I'd walk out the front door and head straight on over to the *Traveler* building. Back in the day it was the Gladstone, a ritzy place with a two-bit Valentino named Phil Garmes who manned the front desk and thought he was as big as the swells who stayed there just because they would exchange a little more than a greeting with him. A favor here and there produced a few cheap dollars, enough for him to impress the local gals but not enough for an imposing bankroll. The mistake was his involvement with Hickey who was not about to trust anyone completely.

When we discovered the body of Heather Devore it shook me up, not that I was able to show any kind of emotion. She wasn't "one of them" and deserved a lot better than she got. Like a lot of guys I met over in France, she was just another casualty but of a different kind of war.

Eventually, I found my way down to the south end of the street, the area near the railroad tracks where I caught Hickey unawares. The surprise on his face was priceless especially when it dawned on him a former buddy from the old neighborhood in the North Side of Chicago wore a badge and pointed a Tommy gun straight at the area where most men have a heart. He played the wiseacre and gave me his best Jimmy Cagney or Edward G. Robinson. It might have been the gangsters learned how to act from the movies rather than the other way around. He had it in his mind we weren't able to hold him in our jail or find him guilty of anything. Just a bunch of palaver from a guy with more bullets than brains. I never learned what he had up his sleeve until we came across the car he was in with George McAllister dead behind the wheel.

The old codger.

It suddenly occurred to me the old guy with the scraggly beard who I thought just ran a still might have been someone who would have helped Jake largely because he didn't like lawmen. He also might have helped members of Hickey's gang escape after the downtown shootout. I first encountered this grizzled man on the county road in between Ark City and Winfield while transporting Will Bell to the Cowley County Courthouse. It was the same road where the fake FBI agent Hollis Burke met his end. They say blood paves the road to hell.

The thing was I didn't have access to a car now I was no longer a policeman. Carl Pearson, the night man at the Elmo, didn't reside at the hotel like other workers. I figured he might have a car on account of him living far enough out of town, unless his wife picked him up and dropped him off at ungodly hours of the night. I asked the current clerk to give him a call for me.

"Well, sure, Baron," Carl responded as though he had just woken up. "Might even get in a little early, pick up some extra hours."

Maybe my luck was changing.

There was no way of knowing how many gangsters and moonshiners traipsed through this area all those years ago. It was still a place that kept its secrets. As I came across a clearing, I had a vivid image of a man in overalls without a shirt and who wore heavy boots that had seen better days. White frizzy hair and a day or two growth of beard. Just chopping wood and sweating to the gills. Out in a clearing with no one or nothing else around. A firm ruggedness lingered in his eyes. He was a man of the land who wouldn't have much cared for either tea parties or barroom brawls. He may have been in his sixties but his meanness scared me just the same. The vague and distant look on his face let you know he was unsympathetic to your plight. It was the element of uncertainty of what a man like that was actually capable of doing.

It was at just this spot we found George McAllister dead in the car. I knew in my gut this was a betrayal, both of George to us and of Hickey to George. I felt worse for a friend and fellow officer who thought the easy way would be better. He found the wrong answer too late. When we realized Hickey escaped and was madder than a bee who lost its stinger, there was no time to mourn right there and then.

Suddenly, from out of nowhere, I heard artillery shells and saw deep green woods and brown mud and rust colored muck, and smelled blood and vomit and death. Was that barbed wire out of the corner of my eye? A blinding flash in the other direction? I needed to run. But no, when I ran the last time, I fell face first into a wall of barbed wire, turned and twisted and struggled, and felt bits of flesh ripped off my face as blood filled my eyes, spat fire like an Enfield rifle from my mouth and snot spew from my nose. I went deaf, a helpless numbness, and couldn't hear anything before the darkness mercifully settled in over me.

Then, at the snap of a finger, there was nothing. I was simply on a dirt county road somewhere between Ark City and Winfield. It was 1948, and I stood frozen, unable to move, not wanting to either. Yet I knew if I didn't, the past would rush up to me, surround me, cover me in the same darkness that would pull me so far down I could never claw my way out. The only thing I could do was press forward. The old codger might still be alive although pushing eighty. There might be some kin who would recall those days. Something. Anything.

I had been asked to do a job for a desperate old lady in need, a mother with very little to call her own except for Hope and Dignity, the last vestiges of a sad legacy. My integrity and sense of honor guided me back into the car. Like a crutch, it was all I had left besides the memories.

Chapter Six

It had been an especially hot summer, the sun bleaching the landscape from golden to a pale white as though all life had drained away. There was no indication anything living would return. The corn harvest left many fields empty and nearly dead. It was like a scene after a battle—no sound except for the moaning wind and the scent of inevitable decay. The only thing missing were the rotting corpses.

About a mile north of the clearing, I came across a narrow dirt road heading toward the east through the remnants of crops and a few withered crabapple trees. Hardly more than a trail, the road was straight yet terribly rocky, suitable only for a tractor or a doodlebug. I hoped I wouldn't wind up damaging Carl's car. In that case, apologies wouldn't do. If I couldn't afford repairs on a policeman's salary, it would be that much more difficult to do so working at the paper. If I weren't careful, this could turn into a costly venture.

The house at the end of the road reminded me of Tara from *Gone With The Wind* but after the war. It was desperately in need of a paint job, a new porch, and quite possibly curtains and furniture. The foundation did not appear stable even from a distance. The windows lost quite a few of the shutters, and hardly any grass remained in the yard. In general, it was a shambled wreck. What passed for a jalopy was barely noticeable sticking out from a decrepit garage next to the house. It was hard to imagine anyone still living there unless he was a squatter.

Nevertheless, I had come all the way out here on a hunch and couldn't back away now. Even if I found no answers, I had to make sure I checked everything out. I parked about twenty-five yards or so from the front door, stepped out of the car, and slammed the door shut to see if it would rouse anyone's attention. Sure enough, a man who must have been in his late thirties stepped out of the house, at first a bit riled at the noise I caused. After a moment, he relaxed his hardened face and was now at ease, as though caught red-handed. My policeman's suspicions rose yet again.

He didn't look much like a farmer. The pressed slacks and Oxford shirt that made him look more like an accountant gave it away. I could see his hands and they weren't rough or calloused. His hair was a bit tousled but for the most part he had a more manicured look about him. I pegged him for a city fella, maybe looking to buy up some cheap property. That being my thought, I figured it was best to feel him out a bit, see what he knew or would be willing to say.

"I don't get many people coming around here. Excuse me for being startled." He spoke with the tongue of a man with education and breeding. I couldn't peg an accent but he didn't sound exactly from these parts.

"No apologies necessary." I looked around, my head swiveling to gather a sound or image that looked familiar. "You know, a while back, I'd say about fourteen years or so ago, I came across a man chopping wood down the road. Big man with a shock of white hair and whiskers. I had some business with him and sure wish I could find him again." I leaned forward as though I were in the confessional of a church. "Truth is, I owed him some money, and my wife thinks I should do the honorable thing." The story didn't sound all that impressive. Heck, I wouldn't have been forthcoming if someone told me such a yarn.

"Where've you been all those years?"

"Just…around." My little fable started falling apart already. I wasn't cut out for this line of work.

His shoulders slumped, again as though caught in some kind of trap. From out of nowhere, a smile appeared on his face.

"That'd be my dad you're talking about."

"Oh. Fantastic. You think I could have a chat with him?"

The smile faded as quickly as it appeared.

"He passed away. A while back." He spat out the words as though there was a rancid taste in his mouth. Then, a gust of angry wind that was fixing to carry us both away broke the silence. He stood there, straight faced, and probably figured the question was asked and answered and didn't require anything further. That is until the same man in question stood at the screen door behind him.

"Who the hell is he?" the man shouted, spittle flying from his lips. The beard was now stubble but the hair was longer as though a barber hadn't come near his head for a decade or more. "You didn't tell me no one was comin' over."

"Sorry, Pop. My mistake."

"Your mother wants you in now. No more playin'

with your friends."

"Yes, sir."

The old man glared at me. To him, I was one of his son's unruly pals, likely to get the boy into trouble by encouraging mischief. I wasn't a police officer worthy of his contempt. Whatever life this man lived was now lost in a cloud. He retreated into the house. He was pretty much stepping back into time and just about took us with him.

There was no more business for me at this place. When I considered what happened to so many other people in my life, this felt the worst. There were enough issues I had to keep my own sense of identity straight. To have lost it completely was something I couldn't imagine.

"He's only been like this the last couple of years," the young man declared breathlessly. "I couldn't see, you know, putting him in a home or anything like that. You think about it, seems like a funny word for a place that's so unlike how it sounds." I heard him gulp and swallow his embarrassment. Maybe it was because his educated mind couldn't accept this or feared it could happen to any of us.

I nodded and started to walk off, ashamed to be there. He ran up to me, got in front of me, and held his hands out as a barrier without actually touching me. I was a real human being with my sensibilities as far as he could tell. Perhaps I was the first straight-minded person he had spoken to in a long time.

"Look, I don't know what all he's done in his life. I left early on, lived in Joplin for many years managing a co-op. It didn't feel right after a while so I came back to make amends and found him like this."

I couldn't think of anything worthwhile to say.

"Whatever he's done, can't he have a little peace now? Huh?"

It didn't seem like all that much to ask. Nevertheless, I was there to get whatever information I could in order to solve a mystery.

"Has he ever mentioned a man name Jake Hickey?" I had to ask, clear my conscience, and do what I came to do. "Or Jack Hale?"

"Not that I recall." He bowed his head in contemplation, shook his head slightly, and then looked over his shoulder, back at the heap in the garage. "Although there was this guy who gave him the car out there in the barn. All my pop had to do was drive him out of town as far as he could. They drove all night to Springfield."

"What happened then?"

"Nothing. Pop dropped him off. The man gave him a hundred dollars, and he drove the car back home. That was it."

"When was this?"

"Nineteen thirty four I think. Late. Fall maybe. Maybe October."

It made sense.

"Did your dad mention the guy's name?"

The man squinted and then looked down at his feet hoping to find the answer there. Without warning, he ran into the house but darted out in less than a minute, overly eager like a puppy.

"I took the registration card out of the glove box so no one would know where it came from." He extended his arm forward as though giving me an offering.

Sean Brennan. I had another name. It was a gift.

I nodded as a partial smile of appreciation glanced across my lips. I turned and walked to my car without looking back, allowing the young man to deal with his own burdens. I left this house and another piece of the past behind.

Two names. More than before but still no closer to an answer.

Chapter Seven

It was 1935, and I stood on a county road east of Ark City with Officer Dave Morton. Between us on the ground was a body covered with a sheet. What appeared to be bloodstains were around the chest and groin area. We uncovered the body and saw the most gruesome sight either one of us ever encountered. Carl Bottomley was stabbed multiple times in the chest with a deep contusion on the side of his head, and his private parts sliced off. While waiting for Dr. Brenz and more patrolmen, we started talking, thinking, analyzing. That's the way we had started and continued through 1938 with the Wichita Ripper murders. I realized that would have to be the way now. This time, however, I was on my own.

As I drove back to town with Carl Pearson's car hiccupping over every rock and pit in the road, I put together in my mind what I actually had rather than worry about what was missing. The dead bald guy in the flower store. Pat McArdle who stayed in another hotel and then disappeared. Sean Brennan who traded his car and a hundred dollars for a drive out of town. These all could have been members of Hickey's gang especially when you considered Brennan left town likely around the same time as Jake's death. Was Jimmy O'Donnell part of the gang as well? According to Mrs. O'Donnell, her son knew Jake and was involved in what she might have thought was some kind of a job. The real notion was they pulled heists and stored the loot in the underground tunnels while they kept their distance from Hallett and Childers. Jake might have a notion to take over the criminal underground in Ark City, considering a return to Chicago was out of the question.

As of now, there was the possibility of locating two others who could help point me in the direction of young O'Donnell. The question was where I would start looking. Brennan made it as far as Springfield. Unless I found an arrest report there, the records from that far back would be as vague as those found in Arkansas City. However, the thought crossed my mind a good newspaperman might have a decent set of archives especially if a bird like Brennan made a big splash in a new city. Would have made for some good copy.

When I called the *Springfield Leader & Press*, they connected me to Archie Gallo whose dad, Joe, had been a long-time patrolman on the police force. He was as interested in criminal history as I was and pleased to know I served as well. It took him less than an hour to review their past editions for 1934 and 1935 to determine there was no one by the name of Brennan involved in any criminal activity in town. He gave me a name for a reporter on the *Joplin Globe* who was around when the police recovered a camera left behind by Bonnie and Clyde during a shootout in '33. It led to a lot of information spread out to the world about that insane couple as well as a bump in circulation. While it was tempting to call, it dawned on me I could make calls to newspapers in St. Louis, Tulsa, Fort Smith, and

Memphis and still not get anywhere. I'd be running up the *Traveler's* long distance bill for nothing.

I changed my thinking. Why would Jake Hickey be involved with McArdle, Brennan, and the bald guy? They might have been disgruntled just like him, having come to hide out in Kansas only to get the cold shoulder from their bosses in Chicago. So assuming they were Chicago gangsters originally, they would have a file on each one from before they left town. I lost touch with Eliot Ness after his failed run for mayor of Cleveland. Besides, he no longer had any connections in the government, and from what I heard, was on the outs just about everywhere else. He was also on his third marriage. A call to him would drag me down the rabbit hole of a long, sad story. Yes, he was still my friend but I was on a mission of sorts and time was a factor. Besides, I figured he might like to tell me his story some time for a long series in my column. Might set the record straight or build him up to heroic proportions.

It was tempting to reach out to Alexander Gordon, the FBI agent who helped capture the escaped German POW and bring down a small team of saboteurs and assassins. He started his career in Chicago and headed off to Washington DC after his brief stay in Kansas. His subtle implication at knowing my true background both scared and fascinated me. If I wanted to get any info on these guys, I knew he would be the only one who could help. At this point, I had nothing left to lose except my reputation, which wasn't all that much anymore.

"It's probably best you retired," he said. "You were getting a little long of tooth there." The tone was of a vaudevillian silencing a heckler.

As I didn't want to appear hesitant, I laid out everything I discovered thus far. He was mostly familiar with the Hickey case but hadn't heard the names McArdle or Brennan prior to my call. Of course, Alex was familiar with the O'Donnell clan although he was unsure if there were records to account for a younger brother.

"I've got a few friends still in the Windy City who I can count on. Tell you what, I'll see what they have and get back with you. But, Baron, it might take some time."

"Seeing as how this was fourteen years ago, I figured it would. You still bucking to be head of the FBI?"

"You're darn right I am."

Just like taking down the fake FBI agent Hollis Burke, Alex Gordon could still line up anything in his sights and strike a bull's eye. I was hoping for as much this time.

Several days passed and I continued writing columns for the *Traveler*. I did a three-parter on the Farmers State Bank robbery in 1925, the first major case in which I was involved. I completed a biographic piece on Dr. Louis Brenz told from my perspective as a returning soldier and detailed how he helped me recover in so many ways. Doctie caught up with me after the article appeared to let me know he was both flattered and embarrassed. I reminded him he deserved the former, and I apologized for the latter.

When Alex Gordon called back a little less than a week later, I got writer's cramp from taking down everything he told me. As these were government files, he couldn't send me copies. I appreciated him just doing as much as he did.

"Patrick McArdle worked for Frank Gusenberg and occasionally his brother Peter Gusenberg."

"The Gusenbergs from the St. Valentine's Day Massacre?"

"The same. After Pete's and Frank's deaths, Bugs Moran took McArdle and your pal Hickey under his wing. They were going to be the new gang. Except at that point, everyone was too scared of Capone and no one from the North Side ever got that big again. McArdle's file shows an outstanding warrant on a gun charge, but he skipped town sometime in 1933, whereabouts unknown. From what you told me, he was probably one of the countless guys hiding out in your neck of the woods. Sean Brennan was with Hymie Weiss from 1925 until Hymie's death in '26. But there are no records of him after that. I mean, his file is completely empty. However, I seriously doubt he retired or became a priest."

"What about the O'Donnell kid?"

"No records there either."

"I've got a woman down here named Regina O'Donnell says he's her son. Could he have somehow been associated with Spike O'Donnell?"

"I figured that as well. But I couldn't find anyone with the name Jimmy or James or Jamie associated with Spike O'Donnell. Nothing from his dad either. Now, he could be a half-brother or a nephew or distant cousin that wasn't involved in bootlegging. But since you're saying this kid bragged about being with Hickey, he just might have the same name and tried cashing in on it. After all, how would Hickey have known otherwise?"

Whereas my suspicions about McArdle and Brennan proved accurate, Jimmy O'Donnell was still a mystery. Alex called me two days later with further news. He found a report on Pat McArdle's arrest in Chicago in 1935 on an assault charge to go along with the old minor gun possession. McArdle wound up on a three-to-ten year stretch in Stateville, and then released after serving the minimum. Brennan, on the other hand, died while in the commission of a bank robbery in early 1935 in Joplin. It was less than four months after Jake Hickey was shot and killed in Ark City. My options and opportunities narrowed each day.

Chapter Eight

I had names but that was all. Heck, I always had names. George "Bugs" Moran. Earl "Hymie" Weiss. Vincent "The Schemer" Drucci. "Crazy" Jake Hickey. The first was in jail; the last three were dead. Neither a headstone nor a prison file contained the truth. A lot of good the names did for me.

The indication was Hickey ran a five man crew including himself. Only two were possibly alive. McArdle was a parolee, and the O'Donnell kid might be out there somewhere, either six feet under, behind bars, or walking around with a new life and a new name. Before I made any effort to locate McArdle, I needed to get everything I could on Brennan's death.

It took three tries, but I finally got hold of Sgt. Brian Archer of the Joplin Police Department. He definitely sounded like a relic with a whole lot of years under his belt but with no intention of retiring any time soon. It was likely he didn't have flat feet and a chief like Walter Gray.

Archer read verbatim from their files. Brennan entered the Bank of Carthage on Main Street just after one in the afternoon on Friday, January 25, 1935. A handkerchief covered his face, and he wore a dark overcoat, dark suit, and dark hat. He carried a Tommy gun, didn't act riled or aggressive, spoke calmly and told the teller exactly what he wanted. He was in and out of the bank within two minutes, just as though the ghost of John Dillinger was in Missouri. He ran out to a car in front and drove off himself. There were no other accomplices seen in the area, and no one in town recalled noticing him prior to that day. Afterward, bank examiners indicated he collected just short of five thousand dollars in a canvas bag. Seems like the ghost of Dillinger was slipping a bit.

A security guard and bank manger immediately ran outside and both fired pistols as the car drove off south while the assistant manager called the police. No one from the bank got in his or her own car to give chase. The desk sergeant at the Carthage station contacted the Joplin police based on the direction the car headed.

On AA Road, just north of the town of Prosperity, of all places, Brennan ran into two cars from the Joplin Police Department, stopped, and fired his gun in their direction. Less than thirty seconds later, two vehicles from the Carthage Police Department came upon the scene and immediately engaged the robber. Brennan, caught in the crossfire, collapsed after both sets of policemen shot him multiple times front and back.

Each department claimed they ended his life. Archer said he only read from the Joplin file and could not advise how the Carthage Police Department would have written it up although he clearly gave me his opinion.

It was definitely the kind of material exciting enough to put into a newspaper column but it wasn't the reason for my call. I asked Archer if he remembered the case.

"Oh my goodness," he started, grabbing a big breath of air as though he were going to break the underwater record. "That wasn't the only one. I mean, we had all kinds roaming through these parts, none so glamorous, most of them roughneck thugs. Of course, Clyde Barrow was nothing more than a thick-headed punk. But that there Bonnie Parker was a certified bitch. Sorry to use them words."

According to him, Sean Brennan was somewhat of a mystery while alive and now even more so in death. After an inquest, the body lay in the morgue for a week, then buried in an unmarked pauper's grave.

I went back to the drawing board and focused all my attention on Pat McArdle. I asked Sandy Clevenger to contact the warden at Stateville Prison, a man named Joseph E. Ragen, to see if I could get any records to indicate what might have become of McArdle. Her voice on the phone had a professional tone, and her reference to me as a star columnist who was a friend of Eliot Ness got me a conversation with the man. If I didn't know better, I'd have sworn she was my PR agent.

Ragen had a long history in law enforcement both as a sheriff in Clinton County in Illinois, and as a penitentiary warden. His memory was phenomenal as he was able to rattle off facts, dates, and criminal records going back to his first prison job in 1933. Once again, I found myself writing as fast as possible to keep up with the oral history of Patrick McArdle.

"McArdle was probably useless to Moran after the Massacre," Ragen began, "largely because he lost his stomach for bootlegging and killing. I personally believe the gun charge he was up on caused Moran to send him away. There was no need to have someone useless around who could have been pinched at any moment when Moran was still trying to go up against Capone."

"So what happened?"

"He appeared almost out of the blue in a dance hall near the California Clipper and apparently started a fight with a colored patron. The police arrived and arrested him after they found the outstanding warrant from 1933. However, because of the assault being unprovoked, the judge sentenced him to a period of three to ten years. This is how he wound up in my domain."

"Do you remember much about him?"

"Well, he certainly was nothing like the other members of the North Side gang. That's for sure. We had a few in here at one time. Others were in Joliet. McArdle impressed me as a working class kind of guy, more used to putting in a day's work at a factory or office. Probably got that from his folks. Matter of fact, he worked in the laundry and then in the kitchen. Very productive. His time here was rather quiet, which is why he was recommended for parole."

I tried my best not to get my hopes up given Warden Ragen was informative and his comments moved in a direction I wanted. It was time for the most important question.

"What became of him, warden?" At this point, I practically held my breath.

I heard the shuffling of papers, a clearing of the throat, and something that might have been a gasp or sigh.

"Ah, here it is. After his release in 1938, he was required to secure employment and stay away from known felons or other criminals for the remainder of his sentence. He secured a job, if you can believe this, as a bartender at McGill's Pub. That's right across the street from Marge's Still. It was not on the recommended employment list. When the owner vouched for him and assured us of McArdle's integrity, we acquiesced. It was better for him to have some kind of job even if it wasn't what we would have preferred. It was touch and go for the first few years, but there were never any reports from the local police."

"Is he still there?" I sensed perhaps a little too much eagerness in my voice.

"He may be. They released him from parole on"— he laughed—"of all dates, February 14, 1945." The irony was thick. I thanked him for the information and for his time.

The *Traveler* had a room with phone books from all over the country. It was what we used for research to make phone calls for stories. I found the one for Chicago and located McGill's Pub. Seventeen hundred sixty-five North Sedgwick Street. In the Lincoln Park neighborhood of Chicago. My old neighborhood. Images ran through my head quickly, blurred and fractured. I was mighty close to being a little boy again.

I made a call to the place, asked for Pat McArdle. The voice on the phone told me he wouldn't be in until five p.m. that night. Asked if I wanted to leave a message, I indicated I would catch up with him later.

He was still there after all these years. Maybe he had nowhere else to go. Or he just might not have wanted to go anywhere beside where he was, where he wound up. None of that mattered. He was still alive, and that's all that counted.

If I were to follow through on my promise to

Regina O'Donnell to find her son, it meant I would have to go home again.

Chapter Nine

The Arkansas City Police Department did not officially sanction my trip when I visited Eliot Ness in Cleveland back in 1938. Then Chief Lester Richardson suggested I take some time off when the Wichita Police Department summarily excused me after they themselves requested my presence to assist in the investigation of several brutal murders. I knew I was on to something and so did Chief Richardson.

However, he recognized it was another city's jurisdiction and could not authorize me to go on a consultation with the creator of the Untouchables. I had to pay for everything out of my own pocket. I took three trains including two locals over a period of about a day and a half and stayed in a rooming house recommended by Ness after I met him and he took a shine to me. As I kept Sandy Clevenger aware of my progress in this current case for use as a major series of future columns, she indicated the paper would cover my expenses. I never determined if Mr. Stauffer was aware of this or if there would be some creative accounting in the expense report. Naturally, this didn't mean I would travel first class or peel bills off a Saint Louie bankroll to impress some Bruno. It wasn't the 1920s, and I never immersed myself in a world of gangsters. I was a newspaperman now, on a lead for a fascinating story. That was all, but it was enough.

I went over the travel arrangements with Sandy and identified what my exact plans were. Half of what I told her was what I hoped to be able to do. Once in the Windy City, things could go awry awful fast. She looked a little pale and sounded short of breath as we spoke the day before my departure.

"I think I'm coming down with something," she responded to my inquiry.

"Well, you better take care of yourself. I'm coming back with the goods, and I intend on getting a great series written up." She smiled back at me but it looked weak and forced. I hadn't worried about her in all the time I knew her. I was likely letting the anticipation of this trip get the better of me.

The Texas Chief started up recently and would make my trip a lot less inconvenient than ten years ago. I packed a small satchel with a couple of changes of socks and undershirts and boxers as well as a clean shirt in the unlikely event I would need to dress impressively. When you consider I was trying to meet up with a former gangster who was now a bartender in a dive bar, it would be an unnecessary piece of clothing. The train was prompt, arriving at 8:15 p.m. and making its way up to Kansas City, Missouri at 12:50 a.m. the next morning. Normally, I would have been on my way to bed but the excitement of the journey kept me awake. I had a change of trains and grabbed a cup of coffee while I waited for a waitress to wrap a couple of beef sandwiches to go. I didn't think much about hunger but knew I needed to keep up my strength not knowing what I would actually run into.

In the brief twenty minutes I was there, I saw the widest variety of travelers. A woman who tried to corral two young children. A well-dressed businessman type with a worn out valise and shoes. A young couple, possibly on a honeymoon, looking more scared than in expectation of a great adventure. It was strange to consider those out and about this time of evening, on a train bound for Somewhere and hopeful it wasn't Nowhere. That was true for me. I told Sandy Clevenger what I hoped from this trip in terms of a journalistic effort. Personally, it was something deeper, not just a task promised to Regina O'Donnell. There were pieces of my life, my real life, my former life, back in that city. I didn't know what I would find or how I would respond. Time has a way of burying memories; this trip threatened to dig them up.

Far more irony washed over me as I looked up and down and all around Union Station. Bank robber Jelly Nash had died in a hail of bullets while in the custody of the FBI and Kansas City police just outside in the parking lot when the darn fools who tried to free him got panicky. That was fifteen years ago. The FBI always thought it was Charlie Floyd, although Pretty Boy denied it with his dying breath. The echoes of Tommy gun blasts, the languid blue smoke, the acrid smell of gunpowder was as present in my ears and eyes and nose as though I had been here that day.

All these years I worked so hard to leave the past behind. Like a blind man with his eyes wide open, I was walking back into it. This was no dream.

I made an effort to get some sleep on the last leg to Chicago but the motion of the train was too busy and too demanding. Restless passengers yawned or got up to stretch. One woman talked the ear off the guy who was with her. From the look on his face, I could tell he wanted to sock her in the puss but probably thought better of it in front of all these people. I had no desire to get to the dining car and mix with anyone else. This wasn't a vacation or pleasure trip. Even the thought of having to explain my facial scars or the reason for my journey was too tiring. People always wanted something from you. It might have seemed simple to them but it could have been everything to you. I finally just stared out the window into the dark night and wondered if I was heading backward or forward. There was no way to tell until the train stopped for good.

It was 9:00 a.m. in Chicago when we arrived at the Dearborn Station on Polk St. I could sense something vaguely familiar about it, like an old friend who aged and gone gray. In an instant, I wondered what would happen if I ran into a childhood friend then quickly squashed the notion when I considered no one would recognize me. Sandy made reservations for me at the Hotel Lincoln on Clark St. as it was the closest place to McGill's Pub. Obviously, it was far too early to go in and seek out McArdle. The best I could do was grab a hack to bring me to the flop so I could catch up on my sleep. It was a swank joint, nicer than anything I ever stayed at, as far as I could remember. Being here, in this hotel, in this city, made my mind wander and changed the words as they went from my brain to my mouth. It took everything I had to remind myself I was Baron Witherspoon from Arkansas City, Kansas, a local farm boy and veteran of the Great War who became a patrol cop determined to protect the citizens of his town.

The desk clerk was considerably more professional than Phil Garmes from the old Gladstone back in the day. This gentleman, in his mid-forties, was generous and complimentary, wanting only for me to enjoy my stay both at the hotel and in Chicago. He came across as a real estate agent selling me on the virtues of buying a home in the nicest neighborhood in spite of my appearance as a less than worthy credit risk. I had a natural apprehension based on years of dealing with con men and shysters. Something about this guy convinced me I was a valued client, even a stranger with scars. He may have limited talents but he put them to good use.

I finally plopped down in my bed about eleven in the morning and figured to get some shut eye, but all I did was toss and turn for the better part of a half hour. This whole trip had gotten me agitated, and I hadn't even yet met up with Pat McArdle. I needed to blow off some steam so I went outside and started walking.

I turned to the right and headed north. I saw signs directing me toward Lincoln Park Zoo and remembered going there as a kid with my ma while my pa worked a second or third job to bring in enough to feed the family. I could barely see Lake Michigan and had visions skating on it in winter, exhaling just to watch my breath in the frigid air. The streets were still the same although some storefronts changed. This city, however, would always be as it was, no matter how much it appeared to change. It scared me to think the memories made me revert to Eric Kimble, someone who I allowed to die in the forests of France so many years ago. It was too late to start believing in resurrection. For that matter, there was no purpose to bring Kimble back to life.

Before I knew it I stood in front of the Werner Storage Company at 2122 N. Clark St. The address appeared more familiar than the name. It was while I got my footing as a beat cop in Arkansas City, Kansas, a brief four years back from the war in Europe, acclimating to my new surroundings and new identity I read news articles of a massacre in Chicago. The assumption was men hired by Al Capone killed seven guys in the employ of George "Bugs" Moran at the S.M.C. Cartage Company. Right here at 2122 N. Clark Ave., the same address where I stood dumbfounded. "Only Capone kills that way," a distraught Moran uttered to break a code of silence among these brutal gangsters. Not even Frank Gusenberg, shot fourteen times, would say anything before he died three hours later in the hospital.

Back then, a chilled shudder ran through me as I thought of how Moran had taken over the North Side gang after Dion O'Banion's death, and how Jake Hickey would likely be right alongside to serve his master. What would have happened had Hickey been one of the seven and never had to hide out in Kansas? And what of Heather Devore? It was likely Hickey with his hotheaded temper would meet his fate somewhere else and a dame like Heather might have hooked up with another beau, someone who appreciated her charms. Fate has a way of bringing everything to its expected conclusion.

I heard the deafening rattle of Tommy guns and blast of shotguns like a heavy rain on a tin roof, even twenty-four years later. Blood spurting from their mouths, the stabs of pain from numerous bullets, they fell like sacrificial lambs on an ancient altar all for a little piece of a territory and in retribution for an imagined wrong.

Peter Gusenberg.

Frank Gusenberg.
Al Kachellek.
Adam Heyer.
Reinhardt Schwimmer.
Albert Weinshank.
John May.

I stood there outside the building with a new name, one that obliterated any sense of its history. In that regard, it and I shared a great deal in common. I needed to be here for a different reason. That much I knew. What it was doing to me made me doubt my own sanity.

It was less than a mile back to the hotel. I walked on bandy legs feeling dizzy and weak, woozy as though drunk on bathtub hooch. A fifty-year-old man, a relic of a time long past, I contemplated where I fit in this world today and as whom. When I got back to my room, I hadn't figured out the answer. All I did was pass out as though I had been on a toot at an all-night speakeasy, dancing with the B-girls, flapping my yap with the sheiks and shebas. I didn't know what I would encounter when I woke. Or who I would be.

Chapter Ten

There had been so many times over the last ten years when I woke up not remembering where I was. It was a feeling of disorientation, like dishwater draining down a sink, something old and used up spinning away into oblivion. This was another of those times.

Al Capone died the previous year in January. By then he was a mumbling maniac drooling like an infant, his mind eaten up by syphilis. A man so powerful and so feared reduced to a quivering mass of Jell-O. For the most part, his demise was symbolic of the entire gangster period. The Commission ran things in a nice and neatly ordered way, and regional rivalries were a notion of the past. The focus was on business instead of ethnic differences. The only color that mattered was green.

Yet as I stepped out of the Hotel Lincoln and looked up and down both ends of the street, it was as though nothing changed. Maybe it was just a vision from thirty years prior burned into my memory and hiding the certainty of today. It was then I realized everyone had his or her own version of reality. Mine filtered through a dead soldier from a small town in Kansas.

I decided against changing into a clean shirt. After all, I wasn't going to The Pump Room. McGill's Pub was essentially a neighborhood dive that served cheap drinks and tasteless hash that temporarily occupied room in a few empty stomachs. Some place where a man could disappear from his drab life for several hours before waking up into the next morning and starting a stale routine all over again. Pat McArdle was no one I needed to impress. However, I hoped he might astonish me with some small piece of knowledge to make this disorienting journey worthwhile. Selfishly, I needed to come out ahead, get something in return for all I was emotionally giving up. The odds were not in my favor.

It was quarter till eight when the sun set, a warm orange glow reflected off the windows of the buildings I passed as I walked down Menomonee Street. I was bathed in a kind of heavenly light, as though this task received a celestial blessing. I needed to feel that finding a mother's son was something good, and that it would somehow redeem me from all my past sins. I certainly wasn't willing to count on the powers of Sister Celeste, wherever she might be at this moment. Certainly, a dive on the North Side did not routinely stock Holy Water. In the end, it all might just be fodder for a series of articles in a small town Kansas newspaper read by a few thousand folks and farmers. There would be no Pulitzer Prize in my literary future and no open welcome past the Pearly Gates.

The odor of damp decay hit me as I walked in, the air thicker than a summer day in Florida. Nothing bright or shiny stood out; the predominant colors were brown and rust. Three men sat at the bar in relative silence. They were all in their sixties or older. Two tables had two men each sitting and talking. Those men were younger and rather animated. I caught a conversation at one of the tables bemoaning the misfortunes of the

Cubs and the White Sox, both of which appeared mired in losing seasons. Perhaps discussing the bad luck of someone or something else hides your own misery, turns your attention away from the fact you don't get to start over in a new season next year.

The man behind the bar was mostly gray haired with a streak of dark specks in a few places. There were bags under his eyes, and his shaggy arms appeared withered as though he were malnourished. Wiping the bar was like a form of exercise. He didn't look up at me when I sat down, just simply said, "What'll you have?" At that point, I was just another chum off the street he didn't have to care about, as long as I had the cabbage to pay the bill.

"Old Grand-Dad."

"Rocks?"

"Neat."

The glass was on the table and poured in less than fifteen seconds. It wasn't done out of efficiency as much out of boredom. I took a sip.

"You Pat McArdle?" I asked.

"Nope." He said it too quickly as though he heard the same question asked a thousand times or perhaps rehearsed it well enough for when it finally came.

"You know him?"

He looked up at me, the look on his face like a tired old lion harassed by jackals for far too long.

"Never heard of him." With a face chiseled out of brick, nothing moved save his lips.

He walked down to the other end of the bar, to one of the older guys who just stared into space, and started a conversation about something to do with a woman. The other man barely responded. The bartender didn't look back in my direction at all. I polished off my drink and threw two bits down on the bar. I didn't know if he was McArdle or simply looked out for him. I would have to find out some other way.

I went across the street to Marge's Still, got a shot of Old Grand-Dad with a beer chaser, sat at a table by the window and looked back toward McGill's. I hoped no one would be able to notice me. It was just like doing surveillance as a policeman, the learned skills imbedded deep within me, the memories of long nights walking a beat bringing a fond smile to my lips. This whole adventure was more like a cop than a writer, the research notwithstanding. I was on an investigation, a search for a missing party. It was a lie I kept telling myself—this was for a good cause. Pushed aside after nearly thirty years, all I could find myself doing was exactly what I had done. Old habits die hard. This time, I was outside the legal jurisdiction of law enforcement. Something about it gave me a sense of freedom. It was exhilarating.

It was slightly busier at Marge's with more robust and upbeat patrons. They might have been the same ones who frequented the place when it was a speakeasy during prohibition. It was certainly livelier than Junior's back in Ark City.

Hardly anyone bothered me as I sat there. It was typical for a place like that, allowing patrons their space. That attitude was a carryover from prohibition where each man guarded his circle meticulously and only invited in those most trusted. Somehow, the hours passed and it was close to eleven. A deep discouraging blue replaced the golden sunset followed by a harsh sinister black that hid all the malcontents and other demons. As there were hardly any lights in McGill's it appeared closed. I knew otherwise. I paid my tab at Marge's and walked diligently back across the street. It was now or never.

A young couple sat at a table. The man tried convincing the girl to go back with him to his apartment and plied her with enough drinks to encourage her. An elderly man with a hearing aid strung from his ear to his inside pocket sat at the bar sipping from his glass. The bartender with the emaciated arms looked up as I entered and watched me as I came over to the bar.

"We close in five minutes," he said. "You can hang around," he added suddenly. His comment caught me by surprise at first until I realized I had a kind of recognizable face. He certainly knew me even though I had never met him.

As the girl started loosening up and giggling, the man escorted her out. The bartender tapped the old gentleman on the shoulder to remind him of the time. The place now empty, the bartender locked the door. I should have been concerned. Anyone from the North Side back in the day would have been in a situation like that.

"I knew you'd be coming for me some day." Did he think I was the Angel of Death?

"You don't even know who I am."

"You're from the past, aren't you?"

I nodded absently, realizing I was.

Chapter Eleven

We stood there staring at each other for maybe a full minute or more. Our faces were empty of anything resembling human emotion, largely because we were two ghosts who had been wrung dry from all the years of reaching for dreams that were just beyond our outstretched fingers. Missed opportunities and repeat mistakes kept us far enough away from succeeding but close enough to know what success was. When he blinked nervously, the spell was broken.

"You're the cop from Kansas?"

"I was." My answer sounded hollow as though I had fallen down a well.

"We all were something once."

"The question is what are you now?"

The small smile that briefly appeared was more a recognition of the truth than a response to something humorous. At least in my case for the better part of nearly thirty years, I wondered who I was at every juncture of my life. I could not presume the same thing for him. He'd have to answer that for himself.

"I'm Patrick Sean McArdle of the Mount Greenwood McArdles."

"South Side?" I was surprised given his connections to O'Banion and Moran. O'Banion grew up in Kilgubbin, known as "Little Hell", a heavily Irish area known for its crime. The Italian mob had their stronghold in the South Side. McArdle nodded with a sense of pride.

"When my pal Frankie Gusenberg introduced me to Deanie O'Banion, they thought I might be able to give them dirt on the Italians. Truth was I never met a Dago until the first time I killed one." I heard such talk from bigger mouths like Will Bell and McArdle's old pal Jake Hickey. This shocking revelation, so to speak, spoken deadpan and calm was intended merely to get a rise out of me. I didn't bite. "How about an Old Grand Dad?" A slight nod of my head and he reached behind the bar for a bottle and two glasses. We sat down at the same table where the desperate guy worked his charm on the intoxicated gal. The seats were still warm. Our hearts were both cold.

"When you came back in '35, you had a minor gun charge on you. You could have laid low. You should have. Yet you started a fight with a colored man and got sent away for a ten spot?" He slugged down the first drink as a way to shake off the dust gathered through years of hiding and stagnating. There wasn't a need to remain silent. He no longer looked like a tough who could take on the world. I guessed he was maybe a couple of years older than me but his face looked like a worn down tire that had seen too many miles.

"Kansas was a bust. Sure, we cooked up a couple of scores, made some dough. It might have been enough for a laugh and a few drinks but nothing that would get us on our feet again and start a new gang. By the time I got back here, Bugs lost all his power. He basically pulled out of town. I figured nothing was left but a nice cozy stay in the big house. Either I could ride out the time based on my rep or a gunsel with something to prove'd kill me. I was fine either way."

"But you got paroled instead."

"Yeah. My luck. The luck of the Irish." A snort of a laugh preceded another shot of booze.

This was a man who was playing out his hand. Problem was he had nothing to bet with. The time of the gangster was long past and his opportunities for wealth or fame by death slipped through his fingers. People would remember Dion and Hymie and The Schemer. No one heard of Pat McArdle or would even remember him. He was an old man who served cheap liquor to bindle stiffs not much better off than him. It was a purgatory for a former gangster who was a good Catholic.

"Tell me about Jake Hickey."

His eyes lit up. A friend, an impressive character, a good egg, a man with a plan. He had to tell Jake that Moran was not going to send for them in six months or a year or three years. They were sent out of town to prevent them from trying to push "Bugs" out completely and grab whatever few beans were left for them. Moran made it sound like protection, but he was only protecting himself and what little remained. Indentured slavery is what Arkansas City, Kansas turned out to be. A place to shrivel up and die if all you did was toe the line.

The funny thing was I felt the same way at one point. I returned to Baron Witherspoon's home and family and was grateful to be taken in long enough to get my wits about me. A year or two passed and I realized I was dying inside trying to be a farmer, something I had no stomach for. Then I got the bright idea to become a cop. It was completely opposite of who I started out as but honorable enough for me to become a new person. Pat McArdle wasn't as fortunate.

"You worked for Martin Childers at Kanotex?"

"Yes and no." I raised an eyebrow wondering if he was trying to play me. "We were on the payroll if anyone ever asked but we never worked there. I walked through there once maybe."

"Was it him who set up jobs for you?"

"No." His response was direct and clear.

"What about Councilman Hallett?"

"I'd heard of him. Didn't know if he ran the show. So far as I knew, a guy named Dietrich was the bean picker before Jake convinced us to rake in dough on the Q.T. to get enough of a stash where we could all leave. Whoever the Big Deal was had the marker on our lives. We owed for the sanctuary they gave us but there was no way we'd get out of debt in a small burg like that. At least Jake gave us a chance to bail out. The problem was the more we kept swimming, the more the water kept rising."

He verified Sean Brennan was part of the gang. He started out rubbing Jake the wrong way until he saw there was a method to the madness and played along without raising any more of a ruckus. He actually showed brains and would take any score that was set up. He identified the tall bald guy, Dietrich, as the one who initially had a list of chores but McArdle didn't know who handed them down. Dietrich was like a foreman in the tunnels, overseeing the loading and unloading cases of hooch and stolen goods, likely at the behest of Childers, although he could never confirm it. Dietrich fell in with Jake as soon as the whole gang idea came together. Perhaps he had always been looking for some greener grass.

I looked at the bottle and it was about half gone. It was as though some radio show had me all caught up in it, and I just kept taking belt after belt due to the excitement. The actions from 1934, when I was on the other side of the street, had a light shine brightly on them. The blank spaces started getting filled in.

"What about the O'Donnell kid?"

"Jimmy? Cute kid trying to be a tough guy. He was like Jake's puppy dog."

"Spike's kin?"

"Said he was."

"I looked into it. Couldn't find anything to say so."

"Probably just looking to get an in. Who wouldn't around Crazy Jake Hickey? I think the kid would have claimed to be the son of Patrick Pearse if it would have gotten him in the gang."

He recounted the plan to help Hickey escape and the shock when George McAllister was shot and killed. That convinced McArdle to leave and forget about any stake at all. Up until that moment, it was all just robberies. Now it was the murder of a cop and that meant the chair. It wasn't something he counted on or planned for. He saw Brennan drive off with the old farmer while he just kept walking until he got all the way up to Winfield, located John Twomey who reluctantly helped him get back to Chicago.

"No one I knew before was around," McArdle continued, "and the few that remembered me from my reputation were unwilling to help. That's when I got the idea to play it safe in jail. At least they wouldn't connect me to some cop killing in Kansas."

He poured the last two drinks into our glasses.

Surprisingly, I wasn't overly drunk or unstable. I listened to his story with fascination as though I had never been a part of it. Even the description of a fellow officer's killing didn't move me to tears. At that point, I looked at my own life through the eyes of a stranger.

I now knew the name of the mysterious dead man from the flower shop. I reaffirmed Jimmy O'Donnell's claim of a relation to Spike although no one knew for sure and no one really cared. Nothing pointed me in the right direction except back home. I identified each card in the deck. I just didn't know what the game was.

"I hope I wasn't keeping you from going home," I said politely.

"Nah. I got a room in the back." He nodded with his head. "A bed, a dresser, and a wash basin."

"That all you got?"

"It's all I need anymore."

Pat McArdle was a man who wanted to be something big, just like all the other Irish and Italian hoodlums fighting over bathtub hooch. He wound up in Kansas, losing himself and any sense of who he was or might have been. Every day was like the one before and like the one to come, assuming the next day would come. It was scary to think how close to him I could have been.

As I started to walk out, he called back to me.

"Did you get what you came for?"

"No. Not really."

"I don't think you will." It wasn't a malicious comment. It had a note of sadness to it, like a bugler blowing taps.

"Why not?"

"You can't wrap your arms around a ghost."

I nodded my head, left, and never looked back. It was time to go home. I had some place to be and something to do and I hadn't quite lost myself completely.

Chapter Twelve

Old Grand Dad may not have had much of a bite the night before but he was sure making his presence known early in the morning. I found a small diner near the Lincoln Park Farmers Market and choked down some eggs, toast, and coffee. Lots of coffee. I was in no mood to compare my breakfast to Daisy Mae's considering the marching band playing John Phillips Sousa in my head, the tubas and kettledrums pounding out a deadly rhythm. For all I knew it was the voices of the past singing a requiem mass. Either way, all I wanted was for the music to stop.

Check out time was eleven a.m. The Texas Chief's scheduled departure out of Dearborn Station wasn't until six p.m. That was nearly seven hours of nothing more than thinking. The hack drove me and my full belly and satchel down to Polk Street and by 11:30 a.m. I sat on a hard wooden bench on the second floor of the head house reading a discarded edition of the *Chicago Tribune.* The White Sox fell to the Boston Red Sox, making it four losses in a row. Meanwhile, the Cubs dropped a close one to the Boston Braves. The beat writer made a big deal of the coincidence. Most baseball fans were still in mourning over the passing of Babe Ruth barely two weeks earlier. In baseball, there was always something to cry over. Until the next game.

The House Un-American Activities Committee

claimed Communists infiltrated various sectors of the US government during the Second World War and the Crest Theater had ads for the latest John Wayne western *Red River* which was a box office smash. The Crest was across the street from the Biograph where John Dillinger watched his last movie. He wasn't around long enough to give the Duke's movie a review.

All I could think of while reading the paper was baseball scandals, crooked politicians, and gangsters of the past. Maybe it was all just being in Chicago. Or perhaps where my mind was and where it had to be in order to fulfill an obligation. It occurred to me all the time I spoke with and listened to Pat McArdle, there was never any reference to Jake and their lives prior to coming to Kansas. No reference to their heyday as big shots in the North Side Gang, how they got the better of Capone on numerous occasions before he finally squashed them. There was no mention of Hymie or the Schemer or Polack Joe or Frank McErlane. Pat was content to let all of that vanish into the mists of time, happy to be a bartender with a one-room flop in the back of a dive bar, waiting for a real death to end the purgatory of being forced to forget but unable to completely do so. That made every waking moment a series of regrets endlessly repeated.

It had been my story as well despite the fact I only had my toes in the water when it came to being a gangster. The time I served in the military gave me a temporary reprieve. The masquerade for twenty-eight years and counting was a study in patience and fear. A good deed forced me to look in the mirror and see who I had been, scars and all. This jaunt up north was a history lesson, a slide show of all that was in the past.

For the life of me, I couldn't quite figure out what the future would bring.

I changed trains again in Kansas City at 1:30 in the morning and was pleasantly surprised to see the same young lady who provided me with coffee and sandwiches working the same shift upon my return. The order was the same although this time I was famished and ate both of my sandwiches before we got to Emporia.

I knew I needed to focus and determine where I stood. The phone calls and now this trip gave me a clearer picture of exactly what took place between late 1933 and October of 1934. I identified three out of the five men. A fourth had a name. The fifth was the mysterious youth, Jimmy O'Donnell, who was the target of this query. The only remaining individual connected to these men in any fashion was Councilman Hallett. No certain evidence existed of his involvement other than the gut feeling of a former policeman who knew enough to trust his instincts. Somewhere outside of Florence, Kansas, I fell asleep. Surprisingly, there were no dreams.

It was as though days passed. However, just a little over two hours later the conductor called out Arkansas City. For whatever reason, I felt rested although my back could have used a good stretching out. There were so many things I thought to do, whether it was heading to the *Traveler* or going back home to my own bed. What I was obligated to do, however, was visit with Regina O'Donnell and let her know what I discovered so far.

That was going to have to wait for a bit. Linda Kuchenberg was waiting for me when I arrived at the

Elmo. She stood up stoically, but I could tell she had been crying.

"She's gone." A simple sentence. Two words. But I realized her sister, my dear friend and co-worker Sandy Clevenger passed away. She told me Doctie figured it to be a heart attack. I never considered Sandy's age or health. She always came across as fit and sharp as a tack. Those last moments before I left made me feel uncomfortable. Perhaps I had a bit of regret for leaving, but I knew I could have done nothing to save her. She helped me track down two killers, recommended me for a job that changed my life, and was able to banter about crimes from past and present with the best of them.

I was lost. The only reason I was working on this case, the only reason I had the confidence to make an attempt was because of Sandy. While I was able to gather some information, at that very moment, I couldn't see myself continuing, couldn't figure out where to turn from there.

Linda let me know when the funeral would be, and that I was to be a pallbearer. That gave me some comfort. I graciously accepted. Right now, I needed to keep moving forward. For my own peace of mind and for whatever sanity I had left. Carl Pearson was still working the front desk. Reluctantly, I asked to borrow his car again. As his shift ended at eight, he generously offered to give me a lift wherever I needed to go. Over the years, I got the impression Carl didn't have too much excitement in his personal life and often worked extra shifts as much for the money as for just staying away from home.

I figured Regina O'Donnell didn't have a phone as she never provided me with a number. It was also a slim possibility I would find her at home since it was Sunday and most people would have been at church. It was a chance I had to take. Carl pressed me for details on the drive up to Hackney, and I felt I owed it to him to let him in on the story.

"You been back up there since the thing on the base?" he asked as though he was ready to turn the page on a pulp story.

"Been no need to. Until now."

"You figure you'll find this kid?"

I didn't answer him largely because I didn't know.

It was one thing to give Carl the synopsis on this adventure but a whole other thing to have him sit in with Mrs. O'Donnell and me. He took no offense to my asking him to wait in the car.

Mrs. O'Donnell reacted to my surprise at finding her home on Sunday. Through her mumbled words I gathered she had issues with either the church or the Holy Spirit. She stayed within herself, physically and emotionally, a pious lady who didn't deserve the cards life dealt her.

I went over the whole thing in absolute detail, leaving out nothing as I owed her everything. I was disheartened to have to confirm her son had been involved in a gang of robbers, and lied about his background in order to make himself more impressive to these older and experienced men. Three of the five men were dead; the other one was living a life of no consequence. After all I discovered, I could not find a trail to reach Jimmy.

"You have simply amazed me, Officer Witherspoon." She referenced me by a title that no longer fit. "At this point you have confirmed my suspicions of his indiscretions." She was gracious in using such terms. "But I have nothing left except for Jimmy. I need to know what became of him." I couldn't fully understand what she sought, especially considering the likelihood was the young man's violent death. "Would you please continue your efforts? No mother would be able to accept the uncertainty. Can you continue? Would you?"

I was tired, not from the long train ride but from the many years I walked this earth. I felt somewhat like Pat McArdle thinking I had done all I could and there was nothing left to do. I did not have a connection to anyone in a personal sense, in spite of my friendship with Dave Morton and my working relationship with Sandy Clevenger. Now she was gone. Nevertheless, I made a promise and I was going to keep it. I was going to honor Regina O'Donnell just as I had honored Baron Witherspoon. To do this, I would have to walk like Daniel into a lions' den.

Chapter Thirteen

There was no need to consult with Dr. Brenz or the late Sigmund Freud to analyze the most recent dream. Dressed as a poor farm boy from medieval times, I tossed some seeds into the ground in hopes they would grow into something useful. My patience turned into boredom as nothing happened; I could only stare at a dry plot of earth, arid and incapable of producing any crop. That is, until I awoke one morning to discover a huge thick leafy vine that reached into the sky. I was weak, afraid of heights, and uncertain as to where this vine went, but I climbed it, nevertheless. At the top upon a cloud was a typical Kansas farmhouse behind a cast iron fence. I passed through a gate to approach the house when suddenly a giant in a suit of copper armor emerged, a sinister smile plastered on his face. He did not utter a word but simply ran toward me with loping strides. He nearly caught up with me when I reached the vine. As I climbed down hurriedly, I fell to the earth below, waking up as I landed.

I would be the giant killer. I would bring down men far more dangerous than I ever had a notion to be. I was going to wind up failing to destroy this menace. Its name was Hallett.

After a few hours of sleep, I went into the offices of the *Traveler,* spoke with some typesetters and other reporters, and stared at the empty desk of Sandy

Clevenger. The witty banter would be no more. I was also scared I might lose the best researcher I had ever known.

Mr. Stauffer wasted little time in getting a receptionist/secretary/archivist. He got a hold of me that afternoon to pass along his condolences and advise me he found the ideal person to further assist me. Mrs. Julia Lindstrom, the retired librarian and widow of Professor Bryant Lindstrom, was at Sandy's desk two days later. She greeted me with courtesy and reserve. The high collar was almost Victorian. Her hands, gently crossed and placed gingerly on her lap, presented a demeanor from long ago. I didn't figure to have as much fun with her.

Because of that dream, I decided I needed to know more about the former councilman than what I thought I knew. My best resource would have been Sandy Clevenger. Fortunately, and surprisingly, Mrs. Lindstrom was equal to the task.

"I've put together a file on the former councilman," she replied to my amazed reaction at her confession. "I wouldn't trust a hair on his head." It was everything I could do to withhold a smirk. She opened up a folder that was a good three inches thick, licked her finger, and strummed through the first few pages. Her verve made me aware a fire and passion still lurked within. "John David Hallett…"

"Heck, I always thought his first name was 'Councilman'." She smiled at my labored attempt at humor.

"Born April 30, 1873 in North Hempstead, New York."

"You mean he's not from Kansas?"

Julia looked up at me, contempt for Hallett in her eyes, and returned to reading from her files.

"He claimed to have served with the 1st United States Volunteer Calvary during the Spanish-American War."

"The Rough Riders? I can't see him as a horseman."

"Neither could I. Eventually I found out, well after his fifth or sixth election as councilman, he contracted malaria shortly upon arriving in Cuba and spent most of his time in an Army hospital. But he used his enlistment as a means of building up his reputation."

"How did he wind up in Kansas?"

"He spent five years after the war working his way up to Vice President of a Morgan bank in New York City. An article from the *New York World* casually mentioned him in conjunction with Herman Rosenthal."

"Who was he?"

"A bookie who complained in the press about a crooked cop named Becker. Darn fool thing to do. A bunch of idiots who thought this Becker would get them off the hook killed Rosenthal. That was too much for Hallett to be associated with so he asked for a transfer to the Kansas City branch about 1913. Nothing else I was able to find there until he winds up down here two years later. Sets up a shingle as a lawyer even though I've never seen a diploma from anywhere worthwhile. Additionally, I've been unable to verify he passed the bar in Kansas, Missouri, or New York. You ask me, I'd say you could have him arrested for impersonating an attorney."

Mrs. Lindstrom certainly impressed me. Her distaste for Hallett was in full bloom although one couldn't tell she harbored such feelings merely by her appearance. She recounted how his first run for public office fell flat when he didn't have enough money to maintain any sort of campaign. That was in 1917, just before the US entered the war. Two years later, he became Commissioner of Public Works after spreading around the lettuce. No one seems to know where it all came from. I thought at first Abram Dutcher, the man known as Der Kaiser, who had a hand in all things illegal in the region, might have been behind Hallett. Then I remembered how Dutcher advised me to forget about the councilman when we were at loggerheads with Jake Hickey. That either meant Hallett was of no consequence or others of even greater power protected him.

"Hallett won re-election in 1921 before finally gaining a seat on the City Council in 1923," Mrs. Lindstrom continued. "It was the position he held until 1935 when he declined to seek reelection." This was, of course, about six months after Hickey had his career and his life ended in our fair city. For the past thirteen years, he returned to private practice although there were no records of any clients he represented or any cases he brought to trial. She could find no mention of him in any newspaper articles. How he maintained his comfortable lifestyle was still in question.

"How many other folks do you have a file on, Mrs. Lindstrom?"

"A few that have rankled me over the years."

"Anything on me?" I asked whimsically, half expecting her to rattle off the name Eric Kimble.

"Officer Witherspoon," she said respectfully, "you've never rankled me at all."

She pulled out clipping after clipping from the *Traveler*, indicating Hallett was the real power in city government and how no one questioned his decisions or judgment. There were whispers of collusion with businesses, both legal and otherwise, but no direct accusations. All the while, he sat in his law office downtown, smoking his cigars, and blowing smoke in the faces of his detractors.

A seventy-five-year-old man, a relic of prohibition gangsters and small-town corruption, he was still feared for the many secrets he held in a vise grip. All he had left was his pride and vanity. That was going to be the way I would confront him.

In my position as a newspaper columnist, it would not appear out of the ordinary to seek an interview and make deep and probing inquiries. I no longer had the credentials of a law enforcement officer so I hoped there would be nothing to fear by his speaking with me. Nevertheless, he was a cagey old codger who left me high and dry many times in the past. We were the only ones left who truly understood the world of the gangsters, how they thought and what made them tick. What we really knew about each other was inconsequential. What we would wind up admitting to was the only way to win.

He no longer had a secretary or anyone working for him, not even a clerk. His office still had a front room where a receptionist formerly sat and decided who would get to see him. The Roman emperors used to have tribunes. Now just an empty desk and chair remained, not even a lamp or blotter to make it appear as though it had any use.

The door to the inner office was open. Hallett sat

behind his large mahogany desk reading the latest edition of the *Traveler*, his ever-present cigar filling the room with a dense bluish smoke that hid the true nature of the man. Only those brave enough to enter might have a chance. As they say, you can't win if you don't play the game.

I stood at the doorway, resisting the urge to cough, and waited. It was obvious he felt my presence but didn't acknowledge it until he was ready. He lifted his head and blew out a cloud of smoke. When it cleared, a politician's smile was on his face. He was ready to grant me an audience. This was the Vatican, and he was the Pope.

Chapter Fourteen

It was a contest, all just a game. The one who spoke first would give in to the other. I figured neither one of us had anything left to lose.

"Good afternoon, Councilman," I said politely, giving him the courtesy of a title he no longer possessed and probably never deserved. He looked back at the newspaper and spoke without looking at me.

"Great article on Will Bell, Baron." By that, he was reaffirming I no longer had the weight of the law behind me. Even when I did, he still acted superior. I was now just an ordinary bug he could crush if he so desired. "The kid was more of a blabbermouth than a criminal, don't you think?"

"He had his share of indiscretions."

"What do you suppose became of him?" It was then he turned back toward me, waiting for an answer into which he could dig his teeth.

"As a police officer it wasn't my concern. I delivered him to the county jail and the District Attorney. That was my only job."

He folded the paper in half and placed it like some holy scripture on his desk.

"Ah, but now you are a seeker of truth."

I shook my head in the negative. "No, sir, only a teller of tales."

The laughter was riotous and heavy, like a violent

thunderstorm. But no gaiety or whimsy was within it at all. Like the roar of Zeus, I was supposed to cower. I chose to stand tall.

"And what tales are you telling now?"

Boldly, I walked up to the desk and sat in the seat opposite him. I decided not to wait for an invitation. In one instance, a singular movement, I showed him no fear remained within me. I knew the dead could not be frightened.

"Oh, I think a lot of our readers are fascinated by those days. You know, the bootleggers and gangsters ran amok all over these parts without any constraints as though their malice was sanctioned."

"A bit of hyperbole, perhaps. I assume you are referring to the home-grown types like Floyd and Bradshaw?"

"Certainly. Those but also the Chicagoans like Hickey."

The smile didn't leave his face. He might have maintained his composure but I wondered how much he would reveal.

"What stories are there left to tell?"

"Well, you know, newspapers are a business. I'm sure you can appreciate that. Selling copy, raising circulation. It is kind of a mandate given to me from Mr. Stauffer. The way I see it is the war is too fresh, too many bad memories, too much loss. I thought a few gangster stories might feel, well, nostalgic. You know, the good old days." The sense of irony was intentional.

"We had our share. No more than Joplin or Tulsa or Wichita."

I leaned forward and rested my arms on the desk, somewhat breathless, like a son hanging on every word of the story his father told.

"You see, what I can't figure is how guys like Hickey and Pat McArdle and Sean Brennan could all just hide out here in our little old town for nine, twelve, fourteen months without being detected at all."

Hallett leaned forward as well, making sure to avoid touching the newspaper. He held his cigar close to his face so the smoke became a curtain between us. Nevertheless, I could still see his eyes.

"Perhaps they had sufficient funds to bribe the right people."

"Leaving Chicago in the midst of all that was going on? Having no contacts within a hundred miles of the city? I sincerely doubt their funds, as it were, would last too long. Let's say for a moment you are correct, who would the 'right people' be, sir?"

"You want me to hazard a guess?"

"By all means, please." I played serve and volley just like Pancho Gonzales.

That politician's smile grew wider. He thought he would weave a tale for me. What he didn't realize was I knew it would be a fable before he uttered the first word. The opulent phrase "Once upon a time…" was something I lived through, and he wouldn't be able to make me believe otherwise.

"Well, off the top of my head, I'd have to say Martin Childers."

"The former president of Kanotex?"

"Yes, exactly. In his position, he could create false employment records and make it appear these men had real jobs. Such actions would eliminate suspicion. After all, you're less likely to suspect a gainfully employed man than you are a hot shot in a silk suit aimlessly wandering around. Especially here in Ark City."

I figured he would target Childers. Since he died ten years ago, Martin Childers was in no position to discredit this character assassination.

"Very astute point. But assuming they were bribing Mr. Childers and had fake jobs, what do you suppose they would do once their money ran out?"

"Are you familiar with indentured servitude?" I scrunched up my brow and pretended to think while I played the village idiot to his lord of the manor. If he wanted to assume my ignorance, I was fully willing to let him fall into that pit. "A man owes a bond to another man. To pay off the debt he becomes a contracted employee, so to speak, unable to leave said employment until the debt is paid off."

"So these guys were forced to work for Childers at Kanotex. Is that what you are suggesting?"

"I would imagine Martin had other lucrative jobs for them."

My eyes opened wide slowly like Stepin Fetchit. I was no vaudevillian but rather someone hearing for the first time a subtle admission of crimes committed within our city of which the former councilman seemed to have an awareness. His familiar use of Childers' first name indicated to me his complicity.

"That makes sense now."

"What does?"

"The unidentified man we killed in the flower shop back in '34."

"How does that?"—I cut him off to indicate I led the conversation now.

"—He was unidentified by Mr. Childers and no one else knew anything about him. No hotel would claim him. We could find no identification on him. Nothing. We figured all along there were a large number of these gangsters hiding out in and around Arkansas City. What I still don't understand is how you, or rather the City Council, who had intimate dealings with many of the refineries and packing plants, never had the slightest clue there were these criminals living among us."

He leaned back in his chair, the smile still held fast on his face, but just unwilling to be as close to me. He was either trying to keep his distance or the truth from me. The troops were in temporary retreat preparing for a counterattack.

"You forget it was the Depression. The city struggled financially. Oh, the refineries and other large businesses were still doing well. However, the drop in the agricultural economy lessened our tax revenue and basic services, such as the police and fire department who were on the verge of needing downsizing in order to survive. Some businesses offered loans in order to maintain these services as well as providing us with rather inexpensive labor. If these men were criminals from up north, we quite honestly never knew about it. I guess we just never asked. Then again, why would we? Those businesses kept us from going bankrupt. We would certainly have turned into a ghost town."

"What would you have done if you found out someone like Hickey was in town and not simply biding his time but actively committing crimes around these parts?"

My face was blank. His was blanker.

"I would have put him down like a rabid dog."

The man was far too serious for this to have been a

way to put me off. I sensed a reality to his comment, a recollection to a moment in either his or Childers' office when they discussed how they lost control of a dangerous Chicago gangster and needed to do something. Yet they never got around to it. Hickey managed to escape but came back to challenge me. I could never understand why he would do that.

As kids, we were more friends than rivals. Perhaps he, too, wanted out of the Market Street Gang and wanted a better life for himself. Then again, I doubted that and decided he was not jealous of me for the life I managed to create for myself. Maybe it wasn't anger or jealousy. Maybe he was just crazy.

I advised Hallett I greatly appreciated his information, and I believed I had the makings of a series of articles. I respectfully requested to visit him again to continue the discussions as he was an invaluable resource. Since he no longer had a fencing partner, I was someone with whom he could parry. While his reflexes may have slowed down a bit, the point of his sword was still sharp.

When I got back to my room at the Elmo, I took a long, hot bath. Sitting in Hallett's office made me feel soiled in a way I never felt as a police officer. I was no longer involved in the day-to-day life of violations and lawbreakers, domestic disputes and public drunkenness. The darker side of life was nothing I witnessed frequently. For me it was all a bunch of pale memories. Hallett, though, was a reminder of a shadowy past, the last vestige of a time when criminals carried more influence than upstanding citizens. Capone was a hero to some. Perhaps many considered Hallett a savior in the more difficult times of this city.

I didn't need to worry so much about exposing him as a corrupt fraud. He could take that to the grave and beyond for all I cared. My only goal was to locate Jimmy O'Donnell.

Chapter Fifteen

Hallett's sinister smile kept growing in my eyes and in my dreams. It was as though he was aware I knew but could do nothing about his transgressions. I could write endless articles but the people of Arkansas City wouldn't believe anything about the man who had a significant influence over the community for so many years. I would be nothing more than a muckraker and a bitter former cop. This man knew the extent of his power.

I wanted to topple him like a great oak tree in a tornado, rip him up from his roots. That bitterness drew me away from the task I accepted from Mrs. O'Donnell, something far more honorable than this sniveling lawyer had ever done in his life. Yet somehow, I felt deep in my bones there was a connection with all of this to Hallett. He knew what Hickey was up to, regardless of whether he sanctioned it or not. It was just as necessary to dig up the dirt on him in order to find the O'Donnell kid. I just hoped I had a strong enough shovel.

Using my credentials as a reporter, I went to City Hall to research old business records. There were two brief mentions of Billy Skidmore, one around the time of Hallett's re-election campaign for Public Works Commissioner in 1921, and the other after his first election as councilman in 1923. Skidmore had been a scrap-iron dealer as well as a bail bondsman with a loose connection to the North Siders. There was no indication of how these two rats came together or even met. An offer of building a scrap-iron business in 1920 coincided with a generous campaign contribution. Whereas the business never saw the light of day, there was definite knowledge on Hallett's part of Chicago mobsters.

I found a contract to hire workers for the packing plant signed by Dorsey Crowe, a Chicago Alderman implicated by documents found in safe deposit boxes of the late Jack Zuta, a known fixer for the North Side gang. On the city side of the contract was the name J.D. Hallett. The connection strengthened. Gangsters funneled out of Chicago and got jobs at businesses in Kansas so far away the local law couldn't get a handle on them. By the time they got down here, their names changed making it nearly impossible to track them down.

The names kept flying off the pages: Dan McCarthy, president of the Journeyman Plumbers' Union; Barney Bertsche, notorious fixer; Judge Joseph Schulman and ex-judge Emanuel Eller, also implicated in Zuta's files. It was all there, in plain sight, in perfect English. No one ever thought to look this up, largely because they were too scared to do so. Or maybe because no one had a good reason to challenge Hallett. Hardly anyone questions people in power, especially if everyone is as happy as pigs in slop. Of course, this was all water under the bridge now. I couldn't see anything the police would be interested in bringing a case to the district attorney. But it did allow me a better footing in this rocky climb.

Night after night, there were images of gangsters killing each other, pointing their guns at me in a threatening manner, indicating they would rip my face off. That scared me more than any dreams I had before. Maybe when I was on the force I experienced the sensation of protection, a badge and a gun the only shield a beat cop disguised as a knight in shining armor would need. Now, a typewriter was my only barricade and not much good at that. Words were much slower than bullets.

I was vulnerable now, and I knew it. I was no Jake Lingle, neither a crusading journalist nor a covert racketeering operative for the Capone organization. Yet other decent and honest reporters died while fighting corruption. Don Mellett in Canton, Ohio. Jerry Buckley in Detroit. Walter Liggett in Minneapolis. I was fighting a memory but concerned about my chances, nevertheless. While Hallett appeared to be toothless, there was no telling what kind of a bite he still had.

Jerome Kirkhart, the Tulsa officer who filed the accident report on Martin Childers' death ten years ago was now a desk sergeant, somewhat like Dave Morton, only for a far bigger precinct. I floated the notion of writing a retrospective on the Depression in my community and looking for info on some of the more prominent citizens. Fortunately, he never asked me why I was so interested in an investigation into a man's death from a decade ago.

As though reading verbatim from a script, he indicated nothing out of the ordinary other than a lack of skid marks. The coroner's report was unable to determine with any certainty whether the broken neck occurred before or because of the accident. There were no other cars involved and the three witnesses either were deceased or left the area.

I remember being surprised hearing about his death within four years after Hickey's. For the life of me, I could never figure out what he was doing in Tulsa. For that matter, I was unable to determine if he was still associated with Kanotex. It might just as well have been an unfortunate accident. In order to rid myself of a nagging feeling, I played it out in my mind.

What if it had been a killing of some sort? Who would have wanted him dead and why? There was always the possibility the Organization considered him to be a weak link that needed to be eliminated. However, considering a good many wayward gangsters were supposedly working at Kanotex, among other places, and with the newly acquired information corrupt Chicago politicians fed these men to the town, the leering smile of Hallett popped before my eyes again.

Like a fire engine alarm bell going off in my head, I returned to thinking about how Jimmy O'Donnell played a part in all of this. If he were in Hickey's gang, he would have fled as fast as he could after Jake bought the farm. Might he have had anything to do with Childers' death? If so, that would have made him an associate of Hallett or perhaps the real Mob that came in after the elimination of the gangsters.

Continuing on the same train of thought, Jimmy was possibly a freelance operative for the Organization as a way to prove his mettle. In that case, he would have nothing to do with Hallett. Based on either notion, the O'Donnell kid did not appear to be on the up-and-up and certainly would not have been the squeaky-clean kid he made himself out to be.

It became more muddled as I gathered further information. I reread Mrs. Lindstrom's files over again and kept going back to old magazine articles. The limited documents at my disposal blurred the more I perused them. The only thing that kept repeating itself was Councilman John David Hallett. In the end, I realized he could keep stonewalling me until he dropped dead and would do so with that sanctimonious grin on his face. I wasn't about to go breaking into his office to search for imaginary secret files. The only viable thing to do was challenge him directly, sink into his pride and confidence, get him to admit what I already suspected, all the while knowing there was no proof of anything.

For him, the greatest torture would be admitting complicity while escaping any punishment. For me, that would point the way toward Jimmy O'Donnell. That was all I needed.

Chapter Sixteen

As I recall, every funeral I've attended was covered in a blanket of gray skies, often a smattering of rain. Perhaps it was appropriate. Maybe there wasn't supposed to be sunshine on a day we say goodbye to friends and loved ones. Sandy's was no different. I performed a sacred honor of carrying her earthly remains to a place where she would rest for eternity. Just about every employee of the *Traveler* and half the police department attended. Father David from Northside Baptist Church officiated. He spoke of Sandy in ways that never occurred to me. At first, I was surprised to learn all the things I never knew about her. Then when I considered my own life, I realized there were hidden corners within all of us. Julia Lindstrom sat beside me and at a point where I felt I was going to cry, she reached over and held my hand in solace. It bolstered me and gave me courage at my weakest moment.

It was truly my intention to take time to mourn and grieve. But it was Sandy who got me this job. She encouraged me to take on this case on behalf of Regina O'Donnell. She had full confidence and faith in me to find the truth. I wasn't about to disappoint her. There would be plenty of time for tears later.

It was never my expectation Hallett would become Shiwan Khan to my Shadow. There was, however, a certain level of annoyance at this elderly man's ability to have everything fall off him like water from a duck's back yet never appear wet. A sense of unfulfilled justice burned inside me, a passion I realized I might never quench. I was not willing to accept that.

The mood in his office was one of a sinister cavern, tunnels running amok where it was too easy to get lost for the uninitiated. Going back there, I would never be able to crack the stone fortress he set up. Where else could I go to make him feel more at ease and perhaps allow a slip of the tongue?

Trying my best to collect my thoughts, I ambled around town of a Friday evening just past nine when an elegant man in a straw boater, white striped shirt, and white linen pants held up by brown leather suspenders walked with a pristine assurance into Junior's. There was a time when I knew and understood everyone who frequented the place. Now I was out of my league. I realized this was my best and perhaps last shot.

A table for two sat near the stage where a piano player tinkled the keys and allowed some quaint melody to fill the room. Tonight, the stage was empty as was the chair opposite Hallett. He saw me as soon as I entered, even before I could see him. He stared straight at me, neither shooing me away nor inviting me over. The seat was conveniently available so I took it.

"I wouldn't have thought this would be your kind of place anymore," he said dismissively.

"I fit in just about everywhere." To be honest, I completely believed that. I looked down at his glass with pale fizzy liquid. "What is that?"

"A Tom Collins."

"Looks too lady-like for me," I responded, shaking

my head and returning the derisiveness. "I'll have an Old Grand Dad." I spoke to him as though he were a waiter hustling for tips and stared at him the same as he did at me. After a bit, he looked over my shoulder and made eye contact with the bartender who came over and took my order. A drink was in front of me in less than a minute. I smiled, not necessarily in appreciation of the drink but more because it was a first step, a small victory I could claim. The problem was we were just getting out of the starting blocks.

We sipped and stared at each other, neither one of us blinking nor giving up the ghost. I remembered a time seeing Jake Hickey with a group of toughs sitting around a table in the middle of this place, laughing and not being as delicate or quiet as the two of us were now. Times had most certainly changed.

"How much does it bother you," I asked him, "that you're not in charge anymore?" You could hear the silence shattering like glass.

"I was one member of the City Council, Baron. Just one man."

"Oh, but you were the main man. You were the one that got things done. You told me as much in your office."

"You give me too much credit."

"I don't think so." I paused for a moment and then blurted out like a dragon spitting fire. "So tell me, are you the grandfather on the hill?"

His smile was more like a smirk. It blurred the line between truth and lies.

"I wish I had been that powerful."

"I kinda think you were. By the time they elected you Commissioner of Public Works, the bigwigs ran

Abram Dutcher out of town on the rails. You had all those loosely connected sneak thieves and good time girls hanging around, unorganized, just waiting to be led by the nose like horses to a trough."

"I suppose," he started smugly, "that a bright and resourceful man could have seen the opportunities inherent in such an opening. On the other hand, that kind of management would be rather precarious for someone just entering public service. A precipitous step to take."

"Not if such a man had a background in finance and prior associations with similar individuals. More like a quiet and smooth transition if you ask me."

"Good point." He nodded respectfully. At that moment, I knew more about him than anyone else.

"And by using a respectable businessman as a cover, this resourceful man could have played both sides of the street to his advantage."

"I hope you are not referring to the late Martin Childers as respectable." I did not hear any contempt in his voice, merely a minor amount of disgust, like bile sneaking up into his throat. I raised an eyebrow in response. "Truth be told Martin Childers had two sexual assault accusations which were deferred by financial compensation. The young ladies in question were amply satisfied, and he considered the matter closed. But imagine Mr. Childers' surprise to learn others knew of his indiscretions."

Hallett continued telling stories of the successes a bright and resourceful man in public service might be able to obtain through coercion, bribery, and manipulation of the cheap labor afforded to him by confederates in Chicago who weren't much concerned about having that labor returned intact. It was almost as though I was listening to an opera with tales of love and woe, murder and madness, anything not specifically tied to him but merely his presence as a character in a fable. He was reliving the glory days of his corruption with someone who might not have fully known but was very much aware.

"What gets me is how someone like Hickey could undermine it all."

That comment was like setting a fuse. He looked as though he had drunk sour milk and his stomach was retching violently. Until now, he had sipped his drink. He suddenly grabbed the glass, downed it, and motioned toward the bartender.

"Don't you think he was a bigger annoyance for you as a police officer?" he said trying to deflect the conversation back onto me, his lips tight, and his teeth clenched.

"We had nothing on him. Didn't even know who he was and what he was doing here. The way I see it, he was tipping someone's meticulously crafted apple cart." Of course, I was referring directly to Hallett as I spoke.

He regained his composure as the bartender brought another drink for both of us. It was as if he was the man back in his office, just without the cigar and the billowing smoke. A measure of control was necessary to exert his power.

"I can see your point," he said, enunciating each word carefully. "But how would someone like that be eliminated, especially if he had not come to the attention of the Ark City Police Department?"

"He would have to be brought to our attention. Yes?"

"Exactly."

"And for something more than jay walking, I imagine." It started to make sense. "Well, he was accused of murder."

"Wasn't it more than an accusation? Wasn't he guilty?"

"We never got to find out." My statement of the facts was a lob back to his side of the court.

"Quite a shame that justice was never served."

I was the one whose stomach churned now. Hallett talking of justice sounded so foreign to my ears, like a mule denouncing stubbornness. As the thoughts and ideas swirled in my head, I no longer wanted to sit opposite this man. I reached into my pocket and pulled out a couple of dollars. Hallett reached over and gently touched my arm. I could feel a burning flush like a hot iron pressed more than just my shirt.

"This round is on me."

I stood up, stared at him until I could no longer look into his face, then turned and walked out. Just as I stepped out of the door, Dave Morton came up behind me.

"I never thought I'd see the day when you and Hallett would be out for a social drink," he said smiling.

"It wasn't social." Dave knew me well enough to tell I was dead serious. "We never made Hickey for the killing of Heather Devore, right?"

"Well, it made no sense. But it was his room and his razor. We had no one else to pin it on."

"Who else would have wanted us to take Hickey out of commission?"

Dave looked at me funny like I belonged in a straitjacket before he looked over his shoulder and realized I sat with the devil himself.

"Yeah, but Hallett wouldn't have done it. Neither would Childers."

"Right. So what about someone close to Hickey, someone who wouldn't have come under suspicion?"

"Like a kid who claimed to be Spike O'Donnell's younger brother?"

"Cute kid who Heather Devore might have trusted a little too much given the fact she wanted out of Ark City so badly and would have done just about anything to see that happen."

A sensation of nausea overcame me before my head started spinning. I calmly asked to visit with Dave in a day or two and then stumbled home. This was turning into a fast ride on a merry-go-round with no stops in sight. What started out as a search for a wayward son became an investigation into an unsolved murder from fourteen years prior. There were few folks left from that time, very little evidence, and I had no connections in the department other than Dave who I was not going to ask to jeopardize his career.

On top of that, I would have to advise Regina O'Donnell her worst fears might be true. I so desperately wanted to wake up from this dream until I realized my eyes were completely open.

Chapter Seventeen

Dave mentioned it would be better if I didn't meet him or show up at the municipal building either when he was on duty or off. I guess a strong suggestion is a recommendation but a stronger recommendation is a warning. Without coming out and saying it, he implied Chief Gray was not fond of me. By that it wasn't a reference to my column in the *Traveler* but rather the fact an aloof former policeman acting as a private dick could potentially cause trouble for his officers. I would be preaching to the choir trying to explain to Dave what I had gotten myself into and how it wasn't the honorable thing to do to back out. So I did what he asked.

He met me a block south and half a block west in front of what I would only call a jalopy. With a formal stance in his uniform, I thought he was ready to give it a ticket. He had a smile on his face as though he were the cat who swallowed the canary.

"Okay, I give." I shook my head in surrender.

"Nineteen thirty-six Pontiac three window coupé."

"I can see that."

"It's yours."

"Come again?" We sounded a bit like Burns and Allen although I wasn't sure which was which.

"Abandoned on the side of the road south end of town. No registration. The wrecker was going to bring it to J.P. Moreland's garage. I gave him ten dollars for it. Figured you were getting out from behind that typewriter a lot more and needed to stop bothering Carl Pearson for rides."

I smiled. This was the definition of friendship. "A sawbuck, huh? Well, the least I could do is buy you lunch."

"For a ten spot, I'd say that was a couple lunches at least."

Early afternoon at Daisy Mae's was plumb crowded but a couple of young guys quit their lollygagging when Sergeant Morton walked in, and we got a booth pretty darn quick. Dixie still had a bounce in her step after all these years. I imagined the hard work of running a diner was what really kept her going. That and half the police department dining there for breakfast, lunch, and dinner.

Dave pulled a folded piece of paper out of his pocket, opened it up, and smoothed out the creases. There were lines and arrows on it going from name to name. He had grown either more savvy as he got older or a touch more daft. Same could be said for me I'm certain.

"I took everything you gave me," he started, "and compared it to everything in the police files. We knew about Hickey. But there are no records on McArdle, Brennan, or the bald guy. We have nothing at all to connect them to Hallett or Childers."

"This isn't about facts, Dave. It is a good old-fashioned hunch. Hallett had a good thing going here with who knows what kind of corruption and graft. Childers was in his back pocket. He didn't have the guts or brains to run an operation like that. Gangsters from up north thought they could find protection in places like Ark City but only wound up being cheap labor. Then Hickey throws a monkey wrench into everything with his attitude and his schemes. About that time, the FBI was shutting down all the desperadoes roaming the country, and the Mob became more organized and business-like. It was almost like they were working together."

"So Hallett figures, what? Get Jake arrested on a charge he won't get out of?"

"Exactly."

"And you're saying this O'Donnell kid was a stooge planted by Hallett."

I thought about it for days after meeting with Hallett in Junior's. It was a good thing I wasn't a cop because then I would have contemplated the notion I had no evidence. I was a newspaperman, a teller of stories, a wordsmith who only dealt in tales. All I needed was a good yarn to spin.

"Well, Hallett is not going to tell you anything and Childers is dead. So where does that leave you?" Dave made his point bluntly.

Like that, the balloon was deflated, the bubble burst. All I had was a story, not even one I could print without me and the paper sued for libel.

It was like old times at Daisy Mae's, mixing it up with the regulars and talking things over with the guys. So many aspects of my life could be traced to one little greasy spoon. I dropped Dave off at the station and had the good sense to stay inside the car, giving up the notion of saying hey to a few old friends. Besides, I had a drive ahead of me up to Hackney.

I parked outside Regina O'Donnell's house until

someone dropped her off, presumably from work. The clunky door of my new car had a tinny clanging sound when I shut it, catching her by surprise. Startled at first, she smiled when she saw me. I wondered how long that smile would remain.

In a clear and precise voice without any emotion, I explained everything I learned, everything I heard, and everything I felt to be the truth, admitting there was no proof one way or the other. While she may have known and accepted her son as a criminal of some sort, to indicate I thought he was a murderer was nothing I relished. To my surprise, after I finished my speech, she nodded softly and simply. She did not hang her head. She did not cry.

"Officer Witherspoon, my late husband was a pious man. He always tried to follow in the footsteps of his Heavenly Father. He had a calling and was asked to preach in many churches and even some places you could hardly call a church. He knew young boys could be rambunctious, but he expected them to be respectful and industrious. He would be rolling in agony in his grave at the thought of his youngest son having broken the fifth and sixth commandments. All I have left is my name, which is not much to speak of, but it is something. When I go to my maker, I want it to be free of any stain against it."

It was all I could do to keep the tears from welling up in my eyes. It had been a long time since I encountered anyone as honorable as her. It was likely it would be longer before I came across one such as her again.

"This young woman, did she have a family?"

"Nothing to speak of. But she had—" I found

myself getting choked up.

"What?"

"She had a dream for a better life than the one she was living."

"And he took that away from her."

All I could do was nod. I walked slowly back to my car thinking of Heather Devore. Like any other flapper or floozy, she ran with the big boys who had gin and guns and fast cars and very little hope for a long life. Until the day she decided she wanted something better than "Crazy" Jake Hickey. I second-guessed myself wondering if I could have been the one to save her and pull her out of the mire. Then I remembered how tall and mighty Hallett was at the time. It just seemed like her fate was sealed. She was merely a pawn, but she deserved more, maybe vengeance or justice. I couldn't tell anymore which was which. Maybe I never knew. To do it, however, I still needed to find Jimmy O'Donnell. At this point, I was not any closer and had no viable leads.

That is, until I got back the offices of the *Ark City Traveler.*

"Sit yourself down, sonny," Julia Lindstrom bellowed in a most unbecoming fashion. "I've got some news for you."

Chapter Eighteen

It was back in 1938 and Sandy Clevenger helped me research multiple killers like the Ripper in London and Fritz Haarmann, the Butcher of Hanover. These were monsters I was only vaguely aware of and would have been grateful not to learn of them in the first place. I was no longer on the Wichita killing case but my curiosity and anger got the better of me. I stuck with it like a hound dog chasing a wild rabbit probably because I was resentful of the initial reason they called me in to consult. It was simply for the Wichita Police Department to save face.

We finally ran out of options in terms of newspaper clippings, and Sandy admitted we needed the help of Mrs. Julia Lindstrom. She was still the chief librarian and looked every bit the part. At the time, she was rather squeamish about such matters. She handed us the books she was able to find on the subject as though some strange disease infected them. I am not certain what transpired in the past ten years, but she embraced the sinister and evil now as though it was a wild stallion, and she was a bronco buster.

"These old files are absolutely amazing," she gushed. "I think I found something worthwhile." Her enthusiasm was infectious. It reminded me of my time with Sandy. "There were numerous articles in the Jackson Sentinel out of Maquoketa, Iowa about Sheriff

Pete Harper's continual run-ins with a kid named either O'Donnell or O'Donoghue. Unfortunately, the articles used both names lending to a bit of confusion as to the true identity of this rascal. The encounters were about fighting, possession of a weapon, vagrancy, even spitting on the sidewalk."

Apparently these were mostly minor charges over a seven or eight month period back in late 1935 and early 1936. Then, at one point in March of 1936, a trio of masked men got into a shoot-out with Sheriff Harper while trying to rob the First National Bank right on Main St. in broad daylight. They eventually got away, but onlookers were certain one of the men appeared shot in the leg. Eyewitness description indicated the leader, a short slender man, was likely the O'Donnell or O'Donoghue boy but there was no positive identification. It was the closest thing we had to a lead in a long time.

"Great," I blurted out. "I wonder if this Harper is in town. He might still be a cop, but even if he isn't, he might be able to remember something."

She apologetically handed me a clipping from late 1942 indicating the former Sheriff of Jackson County, Iowa, Peter D. Harper, died during the Battle of Guadalcanal. I shook my head in defeat. I was back to where I started.

"May I ask why you got my hopes up so high if you knew this was a dead end?" I pondered, a bit of frustration leaking out of me. It felt like I simply dug an even bigger hole for myself. Mrs. Lindstrom wagged an admonishing finger in my direction.

"There's a rhyme to the reason. His widow, Sally, moved here to Ark City in early 1943. She had a couple of cousins and decided to be close to them."

"You don't say."

"I do say. You know that little place on East Madison, La Bella Vita?"

"Yeah, an Italian restaurant, isn't it?"

"Exactly. It's hers."

All of this was a long shot. The fact a punk kid named O'Donnell or O'Donoghue harassed a sheriff in Iowa didn't mean it was the same O'Donnell who was part of Jake Hickey's gang. On top of that, a lawman's widow might not be as aware of his cases nor even remember one from over a decade ago. At this point, it was all I had. That and an appetite for pasta with clam sauce. First, I had to visit a lady in need.

I can't remember the last time I spent any time inside the Ark City Police Department in the Municipal Building. The word was Chief Gray was not very keen to see me around for any reason. However, I had to take my chances for a special cause. Late that afternoon, I walked in and through the hallways with my head held up in pride. I wasn't counting on Dave bailing me out, so to speak. The memories in the building were rich and varied. I spent more time as a cop than anything else in my life. My entire identity, whatever it might have been, was inside these walls. Names flew around my head like characters in a picture show, their faces as bright and vivid as though I had just seen them that day. The place and the job made me who I was.

I passed Clifford Smiley who was surprisingly happy to see me. Cliff worked nights as did I early in my career. He never gave a second thought to my scarred face and felt I was on my way to being the next chief of police.

"How have you been, cowboy?" he uttered using the most offbeat nickname I've ever had.

"Well, no one is shooting at me for anything I've written."

"You're missed around here. You know that?"

"I do now." I slapped him on the shoulder and kept walking, not wanting to show how choked up it made me feel.

Linda Kuchenberg was still behind the switchboard, ever diligent and ever proud of her work. She was the one who continuously reached out to Eliot Ness when he was the Public Safety Director in Cleveland, and with a smooth and professional voice, let him believe I was someone important enough to talk with. She backed me up when I had so little to go on largely because she trusted me to work things out. I stood there at her console until she looked up. It wasn't a sagging face she saw as much as a welcoming friend.

"When was the last time you had lunch at Daisy Mae's?" I asked with a smile plastered across my face like the Cheshire Cat.

"Yesterday." She smiled in response. "But I can't remember the last time I had lunch there with you." Her smile was even bigger.

She wound up getting the open-faced hot turkey sandwich while I uncharacteristically ate a BLT. Two ice teas completed our dainty meal. Just two old friends passing time over the midday meal and reminiscing about days gone by.

"How are you doing?" I asked plainly.

"I've lost my best friend. I've lost my sister."

My heart ached for her. Neither one ever married but no one who knew them would have dared called them "old maids." They were strong and feisty and didn't suffer fools gladly. They were a match for any policeman in any precinct in any city. I never knew much about their parents or upbringing but it was evident some strength of character had been instilled at an early age. I was envious but only because it took me a lot longer to get to such a point. Every Sunday night they got together for dinner; a simple tradition carried over from their youth. It wasn't about the food but more the communion of two ladies fighting hard in a man's world and proving they belonged. The only bond remaining was one of emotion and memory.

A brief moment occurred back in 1918 when I felt something quite similar. The only person who was truly a friend, someone almost like a brother I never had, died while saving me from an exploding German shell. Baron Witherspoon gave his life to save mine. Maybe it was intentional or as likely a desperate act at an uncertain moment. Whatever the case, I took his identity. In the process, it kept his name alive and something people could be proud of. Eric Kimble died the same day as Baron Witherspoon was reborn.

"What are your plans?"

"Remember Gary?"

"Your younger brother, right?"

"Yeah."

"Met him for the first time at the funeral. Nice guy."

"He and his wife got a pretty big house in Joplin. Seems emptier now after their two daughters got hitched. He invited me to live with them."

"You figure on moving?" I thought I heard myself choking up a second time that day. It hadn't happened often, but I started to get used to it more and more.

"Nothing holding me here."

"These boys in blue are going to miss you."

"They'll get along just fine." She paused knowingly. "And so will you."

I started to feel like a molting chicken, people like feathers just falling off and away from me. Chief Taylor. Mrs. McGuire. Chief Richardson. Miss Banister. Marcus Hayes. Evan Cobb. Sandy Clevenger. Now Linda Kuchenberg. It was like I stood in the middle of a corn field while a tornado passed through, whisking away every ear of corn in sight, leaving me within a barren desert. All I knew and found comfort in was gone. Dave Morton was still around as was Dr. Brenz. Everyone else who had ever been important to me was either out of the area or dead. I was a sole survivor clinging on to an invisible life raft in a swirling ocean. I wondered when the seas would ever grow calm again.

I had nothing that was all so important to live for, somewhat like Karla Frankl, and yet no one was getting rid of me. The only thing in the front of my mind was Heather Devore and finding some kind of justice for her. It probably wasn't enough to be a reason to live. At the moment, I couldn't think of anything better.

Chapter Nineteen

La Bella Vita meant "The Good Life" in Italian. From what little I could remember from my years in Chicago, all the South Siders sought the good life and mostly at the expense of the Irish North Siders. I never encountered any Italian soldiers either in the Great War or in the recent war. All I knew was pasta, pizza, and a few words you weren't supposed to say in church.

The thing that struck me the most was the name Sally Harper didn't sound really Italian to me. Her cousins, Rosa DeFrancesco and Anna Pascuale, must have come from a different part of the family. I guess if I knew her maiden name it might make sense getting married to a non-Italian like Pete Harper. At this point, I wasn't overly concerned about ethnic origins. I needed to know if her late husband had any files on the kid that wreaked havoc in his town all those years ago.

The place was located on East Madison, just on the other side of the Walnut River and near the intersection of Pin Oak Drive. It was a two-story white clapboard house with a porch wrapped around about three quarters of the way. It looked like it could do with a fresh coat of paint but overall was not in any state of disrepair. As it was devoid of much landscaping, it appeared to be less of a house and more of a business. A gravel area served as a parking lot. The only sign was above the door. It appeared hand painted in a classic script in a schoolhouse red. A warm glow came from inside through the window on the heavy oak door creating a shimmer on the elegant silk curtains. Initially from the road, it appeared rustic with a quaint country charm. Getting closer made you feel like you were visiting family.

Perhaps Saturday night was not the most ideal time. With half a dozen cars parked in an orderly fashion, the sound of voices and the clanking of dishes filled my ears as I walked in, a bell above the door announcing my entrance. A woman with very black hair and bright red lipstick came from seemingly out of nowhere. She wore a white blouse and tan slacks covered by a decorative apron. She took a quick look at me, walked past, looked into the main room, and then back over her shoulder.

"Should be about ten, fifteen minutes, if you don't mind waiting." She nodded in the direction of one of two chairs in a small alcove in the foyer. I nodded in return and sat down patiently as though I were in a church.

I couldn't make out any of the conversation inside but the aromas coming from the interior room made me realize this place might give Daisy Mae's a run for their money, not that I would ever admit it to Dixie. It was odd I only heard of this place once in a while and none of the other policeman I worked with even mentioned it. From all appearances, it was a thriving business. My guess was Sally Harper threw herself into this body and soul after her husband died in the war.

A dark complexioned couple in their forties came from the main room. He adjusted his tie and she fixed her hair in the mirror on the wall just to the side of the main door before walking out into the night. The dark haired woman from before stood in the doorway and motioned me in with a nod of her head.

The menu was not much more than a piece of cardboard on which was hand-written three entrees and a notification the dinners were served with a salad and an Italian bread called focaccia, something I never encountered before. I looked around and was able to see all the available meals on the plates of the folks around me. There were also small glasses that appeared filled with wine. I wasn't sure it was the warmth from the kitchen or a feeling of liveliness coursing through me. I almost forgot the reason I was there.

The big boned woman suddenly appeared over my shoulder. She had on a light pink blouse with a white collar, tan slacks, and another of those decorative aprons with the name SALLY stitched on it just over her heart. She looked down at me as I looked up. Her eyes squinted as though she were having difficulty seeing me through the candlelight in the darkened room.

"You know what you want?" she asked plainly.

"What would you recommend?" I smiled. I didn't get a smile back in return.

"Spaghetti and meatballs." She said nothing further to enhance her comment.

"Sure. Okay."

She grabbed the cardboard menu and started to walk off before turning back.

"You want wine with that?"

"Yes, please." The smile remained squarely on my face. I thought her lack of response was due to my appearance although she did not impress me as the type to back down from anything. Perhaps she knew who I was, either as a former policeman or a newspaper writer. For the life of me, I couldn't figure what made her so cold, unless that was how she acted around all strangers.

I kept looking around like a happy-go-lucky child reveling in this new atmosphere. For a while, it didn't feel like I was in Arkansas City or Wichita or anywhere in Kansas. Maybe a bigger city. Maybe New York or Chicago. Just a mile or so out of town, and I felt like this was an entire world away. Even though it was an appealing notion, it was also uncomfortable in some way. I realized I wasn't always going to wind up in familiar places. The journey into an unknown past was as concerning as reliving old dreams.

Like a ballerina, Sally came by with a tray that held a plate of salad, a carrier with oil and vinegar cruets, and a basket of bread that was warm to the touch. Less than thirty seconds later, she dropped off a small carafe and a short red glass. The greens of the salad were crisp as though plucked from the ground just a moment earlier. The tomatoes burst in my mouth like a flood, a kind of sweetness I never knew existed before. An element that was herbal, raw, and earthy came out as I chewed the bread. The wine tasted of the fruits of the Garden of Eden. A meal seduced me in a way I never experienced before. It was something I wanted to get used to.

As soon as my salad plate was empty, Sally brought a bowl of spaghetti with two large meatballs, the whole thing covered with a thick rich sauce. Everything smelled fresh as though made especially for me. I ate slowly, as much to savor these new delights as to allow all the other diners to finish their meal and depart. Somehow, I had shaken off of this culinary reverie to remind myself I was on a mission of a greater calling.

One young couple remained, sitting at a table in the rear near a window. They sipped wine while they held hands. I could fully understand how the dim lights and candles on the table leant this place a romantic atmosphere. It was only when I wiped my mouth with my napkin and laid it gently on the table that Sally came by.

"Everything okay?" she asked, not expecting anything to the contrary.

"Just fine. I'm quite impressed."

She started to take the empty bowl but then stopped to look at me, a kind of recognition coming over her face.

"You're the cop, aren't you?" It appeared she did recognize me after all. I hoped that wasn't a bad thing.

"I used to be. I write a column for the *Traveler* now."

"Oh, yeah. So you gonna write about this place?"

I smiled again, trying to be gracious knowing I would disappoint her with my answer.

"I'd certainly like to but unfortunately I don't write that kind of column. I write about my experiences as a cop, about crime. I heard your late husband was a lawman."

She swallowed whatever smile she might have been holding back. The strange thing was it looked more as though I angered her rather than brought back painful memories. She grabbed the bowl and the empty carafe and walked away brusquely. In a short span of time, she came back and placed the bill roughly on the table.

"You can leave your money at the table. And don't worry about leaving no tip."

She turned sharply.

"Mrs. Harper," I said, my voice like a foot stomping down on the floor, "I need your help. A woman asked me to find her son. I think your husband encountered him many years ago. Back in Iowa."

"That's in the past. It is buried with him." Her face was smooth and cold. No heat, no emotion, nothing to indicate how she felt other than being drawn back to a possible dark past by my question. I could completely understand how that was. There were many hidden rooms in my shrouded dreams but none I wished to enter. I was desperate and her response made me realize she would be the key.

I put a dollar bill on the table even though she indicated I shouldn't tip her. For now, I wasn't going to push the matter. I had no guarantee she would know or remember anything that could point me in the right direction, but she was all there was at this time. While I needed to back away, I couldn't back down. One woman lost her husband; the other lost a son. It wasn't fair to weigh them in the balance. I could only hope one might help the other.

Chapter Twenty

Over the course of the next several weeks, I learned to enjoy several Italian delicacies: linguine with white clam sauce, stuffed manicotti, lasagna, osso buco. I probably gained close to ten pounds from eating more than I typically did. Not even the hamburgers and chili at Daisy Mae's had been able to do that. Sally Harper served as the waitress each time I went. She was never rude or condescending, but did appear slightly annoyed. She didn't return any of my smiles. As a matter of fact, very few words passed between us. I gave her no reason to refuse me service. I never made any further inquiries or brought up the subject of her late husband. Nevertheless, she knew I was looking for answers.

At the same time, my column was a multipart series of the lesser-known lawmen that fought gangsters in the mid 1930s. As the FBI developed, local lawmen stood up against the men and, in the case of Bonnie Parker, women who ran wild throughout the country. Mrs. Lindstrom helped me find some fascinating stories of sheriffs and constables from Nebraska, Missouri, Indiana, and Arkansas. Among those I featured prominently was Sheriff Pete Harper of Jackson County, Iowa. I got a telegram from Mr. Stauffer in praise of my writing and commented on a possible nomination for a Pulitzer Prize. The regulars at Daisy Mae's gave me a thumbs up on my insights. Dixie named a sandwich after me. The Baron was a thick medium rare hot roast beef sandwich with melted Swiss cheese and spicy dill pickles served on rye bread. Despite the professional commentary, the local praise, and the culinary fame, none of the articles were able to secure Mrs. Harper's attention.

Small farms started the fall harvest. Root vegetables, like beets, turnips, and carrots, along with broccoli, cabbage, and cauliflower showed up in stores and at the weekly Saturday Farmer's Market. The change of the season brought to my mind the passage of time. Planting and harvesting were all about renewal and growth yet nothing felt renewed within me, no growth other than more gray hairs and clouded memories, eyes that needed more sleep than was possible to have. I grew tired and became weary as I wondered where this O'Donnell kid might be. I was utterly incapable of honoring a pledge to an even more tired and weary mother. I felt more and more like a failure.

To her credit, Regina O'Donnell never reached out to me or pressed me for any kind of a progress report. She knew I understood her fully and was aware of my limitations. Her faith guided her, and in some small way, it guided me as well.

It was shortly before Thanksgiving. Mrs. Lindstrom offered to share her meager meal with me because neither of us would be sharing our limited blessings with anyone else. I offered to buy whatever food she requested if she would prepare it, knowing full well I was good for a can of beans and maybe a box of Jiffy mix. It was while I was in Vrendenburg's Grocery I ran into Sally Harper. She carried a wooden crate filled with boxes of dry pasta and cans of tomato sauce. To me it appeared as though she were struggling with her load. I discovered otherwise as I went to what I thought was her aid.

"I can manage," she said curtly.

"I didn't think you couldn't," I responded with a smile. "I was just trying to be courteous."

Maybe the icy stare started to melt but only somewhat. She allowed me to walk alongside her, each of us carrying our respective boxes with food and supplies. While mine definitely appeared to contain traditional Thanksgiving fare, hers did not. She noticed my inquiring glance but said nothing in response.

"A different kind of Thanksgiving meal, huh?" I chided.

"I do not eat a Thanksgiving meal. Not since Pete died."

It finally dawned on me she still mourned his passing. Anything that reminded her of him created a profound sadness. I could only guess she ran a roadside restaurant and worked long hours to ward off stray reminders of her life before. The strength and discipline to do that was incredible. It was something I could easily relate to, having returned from a trip to Chicago after a thirty-year absence. I had been Eric Kimble. Roaming around the North Side brought images to my mind of a young man on the verge of a wholly different life. Were it not for the recommendation of Dion O'Banion, the toughest of the micks, my end would have come in gang warfare over a few square miles of what we called "territory" that contained illegal rotgut booze. It would have been an unglamorous death. Either that or sent far away to Kansas to hide out. Fate played out exactly as it had been destined. The journey was slightly different.

"I am sorry for any heartache I might have caused." Mine was the voice of a penitent sinner in confessional with a parish priest. "It was never my intention to bring sorrow into your life. I made a promise to a grieving mother. I'm only trying to fulfill that promise."

We got up to the front counter and the clerk rang up her purchases. She pulled out her purse and made her payment. She started to grab the box but stopped and turned back toward me.

"You didn't bring any sorrow into my life that hadn't already been there before. Look, things have been difficult. Not just since Pete's death but before. We had to make a lot of sacrifices. And you get to a point where you ask yourself when is it going to be your time. When do I get my reward? Sometimes it seems like it is never going to happen. That is where the sorrow comes from."

I couldn't argue with her because I felt the same way. You think it is going to be tomorrow or the next day or the next. Time passes. Years pass. Your life winds up resembling dirty bath water that remains in the tub.

"I'm sorry for this mother. I really am. But I can't help her. So she's going to have just go on grieving. Like the rest of us."

With that, Sally Harper walked out, a firm stride carrying her farther away, as though I might not ever encounter her again even in our small community. Jake Hickey did not face a judge or a jury of his peers. Neither did Natalie Dixon nor Ronnie Roché. The kind of sentence Eihann Hammerschmidt received was not enough for the harm he caused. Ralph Houseman and the fake agent Burke were just more examples of what I now had to consider failures in my life. The image of justice, a blindfolded woman with a sword in one hand and scales in another, mocked my dreams with a sinister smile on her face. However close I might approach the concepts of Law and Order, the Chaos of the world would snatch any satisfaction from me.

Regina O'Donnell thought enough of me and my career as a police officer to entrust me with a solemn task. While it may have seemed like an insurmountable obstacle, there was information and resources readily available. The truth, near as it might have appeared, now slipped through my fingers, perhaps to be lost in the desert sands of time.

A cold blast of early winter came through the first week of December. It did not chill me as much as the dawning realization I would wind up disappointing a woman who had even less in life. The shorter days made me feel more tired. I slept longer, dreamed more, and started to grow haunted by reminders of things I had long since forgotten. I rewrote wire service articles about various crimes throughout the country, having become too lazy from being overly tired—nothing motivated me. I just didn't care anymore.

It wasn't until after the first of the year, early January of 1949, I got a call at the office from John David Hallett, the former councilman of Arkansas City, Kansas. He referenced a desire to go to the upcoming inauguration of Harry S. Truman on account of his Midwestern roots. I took it all for what it was worth, never encouraging the discussion. His bloated attitude bored me. At the very least that meant he had no more power over me.

"I'm old, and I'm tired, Baron. I'd like to meet my maker with a clear conscience." I couldn't tell if this was more politically guided talk or a desire to confess his own sins. All I could do was to let him continue the palaver. "Why don't you stop by my office later this evening for a brandy? We'll reminisce about the good old days." A snort and a chuckle came from the other end of the line. Whether there would be any semblance of the truth was yet to be determined.

Chapter Twenty-One

In winter, it is typical to feel warmer when you enter a building from the chill outside. However, anything associated with Hallett remained cold, a frigid air that stopped everything in its tracks. It wasn't nearly as appealing as anything Mr. Birdseye created. The main door to the Hallett Law Offices was open. As usual, the lack of a receptionist was inconsequential. Missing was the ever present smoke from his ominous cigar, the perverse symbol of his authority and dominance over individuals deemed lesser in his eyes. In its place was the smell of stagnation, as though that already foul smelling cigar burned like a brush fire for days and the ground beneath it scorched to cinders. It was the odor of decay.

What was readily apparent from my entering his inner office was the former councilman was dead. The smoldering cigar was in the oversized glass ashtray. Hallett's arms hung loosely by his side and his head had fallen back like it lost the power to remain alert and upright. In approaching the desk, I saw a look of surprise as though the black robed figure with the long scythe made an unexpected appearance. I always thought nothing could surprise Hallett, not even Death.

As a former policeman, my first instincts were of homicide. This scene was nothing like how we found Carl Bottomley back in '35 on a dusty county road outside of town. There were no stab wounds or dried blood. It was obvious there was not a shooting by looking at his head or chest area, the usual places for a homicide. I did not see any beverage on the desk so poisoning was not a likely possibility. Regrettably, old age and a profligate life caught up with him and squeezed his heart until it just plain stopped.

I quickly perused the rest of the desk, the waste basket, and anything immediately within my field of vision. The police would be involved shortly. I wanted to honestly admit to not rummaging through the files or disturbing the scene in any deliberate manner. Whatever Hallett wished to "confess" was to be verbal and not as a written document. He was far too clever to leave a permanent record behind of his indiscretions and thus sully his reputation and legacy. Now it finally appeared I was at a brick wall, unable to proceed any further into this inquiry for Mrs. O'Donnell.

Using my handkerchief, I picked up the phone. I had the slightest sense of being a criminal.

"This is Baron Witherspoon. I'm over at Hallett's law office on Main St. Mr. Hallett appears to be deceased. You better send someone over. And don't worry. I'll be here." It was the obvious thing to say.

Someone must have contacted Sergeant Morton because he appeared less than five minutes after the two patrolmen arrived. Dave wore a white shirt and work pants that were hastily thrown on. He might have worked a long shift and was asleep for all I knew. He looked at me like Hardy used to look at Laurel bemoaning another fine mess I had gotten myself into.

Dr. Brenz came as Dave guided the patrolmen through a review of the office. One of them took the outer room while the other worked with Dave looking through file cabinets and finally the desk drawer. I stood in a corner, erect and silent, my face twitching in time with a Sousa march, initially unaware of how the stress of the situation affected my many scars. Dave looked down into the desk drawer, then up at me, and finally to Dr. Brenz.

"Doctie, come take a look at this."

Dr. Brenz took out his own handkerchief and removed an empty hypodermic needle. He sniffed at the tip and then placed it gently down on the desk. He examined Hallett, opening his eyes, feeling his forehead, and then strangely rubbing his fingertips together. He also reached under one of Hallett's arms.

"Poison?" Dave asked.

"No. I don't think so. Although he appears to have been distressed and there is a trace of perspiration on his forehead and armpits." He looked over to me. "Is this the way you found him?"

"Exactly."

"When was the last time you saw him or spoke to him?"

"He called me about two hours ago."

"How did he sound?"

"Like his usual malicious self." I know you are not supposed to speak ill of the dead but I think in this case Hallett would have appreciated the description.

"Did he have any illnesses you know of?" Dave asked Brenz.

"I wasn't his physician. I believe he was seeing Dr. George Bartlett up in Winfield."

"Why would he go all the way up there for a check-up?" I pondered. "Unless he didn't care for you,

Doctie, or he had something to hide." That was my former police self speaking up, from a time when Chief Richardson entrusted me to use whatever means I could to find a demented killer. That was the expectation back then. Now it was just the mind of a fact-finding reporter.

They brought Hallett's body, like so may I had seen before him who died under suspicious circumstances, to the offices of Dr. Brenz in his capacity as medical examiner. Sergeant Morton requested I accompany him and the patrolmen to the Arkansas City Police Department to provide a statement. It was a strange feeling walking into the building on the other side of law enforcement, a regular Joe who, though not a suspect, was there for questioning. I knew the drill, and I didn't have much to hide.

So as not to appear as someone provided with special treatment, I sat opposite Dave at his big desk just outside Chief Gray's office. He had the standard form we used to take witnesses statements. I caught myself saying "we" in my mind as though I were still part of the fraternal order of law enforcement officers. Perhaps part of me would never stop being a cop much in the same way we would always think of Hallett as a councilman. I made sure to respond to Dave as directly and honestly as possible without coloring my comments or elaborating on anything I knew he would deem unnecessary.

"I know you met with him in his office before," Dave started, "and of course, I saw you with him at Junior's. What was tonight all about?"

"He called me with some malarkey about wanting

to clear his conscience before going to his maker."

"Talk it out."

"What?"

"Like we used to."

Dave gave me the opportunity to assist in this case, and perhaps my own research into Jimmy O'Donnell, by using the skills from the past. For the moment, Chief Gray wasn't there and didn't have a say in the matter. Like any good cop, Dave employed all his best resources. I just happened to be one of them.

"I took the comment to be the guff. Just another way to string me along."

"But he never talked about dying before."

"No, he didn't. Even if he were sick, he certainly wouldn't have shared that with me. I was like a ball of yarn, and he was a feral cat toying with me. By the same token, I can't see this as being murder. Even if it was poison, what killer would just leave the hypodermic there and allow us to find it?"

"And of course, what victim would allow himself to be injected?"

"So what are you thinking?" I asked Dave.

"I don't know. Suicide?" I shrugged my shoulders at his suggestion.

"You're going to have to get a hold of this Dr. Bartlett," I said, deferring all the lawful responsibility to the proper authorities. Whereas I would have liked to interject further and speculate, I didn't want either one of us getting into a mess we couldn't get out of.

I didn't have a problem sleeping that night. No dreams, no demons, no worries. Of course, a minor twitch here and there. Other than being unable to fulfill my promise to Mrs. O'Donnell, and in some small way,

Heather Devore, the issues of this mysterious death did not fall into my circle of responsibility. At some point, it would afford me the opportunity for several columns, including a glowing tribute to a man that devoted himself to public service for our city, or some other tripe I could come up with that would sell copy.

After a hearty breakfast at Daisy Mae's, I ambled over to visit with Dr. Brenz. He wasn't as much of a stickler for propriety Dave had to be. The unfortunate thing was there had been no definitive answer. From all appearances, Hallett died of a heart attack. However, Doctie found several injection marks on his arms indicating prior use of the hypodermic needle. Having never exhibited signs of narcotic intoxication, Doctie could only assume some form of medication from which he might have accidentally overdosed. Then again, considering the amount of marks on his arm, it was difficult to imagine someone as intelligent and in control taking too much of a required medication. This was when Dave's suggestion came back to mind.

After Dave arrived, somewhat surprised to see me there, Dr. Brenz delivered the preliminary report. We agreed a visit to Dr. Bartlett in Winfield was necessary. Doctie commented on a matter of medical ethics.

"He may decline to speak with you as a matter of his Hippocratic Oath."

"Doctors do have a responsibility to their patients," Dave acknowledged. "This one is dead." Dave was determined to get an answer. After all, he wasn't willing to allow a high profile member of the community to pass away under such circumstances and provide fodder for muckraking journalists.

We drove in silence up to Winfield along the same

county road where George McAllister and the fake agent Burke died. From lack of use, weeds grew in the ruts and large divots caused the car to bounce unbearably. Maybe this was Dave's way of reminding me why I retired, and why I should not be involved in such cases. If that were true, I wasn't sure whether to thank him or tell him to mind his own business.

Dave called the doctor's office prior to our departure and found out he was making rounds at William Newton Hospital. The three-story brick building stood like a massive ocean liner in the middle of the plains. The receptionist guided us to where we could find Dr. Bartlett.

"Gentlemen," he started after Dave showed him his credentials, "you do realize there is a certain confidentiality between a physician and his patient."

"Certainly," Dave responded professionally, having acquired a calmness and control that had been lacking in the past. "However, this patient is deceased, and his passing coming under what we consider questionable circumstances. Additionally, he has no living relatives or offspring, his estate is intestacy, and this is largely a case of *ad vitam aut culpam*, allowing that your, shall we say, commission as his doctor died with him." I always thought Dave wanted to be the next chief of police in Ark City. With this dissertation, it appeared he was bucking to be the next Clarence Darrow.

Dr. Bartlett, for all of his professional ethics, realized he would need to acquiesce. The next item on his agenda might be a subpoena to testify before a Grand Jury. That would not only be time consuming but might place a black mark against the good doctor simply by his attendance at such an investigation.

"Mr. Hallett became diabetic in the late 1920s. He came to me as a specialist after learning I had done work with glycemic control."

"You mean insulin?" I questioned, having done my own research to make sure Dave was equally impressed.

"Exactly. By the judicious use of insulin therapy and a highly managed diet, Mr. Hallett was able to maintain good health. However—" His voice dropped off. Dave felt so close to the answer he needed to prod Dr. Bartlett to get to it.

"What happened?"

"He was recently diagnosed with cancer of the lungs. Given his age and already compromised health, he had limited time."

"Doctor, can you describe what occurs when an excess of insulin is introduced into the bloodstream?" Dave and I both thought the same thing. I just happened to be the one to ask.

"The individual would become disoriented, nervous and shaky, perhaps feeling hungry. They would be sweating profusely before becoming drowsy and perhaps unconscious. Without immediate medical attention, they would lapse into a coma and die."

There was nothing either of us needed to say on the way back to Ark City. Hallett held all the cards and would carry his secrets with him to the grave. After inviting me to what he called a discussion of the past, he injected himself with an overdose of insulin and departed this world. Perhaps he wanted to leave a smile on his face as a final indignity to me when I found him. I was angrier than I had ever been in my life.

Chapter Twenty-Two

I was a failure. A desperate woman sought my assistance based on my professional experience in locating her missing son. I dug as deep and as hard as I could into the past, part of which was my own. While I discovered some names and a few stories, this kid was more like a ghost. Perhaps he was dead, and I was merely chasing a dream.

When I left the police department, I initially felt forced out of the warmth of familiarity, the comfort of something I had done for so long, and into a desperate unknown. Sandy Clevenger guided me into the next chapter of my life. I could settle down into a new career for perhaps ten, fifteen, maybe twenty years and become the elder statesman of regional journalism, no one as important as Mr. Stauffer but someone remembered as a storyteller of note.

These days I would go into the office and type up an article as though I were a machine at one of the refineries. It was getting so anyone following me around could figure out what I would be doing at any single moment given how exact my life had become. Waking, getting to the office, taking lunch, going home, listening to the radio, maybe reading the paper or doing a crossword puzzle, sleeping. Every moment as precise and ordered as the day before. Long walks on the weekends, coming across familiar places, dredging up memories that no longer exerted any influence on me because I had grown numb to them. In my mind, I was just as dead as young Jimmy O'Donnell must certainly be.

I felt bad avoiding Regina O'Donnell but nothing I could do or say other than to apologize and admit I had gotten in way over my head was all that was left. My jalopy sat in the alley of the Elmo collecting dust. Such a gracious present from Dave Morton going to waste. I had nowhere to go and no rush to get there.

It was just before the start of spring when I encountered Sally Harper while I was shopping for groceries. She appeared different, perhaps more of a bounce in her step, as though the flowers in bloom warmed her heart. She actually smiled when she saw me.

"What's the matter? You don't like my food anymore?" I could sense no anger behind her words, just a kind of friendly camaraderie. My face could not hide the somber cloud I languished behind.

"Work has kept me rather busy."

"Yeah, I can tell." I looked at her with a question mark on my face. "You've gone from three columns a week to five." I never knew she was an avid follower of mine.

"Circulation has increased although I'm not taking any credit for it." My smile was lukewarm and forced.

An awkward silence hung around for a bit. It was as though she tried to engage in a conversation with me but didn't know what to say, not really knowing me all that well other than a writer for a newspaper who was once a policeman and a guy who pressured her to open up about her own past.

"Did you ever find what you were looking for?" she asked, the words coming in muffled pieces.

"How's that?"

"You know, back when you were asking…"

"Oh, yeah," I interrupted, not intent on her feeling uncomfortable talking about her deceased husband. "No. I didn't. I…stopped looking."

"Well, maybe I can help." The comment caught me completely off guard. As far as I knew, she was a dead end just as most of this investigation had been. "Look, why don't you come on by the restaurant tonight. At nine."

"Don't you close at nine?"

"Yeah." This time she forced the smile as though whatever discussion we had would be uncomfortable. Then I considered she would potentially allow me to see that pain and was touched she felt she could trust me. A sliver of light appeared through a crack in a window.

When I showed up at nine, the last customers were leaving and the light over the door was off. I wondered if she still wanted me to visit. The scent of flowers overcame me as I approached the door, giving me a warm feeling. That was followed by a shudder thinking how there would be the possibility of digging deeper into the past and the noxious odor of decay.

I knocked quietly on the doorjamb until the door opened. Through the screen, blanketed by the darkness of the foyer, Sally Harper stood as a spectral figure, ready to take my hand and walk me on a journey into the unknown. The dining room had one table set up with a lit candle. Two bowls, two glasses, and a carafe awaited us.

"It's just spaghetti and meat sauce. I hope you don't mind."

She was very self-effacing, a side of her I had not yet seen. Perhaps she clammed up after I first accosted her to tell her of my needs and took away the chance for me to see who she really was. It brought to mind my sense of failure all over again. My social clumsiness influenced a great deal of my life up until this moment.

I held the chair for her and then took my place across from her. She spoke silently, a prayer I believe, and then genuflected. She looked up at me as an invitation to start eating. We didn't speak at all during the meal. I slurped spaghetti but tried to keep from doing so in order not to appear uncivilized. She refilled my wine glass, and we looked at each other once or twice. I could hear crickets chirping outside, a strong wind blow through the trees, and my own belabored breaths. Though I enjoyed this dish as all the others I had there, I felt self-conscious wondering if this was the last meal of a condemned man.

"Have you ever wanted to write a whole new story for yourself, make up a different background, just to forget what actually happened and try to be happy?"

It was yet another surprise comment from her. In essence, it was the story of my own life. I started to feel the twitching in my face and hoped she wouldn't take it as some kind of admission of guilt.

"Losing your husband must have been difficult. I can't possibly imagine what you have been through."

"All the time he was a sheriff, that's when I was worried. Those punks running around, shooting up the streets, robbing banks. Their lives weren't worth a plugged nickel. They didn't care if they lived or died or who went out with them. You know, like Bonnie and Clyde. When Pete enlisted, I knew his experience and skills would take care of him." She stopped dead in her tracks, a balloon whose air escaped. "I was wrong."

I couldn't respond because I didn't know what to say. She invited me here. This was her show. The next act was hers.

"I honestly don't know anything that could help you. It was too long ago and Pete didn't fill me in on all the details of his job. He was just happy to come home to a nice cooked meal."

"I can see why," I said smiling, hoping to make this easier for her.

"Pete's not coming back. Maybe this woman's son isn't either. But there's a chance, right?"

"I don't know. I guess there is always a chance." I wanted to believe in a light at the end of the tunnel and convinced her I did. However, my vision was not too clear in this matter. That I was here with her was something. Yet so much had been lost over time there was little to actually hope for.

"I'll talk with you. I'll tell you everything I remember. Maybe it'll do some good. There's only one thing I want from you. I want to be in on this from here on in. If Pete's experiences in any way help you out, then it'll mean his life meant something. I need that."

It was strange for her to say that. As a sheriff, it was almost a certainty he impacted the lives of the people of Maquoketa. Of course, as a soldier, he served honorably to defend our country. I couldn't understand why she would feel this way, but I respected her comments.

I could see no problem including her in on the

investigation as most of it was a matter of public record. I wouldn't be divulging my history with Jake Hickey as kids or the murders I investigated in Ark City and Wichita to any degree. I realized I needed to show her some trust if I expected it in return.

Despite insisting otherwise, I helped her clean up in the kitchen. She poured more wine, and we sat back down at the table with the candle flickering between us, almost burned out.

"Tell me about the scars." She was direct, but her tone was not prying. She sounded more concerned than anything else.

Much as I would if I were writing a column for the *Traveler*, I recounted the events in the Great War when a shell exploded behind me, sending me in a panicked frenzy toward a wall of barbed wire, twisting and turning like a rabid dog trying to get out but only becoming more entrapped. I clinically described the new surgeries I went through in an attempt to make me appear more human despite the fact I couldn't quite recognize myself in the mirror. I explained what Dr. Brenz told me about the nature of the surgery and the repercussions nearly thirty years later. Finally, I calmly indicated what the prognosis would likely be for both my face and my life. It was as openly honest as I could be with someone I barely knew. When I thought about it, I hadn't discussed my injury as in depth with anyone else before.

"Why didn't you and your husband have any children?" I asked after a brief moment.

"Prior to his job as a sheriff, our lives were always on the go, trying to make ends meet." She was reflective, providing me a narration without commenting on it. A variety of opportunities came and went, none of which she went into any detail. It was too much of an uncertain life to bring children into the world. When things became stable in Iowa, Peter figured it was time to start a family. Sally, however, became fearful she would wind up as a widowed mother. His death in the war ended all hopes.

I didn't ask her why such a beautiful, strong, and determined woman didn't remarry. It would have been an insult. I could have guessed a thousand reasons, and they might all have been wrong. It was something too personal to discuss at this time.

"Stop by the office tomorrow," I said. "I'll tell you everything I have so far. Something might make sense or bring back a memory. Like you said, it is a chance."

She nodded. I stood up to leave and looked at her in recognition of her bravery. Her eyes were glassy.

"Thank you." I had no idea why she was thanking me considering it was I who sought her help. I could only nod in return.

The wind died down but the smell of the flowers reminded me again of renewal. It was nearly midnight. A new day was just around the corner.

Chapter Twenty-Three

Had I worn a tie and Sunday-go-to-meeting slacks, I would have appeared as professional as Jeremy Jarman, our local insurance salesman, who acted as though he was always be on the job, even at a Fourth of July picnic. Instead, I wore a wrinkled shirt and work pants worn at the knees. No one could accuse me of being a professional.

Sally came early before I finished my first cup of coffee and Mrs. Lindstrom arrived at work. I invited her back to the office of the managing editor that was notoriously late.

"Can I get you anything?" She nodded negatively, a small smile appearing at the corner of her mouth. I started right in. "Nineteen thirty-six. March. The First National Bank robbery." Her eyes grew wide. "What do you recall?"

"There was a shootout on Main Street. Pete was a good shot. He had always been. He told me that night the fellas who were involved were so disorganized, the furthest thing from Johnny Dillinger you could imagine. It was as though because they had guns, they could puff out their chests. Seems it was all they had."

"Did he recognize any of them?"

"They all had their faces covered with handkerchiefs. But Pete said the ringleader kind of reminded him of the O'Connell kid."

"Don't you mean O'Donnell?" I asked perplexed.

"As I recall, the kid he had the run-ins with was named Jake O'Connell."

At this point, I was confused. I was either way off base or it was the same kid using his idol's first name to cover his tracks. All along, I thought he was just a young punk simply looking to make a name for himself. I never considered, even at a young age, he was wiser than his years. Dave Morton and I speculated Hallett somehow hired the kid solely for the purpose of infiltrating Jake's gang and finding a way of getting Hickey arrested. One thing would have been to turn him in on the robberies they committed. The other would have been to frame him for murder.

"Now these run-ins you talked about, what were they like?"

"Nothing major. Vagrancy. Starting fights. He had a switchblade. I can assure you he wasn't whittling with it."

"So then what made Pete think the ringleader of the robbery was this kid?"

"Something about the way he acted, the way he moved. Like a strange way of walking and that is what Pete noticed."

"He was the one who was shot?" She nodded. "And Pete never saw the kid again."

"No."

Using a little bit of logic, all of it added up to the kid in Iowa being the same one from Ark City in 1934. He moved around, working his way up in hopes of being a big time gangster, and apparently failed. However, nothing got me anywhere closer to finding him and Sally realized it.

139

"So where is he now?" she asked, sounding as though she disappointed me.

"Well, let's think about that for a moment." I sounded an awful lot like a college professor just to validate her being there. "If he was shot and didn't get fixed up, he would have died of blood loss. Unless his gang was as conscientious as Dillinger's, he would have been found somewhere by someone."

"Okay."

"So he got help and moved on. Where?"

"Might have had to lay low, get a new gang."

"Or he might have gone straight." I didn't believe it either, but it was an idea that I had to mention out loud if only to throw it in the waste basket.

"That would be the worst thing."

"Why?" I asked.

"You'll never find him."

"But if he'd gone straight, he might eventually, I don't know, repent and want to make amends with his mother, she being the only family left. They were a rather pious family."

"Good point."

"So he hasn't gone straight. He's committed sufficient crimes over the course of the last dozen plus years to stay alive even though he's not living like Rockefeller. He's not skilled enough to pull off a big enough crime to have him set for life. Eventually he's going to be at his wit's end. No one trusts him. He's practically a derelict. He's out of options. Where does he go?"

"His mother."

We looked at each other, both with blank eyes. All I was doing was riding the roller coaster at Coney

Island, going up and down and twisting and turning. When the ride finally stopped, we both came to the same conclusion. At best, it was all speculation. Between my background and hers, everything we had thrown out as ideas led to a natural end. The question now was when Jimmy O'Donnell would be desperate enough to reach out to his mother for help. The answer came sooner than later.

The next day, I got a call from Regina O'Donnell while she was at work. It sounded like she held the phone close because her voice came across as muffled. She indicated she received a disturbing letter and wanted me to see it. I contacted Sally at La Bella Vita while she prepared a large batch of sauce for the evening crowd. As she indicated she wanted to be a part of anything that happened, I invited her to accompany me.

Despite her own simple lifestyle, Sally appeared surprised at the shack Mrs. O'Donnell called a home. She made no comment but walked with head hung as we approached as though we entered a cemetery.

I introduced the ladies and declined her gracious offer of coffee. The envelope had no return address but the postmark was from Winfield. The note bore block letters as though written by someone who had not practiced the fine art of penmanship.

MA ITS YOUR SON. IM IN TROUBLE BAD. NEED TO GET TO MEXICO. GET WHATEVER MONEY YOU CAN. ILL WRITE AGAIN.

"Is it his handwriting?"

"I don't know. It has been too many years."

I looked over at Sally. She shrugged her shoulders.

"It could be him," I said, "or it could be a fakeloo

artist pulling a scam."

"What do I do?" Mrs. O'Donnell beseeched.

"Well, if it isn't Jimmy, we've got to grab this guy and find out what he's up to. If it is him…"

"I understand." She hung her head.

"Let me know if you get another letter." I touched her arm softly. "We'll figure something out."

Sally and I left. On the drive back to the restaurant, I could feel my face twitching. Apparently, it was noticeable.

"Does that happen a lot?" Sally asked.

"Only when I'm stressed."

She came around to the driver's side of the car and leaned in, touching my face tenderly.

"I'm in this with you until the end." Her smile made all the twitching stop. What she couldn't notice was my heart racing trying to figure out what to do next.

Chapter Twenty-Four

The smart thing to do would have been to report this to Dave Morton. Desk Sergeant Morton of the Arkansas City Police Department. Then again, there were countless reasons it wasn't the smart thing to do after all.

Chief Gray made it clear he no longer trusted my instincts as a cop and felt I was too old to pound the pavement. Probably figured I'd get an honest citizen killed. I wasn't sure what his attitude was toward the press, but I assumed he preferred not to have anyone who wasn't a cop sticking their nose into police business.

Dave had been gracious enough to gift me an old jalopy. It dawned on me I had the freedom to move about and do whatever investigating I needed to without drawing him in and jeopardizing his job. Maybe that was his intention. With the exception of running into him at Junior's after my encounter with Hallett, he had no reason to have me tailed as long as I did my job at the *Traveler.* On top of that, the Ark City Police Department didn't have that kind of spare manpower.

But most of all, there really was no case, no crime, nothing that required the attention of law enforcement. At best, we had an unknown someone requesting money from a tired old woman who just wanted a little peace in her life. It couldn't be considered extortion if it was indeed from her son. That was certainly not a crime and no need to arrest or question anyone for that matter.

I knew that time wasn't now but it would come soon enough. It started with a frantic call from Regina O'Donnell while I worked on next week's column.

"Somebody gave an office boy an envelope for me," she said, her voice just above a whisper and filled with creaks and tears. "He was here, Mr. Witherspoon. He was here."

I advised her to leave work immediately, tell her boss she was sick and had to go home. I called Sally and told her what happened, asked if I could pick her up on the way out to Hackney. She waited for me outside. She jumped in the car and sat silently until we got to Mrs. O'Donnell's house. She touched my arm right before I got out of the car, looked at me with apprehension, but didn't try to hold me back.

My knock on the door grew louder as moments passed. I could imagine the occupant holed up inside, afraid of what might be waiting. The door opened slightly. I couldn't see too well behind the screen. When Regina saw me, she unclasped the latch. Sally and I entered quickly, then closed and locked the door behind us.

With a trembling hand, Mrs. O'Donnell handed me the envelope. Written in bold letters on the outside was R O'DONNELL. I read the note inside. The writing was precise with all thoughts indicated clearly.

SELL WHATEVER YOU HAVE TO. ITS GONNA TAKE A LOT TO GET OUT OF THE COUNTRY. I'LL BE BY IN THREE DAYS FOR THE CASH. AFTER THAT YOU WONT NEED TO SEE ME NO MORE.

"Did the office boy describe who gave this to him?" She shook her head harshly. "Did the man say anything?"

"The boy said the man whispered, 'Hey,' and then pushed the envelope in his hand."

"I don't suppose he saw him leave, get into a car, anything like that?"

"No, sir." She stood there, mouth open, eyes blinking rapidly. "What am I to do?"

I looked at Sally helplessly. I had been so sure of myself until now. I no longer had the weight and authority of the police department behind me and was certainly not physically capable of warding off someone a good twenty years younger. That thought alone justified Chief Gray's assessment of me.

"He's made it so you won't know when he'll be coming. That won't make it easy to catch him. Unless…"

"Yes?" Mrs. O'Donnell asked apprehensively.

"Well, I've got to be here when he comes. I can just grab an admiral's watch on your sofa. He won't be expecting anyone else but you here, whoever it is. They were counting on you being a soft touch."

"But, Mr. Witherspoon, if it is him, I've got to do what I can to help him."

"After fourteen years? And the things he's probably done?"

"I'm still his mother."

What was the point in arguing with her? I guessed she felt guilty, perhaps even already dead, a shell of the person she had been when a loving husband and a family and the future looked bright and promising. It is funny how you can look back upon your life and remember all of your grand plans, then turn, look in the mirror, and realize it was all just a dream.

I certainly wasn't going to step on her toes as far as her desire to be a good mother. However, if there was any chance he was guilty of murdering Heather Devore, I needed to do everything I could to bring him to justice. Maybe it was my own sense of guilt at not doing more to squash Jake Hickey when I could, even if it meant revealing my identity and jeopardizing my life and career. Whatever it was, I needed to act this time.

Sally stood in front of the driver's side of the car blocking me from getting in.

"Why don't I stay inside with her, and you can be on a stakeout in the car? I think she'd be more comfortable with me in the house. Don't you?"

"I said I would include you in on the investigation, but I can't let you be in on this part of it."

"Why not?" She was just short of releasing that fiery temper she advised me about.

"This is too dangerous. I'm not going to risk your life."

"But you'll risk yours?"

"Yes." My tone was emphatic, almost coughing out the word.

"I was married to a cop. I learned how to take care of myself."

For the second time in less than five minutes, I found myself ill equipped to counter the arguments of a woman stating a passionate argument. My experience consisted solely of being a protector to the likes of Beth Handy and Natalie Dixon. I never encountered women of rare and exceptional strength and therefore, could not properly counter their intentions.

I left Sally with Mrs. O'Donnell while I drove back to the Elmo, grabbed a small valise with a change of clothes in it. I also dug into my chest of drawers for a .38 snub nose Smith & Wesson Model 10 revolver. It was my personal piece and not one I used as a beat cop. I didn't want to think I would need it, but I knew what I would be up against.

When I got back, I found Sally and Mrs. O'Donnell sitting over a cup of tea in the parlor. Sally rose and walked past me and out of the front door.

"You can check in periodically," I said firmly, "but you're not going to be parked outside here with me."

She just stared at me for what seemed a lifetime and then nodded lightly. I drove her back to the restaurant and let her out. All the while, I was thinking of something to say, something brave and noble. It was useless. Words failed me. At that moment, it wasn't as important to hone my skills as a columnist so much as dredge up my old instincts as a cop. Regina O'Donnell would need it and then some.

Chapter Twenty-Five

The first night the lady of the house treated me to a dinner of cornbread, fried chicken, and mashed potatoes. It was the kind of meal I could have expected from Daisy Mae's but somehow this tasted different. It was as though Regina O'Donnell waited for an opportunity to turn her humble abode back into a home again. The only remaining family member was a son who became a gangster, a man intent upon surviving by breaking any law necessary, including the Fifth Commandment. We spoke little after the prayer over the meal and kept our thoughts inside. Fear and apprehension washed over me as well as eagerness and obsession. I had no idea what was inside the pious woman, forced to be my hostess.

I slept on a sofa in the parlor the first night. It occurred to me I could be easily seen through the sheer lace curtains. If Jimmy, or whoever the letter writer was, had a notion to monitor the activity of the house, he would never approach knowing there was a strange man sleeping inside. I opted to sack out in my car the next night, parking it unnoticed in a dense clump of woods in the back. It didn't offer the best vantage point, but I had no other options.

Sally came by just about dusk on the third night under the pretense of a visit with Mrs. O'Donnell. I snuck in the back door to greet her. Sally looked sad, almost withdrawn, perhaps at not being able to help any more than I needed.

"You look awful," she said blankly.

"That old heap makes for a bumpy ride and an even worse bed."

"When will this all be over?"

"Soon." And then I added, "I hope."

I expected something that night especially given what the note said. Then again, there was no telling exactly what was going on. As far as I could figure it, the letter writer had to be Jimmy O'Donnell. No one would have chosen this woman out of the blue to demand cash knowing she had very little to her name. It was unlikely it was a friend of Jimmy's figuring to score a quick fix, especially in light of the fact most of his known associates were nowhere around. From all vantage points, this looked to be the act of a desperate man who knew only one resource was left to him. I couldn't imagine the trouble he was in, but I really didn't care.

A car approached just before 7:00 p.m. As it came around to the side of the house, I noticed it was a police car. Out stepped Dave Morton. He went around to the front of the house, was there for about three minutes or so, and then came strolling around the back.

His walk was casual, almost deliberate. He didn't appear to be checking windows or doors, more like the adjacent area. At one point, he appeared to look right at me even though I thought the car was well hidden and unidentified in the approaching darkness.

He continued his sweep around the back, up the other side, and back to the front. After a couple of minutes more, he drove away. I waited long enough to go into the house through the back door.

"What did Sgt. Morton want?"

"He said he'd not heard hide nor hair from you in three days and was worried. Said he remembered you talking about Jimmy and figured he'd just come by and check up on me."

I nodded to her and left to go back to the car. Was it just Dave's instincts or had he actually seen me and knew what I was up to? There was no time to find out. I had to stay the course.

The third night came and went and no sign of anyone other than Dave was apparent. Regina went to work, and I went back to the Elmo to take a shower and get a little shut-eye. I stopped by La Bella Vita in the afternoon. Even though they weren't open for lunch, Sally fixed me up a plate of lasagna and garlic bread. She kept talking to me and asking questions while I ate.

"You think this is a bust?"

"No," I said between chews. "You don't go to all this trouble with the notes just to scare a tired old woman. What is the point?"

"So?"

"My guess is he's trying to make sure the coast is clear. Whenever he does pull his move, he'll grab the cash and hightail it out of here. I figure he'll go through the panhandle of Oklahoma and weave his way through as many small towns in west Texas until he gets to El Paso or some other small town where he can cross into Mexico."

"By then, he'll be long gone."

"I don't intend to let him get that far."

At that very moment, I knew with absolute certainty what my mission was. There would be no going back to those woods in France and the barbed wire that effectively changed my life forever. However, I did have this one opportunity, almost like a miracle, to put to rights all that had gone wrong back in 1934. Everyone from that awful time, except Pat McArdle, died or paid their dues. Perhaps Pat was in his own form of purgatory at this point in his life, a fate worse than death itself. The only one left, the only one not brought to justice, was Jimmy O'Donnell. Heather Devore deserved that.

As desperately as Sally wanted to help, this was my assignment to complete. She had no horse in this race.

It was late in the afternoon on the fourth day, after a hearty Italian lunch, I drove toward Hackney. I circled around Regina O'Donnell's house a couple of times looking for any vehicles or telltale signs of someone else watching the area. After I was satisfied it was clear, I pulled back behind the small clump of trees that had been a temporary home for me. It was about thirty minutes before I expected her to arrive home from work.

She entered her house, and I could vaguely hear the clinking of dishes as she made dinner for herself and cleaned up. Then it was quiet for a long time.

It was close to ten when I heard a door open violently followed by the muffled sounds of movement. I ran from my car to the back door.

As soon as I burst through, Jimmy O'Donnell grabbed his mother with whom he had been jostling. He held her close in front of him. Right then, it looked like "Crazy" Jake Hickey grabbing and holding Beth Handy. The thought sickened me, and I could have easily fainted from the shock but I maintained my resolve.

His gun was against her ribs. I had mine drawn just as when I was a cop.

"You don't want to do this, kid."

"I need the money. I need to go."

"Where? Where are you going to go?" I didn't realize I had been yelling, somewhat like an angry father.

"Mexico. I can live like a king down there." He was smug, assured he would come out ahead.

"And then when the money runs out? What then?"

He looked at me, to the left, then to the right, and quickly behind him.

"You're not going to stop me."

His arm started to move. Maybe he was dropping it to his side or maybe he was lifting it to aim. I couldn't tell which. My instincts were off. Chief Gray was right.

I fired toward his exposed right shoulder but missed. He moved slightly.

Regina O'Donnell pushed harshly back against him, pulled free, moving the only way she could which was toward me.

It was then Jimmy fired back, right as Regina was halfway between him and me. A bullet struck her in the mid portion of her back. The force drove her forward, and she eventually collapsed on me. We fell to the floor.

Jimmy ran, concerned more about his own pathetic life than the money. Two shots rang out. I got out from under Regina and ran toward the door. Standing outside was Sally holding a Smith & Wesson .38 with what looked to be a four-inch barrel and a pearl handle.

Jimmy O'Donnell, on the ground, clutched his leg and hip. I couldn't help but smile.

I ran back inside. I could see a pool of blood forming on Regina's back. I kneeled down and slowly turned her over. She grimaced in pain.

"I'm sorry. I'm so sorry." I gave her the apology her son would never have offered.

"God's will be done."

She reached up and touched my face. It was a kind of blessing. Her hand fell to the side. She was gone. I crossed her arms over her chest. It was the image I had seen at so many funerals. I hoped she was at peace.

I walked back outside with my head hung. Sally didn't have to ask.

"Drive into town and get the police. And an ambulance."

Sally nodded. She knew what the procedures were. It would probably be a good hour before anyone would get here. Plenty of time to think. But I had grown tired. I wanted it all to be over. Maybe it was too much time.

Chapter Twenty-Six

The nurses at Mercy Hospital were rather impressed with the tourniquet I fashioned on Jimmy O'Donnell's leg and the compression bandage I applied on the soft flesh of his hip. After a bit of fanfare they credited me with saving his life. It was not a designation I was eager to accept.

Dr. Brenz received Regina O'Donnell's body for a post-mortem medical examination per the legal requirements. Jimmy received excellent care at the hospital before the handcuffs secured him to the bed. Sally and I went to police headquarters. We started with the soothing tones of Sergeant Dave Morton who urgently advised us to cooperate in light of what appeared to be a private investigation and perhaps something that a District Attorney could construe as entrapment. I was in no mood to argue with Dave, knowing he was looking out for my best interests. By the same token, I had no desire to confess to any kind of felony simply to have an easy end to this situation.

It was when Chief Gray stormed in I realized his dislike for me increased tenfold. His rolled up white shirt sleeves made him look like a man getting ready for serious business, like maybe swinging a sledgehammer on my head. His pale blue tie was too short and his dark brown hat barely hung on his head. His brown shoes were scuffed and worn. Fortunately, he secured the gun on his hip holster.

"You do realize, Mr. Witherspoon, you are no longer employed by this department?" Just the slightest bit of spittle gathered in the corner of his mouth, but I figured the louder and angrier he got I might be subjected to more of a shower.

"You are correct, sir. And you are currently in violation of Ordinance 12-105. Treatment of the Public, Section 5, which states: *That it shall be the duty of the chief of police and every policeman to be courteous and obliging in his intercourse with the public, and shall not use or exercise unnecessary force—"*

"I am aware of the statute." His volume increased, as did the amount of spittle.

I knew it wasn't a good thing to intimidate him but after my summarily forced retirement, it was my intention to make him aware I still knew what I was doing and wasn't just flying by the seat of my pants. I may not have had a badge pinned to my chest but the notions of Law and Order were squarely in my thoughts.

"Well, how about 9-402 Assault, Section 39. 9-403 Assault and Battery, Section 40. 9-405 Weapons, Carrying, Section 42. 9-408 Firearms, Discharge of, Section 45." I thought he was going to run out of fingers with his counting. "And while we're at it, my personal favorite, 9-414 Impersonating an Officer, Section 51."

We played pat-a-cake with our respective knowledge of local ordinances. Obviously, his had more substance than mine did. It was time to get serious in order to get this man off my back.

"State of Kansas Statute 22-2403. Arrest by Private

Person." I delivered my recital in monotone, a flat yet certain commentary with an unwillingness to bend. *"A person who is not a law enforcement officer may arrest another person when a felony has been or is being committed, and the person making the arrest has probable cause to believe the arrested person is guilty thereof."* I stopped and remained silent, staring at him, daring him to push me even further. "I had every reason to believe Regina O'Donnell's life was in jeopardy from her son or someone falsely representing to be him."

Now it was a staring contest. I one-upped him with a state statute that had me squarely in the right. In this particular case, the Law was on my side. If only for a moment he considered what I had actually done rather than allow his distaste for me to fester, we might have come to a quicker agreement on this.

"There's going to be a thorough investigation of this, Witherspoon. We've got a woman murdered in the commission of a felony. This thing has your prints all over it."

Gray turned and stormed out, slamming the door behind him. I didn't completely realize until that moment how much he hated me. Sally, for her part, didn't seem the least bit fazed. She had a slight smile on her face, one of pride perhaps. Dave looked at us like a teacher who wasn't buying our excuse for not doing our homework.

"Junior's. Tonight. Eight o'clock." His index finger wagged back and forth. "Both of you."

He walked out without looking back. I think he just didn't want me to see the smirk on his face.

"What now?" Sally asked.

"Well, I guess I'm buying you some drinks at Junior's tonight."

"But the restaurant?"

"Your cousins can handle it for a night. This is a murder case now. It is just getting started."

I regretted having to say it to her like that, but I wasn't going to remind her she wanted in on this all the way down the line. She knew it. One way or another, both our lives were going to change.

Sally looked worried when I stopped by to pick her up, perhaps feeling a tad guilty at running out on what had been the most important thing in her life after her husband died. I couldn't blame her, but I also fully knew there would be a trial. Because of her stubbornness at wanting to be involved with this as well as her stopping Jimmy O'Donnell from escaping, she would be a witness just as I would be. This simple evening outing would be short compared to what would come next.

Either the traffic was lighter than I expected or I drove faster than I thought but we got back into the city about a quarter till eight. We decided to go ahead on into Junior's. She ordered a whiskey neat, and I followed suit. Calling back to the waiter, she added, "Just bring the bottle." He looked at me, and I nodded. My reputation still carried some weight, at least with a waiter in a bar.

"Isn't this case open and shut?" she asked desperately, after slugging down the first belt.

"Nothing is open and shut anymore," Dave Morton responded, standing right behind her. He pulled up a seat and joined us. "This could be made to look like entrapment if the kid gets a wily mouthpiece. You know, Baron trying to draw him out into the open when all he wanted to do was stay under wraps. That kind of thing."

"But that's not the way it happened." Sally came to my defense and it made me proud.

"I know it and you know it," Dave continued, helping himself to a glass from the bottle. "But all it takes is a little of the old reasonable doubt, and a jury lets him get away with manslaughter."

"Dave is just being cautious," I explained. "Jimmy O'Donnell's crimes go all the way back to '34 with Hickey's gang. We figured he's responsible for the murder of Heather Devore…"

"Hold it right there." Dave put his hand up like a traffic cop. He probably hadn't done that in years. "Don't even try putting that on the table. You'll just muddy up the waters."

"He's got to pay."

"Listen to me. It is as clear as a bell he killed his mother. All the evidence will prove it. You start trying to squeeze in something from fifteen years ago and you'll have everybody's heads spinning. Now, I know what this means to you, Baron. You forget I was there with you. A lot of water under the bridge. We can get Jimmy on Regina's murder. Just leave it where it is." He poured another drink and shot it down fast. "Thanks for the drinks," he said as he stood up to leave.

Everything was starting to unravel for me. My job or task or mission, however it appeared to folks outside of my circle, was to locate a woman's long lost son. I discovered he was an untrustworthy criminal who did anything he could to make it in that shady world. I figured he was responsible for the death of a woman caught up with the wrong man. Ultimately, I led this evil man to his mother who he wound up killing. Not a lot for me to hang my hat on.

Sally reached out to me across the table. She held my hand in hers. I looked up and at that very moment I was at peace. I no longer felt like a failure. We knew of a road ahead of us, a task to be completed. I figured it was primarily my journey, but she climbed onboard the same bus for the same ride. I wasn't sure where it would end, but we would be together.

The phone call I got at the office later that week was an indication I was more than just a witness at this trial.

Chapter Twenty-Seven

Oscar Stauffer, the publisher of the *Arkansas City Traveler*, as well as the *Peabody Gazette-Bulletin* and the *Topeka Capital-Journal,* called me personally on Friday morning. He didn't reach out to William Frailey, the editor, or even James B. Austin, the business manager. He asked for me directly.

"I'm sorry to hear how this adventure turned out, Baron." He seemed genuinely concerned for my well-being. "But I have it on good faith Harold Fatzer, the state's attorney general, will seek the death penalty on this one."

"Really? Why?" In all my years as a policeman, there weren't too many trials I was aware of that were as heavy handed as this one was apparently going to get.

"The boy killed his mother. It reeks of evil, not to mention a kind of Biblical overtone to it. There are many church going voters who want blood." This was headed down the road of the political, and it started to make me feel uncomfortable. "They're going to be trying it in the 19th Judicial Court up in Winfield. You and Mrs. Harper are the star witnesses for the prosecution. You also happen to be my premier columnist who has a devoted following."

"Thank you, sir." I could eerily sense what he was going to say next.

"Now, I want you to stay up there in Winfield for the entire trial. Even beyond your testimony and that of Mrs. Harper. The *Traveler* will cover your expenses. Both of you. Every night I want you to call in a column to Verna Sharer."

"But she's the Society Editor, Mr. Stauffer."

"For the purposes of this task, she's nothing more than your secretary and transcriptionist. She's been made aware of her responsibilities."

It seemed I hit the big time in journalism at the expense of the late Regina O'Donnell and her desperate son, Jimmy.

"This is the biggest trial we've had in years, and we've got one of our own reporters involved up to his elbows. I guarantee you circulation should increase by twenty to twenty-five percent."

Dollar signs floated around like wisps of clouds to the tune of cash registers ringing. It was straight out of a Busby Berkeley musical, if they made them anymore. "Well, this is a pretty open and shut case, Mr. Stauffer. I don't suppose it'll last more than a week at most."

"Perhaps. But there is the appeal process. That will likely be in the 18th Judicial Court in Wichita. And you'll be there to cover that, too."

I was fully aware of what the inevitable conclusion to a murder trial with the death penalty was, but I didn't ask him. Then again, I didn't need to.

"And certainly, when they carry out the sentence in Lansing, well, if there's a sentence to be carried out I should say, I'll want you there as well." His confidence in all of this was overwhelming.

I didn't rightly know how to feel about all of it. I'd investigated brutal murders and seen tortured bodies. I had given testimony in far smaller cases. Outside of watching fellow soldiers killed in the war or the shot up bodies of Ralph Houseman and a man impersonating FBI Agent Hollis Burke, I had never witnessed an execution. My intent was to seek justice without fully comprehending I would have to ride that train to the end of the tracks.

When all was said and done, that was okay for me. There would be a lot to get through. When you force yourself to come face to face with your past, you want to puff out your chest and act like the hero. Sometimes it meant a baptism of fire such as what I seemed to be looking ahead to doing. I just wasn't all that comfortable dragging Sally along with me, even though she wanted to be part of it as retribution for her fallen husband. The Japanese, not a know-nothing punk trying to be a gangster, killed Sheriff Harper. Sally wouldn't look at it that way. If Pete Harper had stopped Jimmy O'Donnell back in Iowa, none of this would have happened, or so she thought. I was the classic example of not knowing where your life would wind up. I couldn't agree with her on that count.

I probably should have spent a quiet evening at La Bella Vita or better yet just gone back to my small abode at the Elmo. I needed something that reminded me of better times despite the fact I couldn't count too many on the fingers of one hand. A big fat juicy burger at Daisy Mae's and some small talk with a few good old boys and fans of my column would probably be uplifting enough.

Tabatha was still around after all these years. She left when she had her third kid and came back because it was quieter in the restaurant than at home. Dixie never did hire another busboy or maintenance man after Ralph Houseman was determined to be an enemy agent working with the Germans. Larry Hammer, on the other hand, permanently retired and spent most of his time giving his two cents on anything and everything to anyone who walked in the door. He sat opposite me as I chewed.

"You get stuck in the middle of the worst jams without even trying." A slight snort in his voice passed for a laugh.

"Guess it's my nature."

"You gonna be reporting on it?"

"Yep." I nodded. "Along with being a witness for the prosecution."

"How's that gonna work?"

"We'll see."

I knew I needed to talk to Sally, but I really felt like drowning my sorrows in hooch. That wasn't going to do anyone a bit of good. I just hung around downtown until it got close to closing time for her place and drove on over, stepping up to the door when I saw the last car drive away. She had an expectant look on her face in response to my timid knock.

Her cousins were still cleaning up as we sat at a corner table looking out the window where a small carafe of wine and two glasses waited for us. I still didn't know what I needed to say and was grateful when she spoke first.

"I know how this works, Baron. Pete testified in a few trials. It was rough because he knew he was in the right, and the defense lawyer tried to make him look bad."

"I'm not worried about that." She looked at me

quizzically. "Mr. Stauffer wants me to report on the trial every night. He's going to spring for hotel rooms for us to stay up in Winfield."

"Why me?"

"I don't know. Maybe he thinks you're kind of special."

"Yeah, but what do you think?"

I looked at her in a way I hadn't before. Her deep rich eyes were captivating and her fiery red lips utterly inviting. Up until that moment, I admired her strength and courage as well as her cooking. Sadly, there wasn't a time where I considered her as a woman, perhaps too afraid to disrespect the memory of her late husband.

Now, this one event that drew us together also helped us ride at full gallop away from our respective pasts. Looking forward, I caught sight of a glimpse of a future with her.

"All I know is we've got to get through this. Together. If he's found guilty…"

"He will be."

"If he's found guilty, there will be an appeal. And after that…"

"Yeah. I know." For about ten or fifteen seconds, we were enveloped by the silence of the tomb. "Would you go up there for that?"

I nodded affirmatively. It wasn't an eager nod. I had no desire to wish death upon Jimmy O'Donnell in spite of the fact he callously killed his mother and most likely killed Heather Devore because a crooked businessman and corrupt politician needed to get out from under a raw deal. Jimmy O'Donnell was a tool that was used by far more evil men who passed before him. All this was to be was his reckoning.

"And after this is all over?" she asked quietly.

I lifted my head, proud and firm, felt my chest puff out like a hero.

"I would introduce myself to you, let you know who I am, hope maybe you might like that person. Then, maybe, I can get to know who you are."

"I'd like that very much."

For the time being, we would just have to continue as strangers.

Chapter Twenty-Eight

It had been a long time since I wore anything resembling a suit. As I recall, it was 1935 and I stood just outside the First Baptist Church as Beth Handy entered and strolled down the aisle to marry Frank Appleby. After everyone entered, I took a step or two inside the vestibule because I still felt like an outsider, as though a house of worship would not accept a man with such a scarred face. It was also when I met Natalie Dixon and convinced myself I might have been in love with her before her sense of vengeance got the better of her. Yes, that was the last time I wore a suit until today.

Sally and I drove up to the Cowley County Courthouse two weeks prior to the trial to meet with Assistant District Attorney Gregory Freeland. He was barely thirty, and a very eager man who appeared to be an efficient lawyer. It was apparent the district attorney considered this was such an open and shut case he didn't need to assign anyone with a greater deal of experience. The meeting was to go over our part in the trial.

"Your testimony, Mr. Witherspoon, will lay the groundwork for our case. We want to show Mrs. O'Donnell was concerned but at the same time scared of what her estranged son might do, and in fact, wound up doing." He stopped suddenly, hand on his chin in contemplation. "Should I refer to you as Officer

Witherspoon?"

"I think it might confuse the jury. I'm just an ordinary citizen now."

"Yes, but with a background in law enforcement." He wrote something on a legal pad before him before turning his attention to Sally. "Mrs. Harper, you needn't worry about any charges associated with shooting Mr. O'Donnell."

"I should think not," she responded boldly.

"Well, we have a Kansas statute that states: *A person is justified in the use of force against another when and to the extent it appears to such person and such person reasonably believes that such use of force is necessary to defend such person or a third person against such other's imminent use of unlawful force.*" He looked up from the law book he read from and smiled. Like Sally, I didn't speak the language but understood it meant she was in the clear.

My heart beat a little faster, and my breath was hard to catch. It was a sense of worry even though I accepted everyone else's notion of the case. A persistent fly buzzed around in my mind and wouldn't quit.

"O'Donnell is also responsible for the death of a woman named Heather Devore."

"Oh. When was this?" Freeland asked, somewhat surprised at this revelation.

"Back in 1934. He had done it at the behest of the late Councilman Hallett of Arkansas City."

"A contract killing set up by a local politician?" I nodded. "How do you know this?"

"I had conversations with Hallett over the course of the last several months, and he implied…"

"Mr. Witherspoon, what evidence do you have?"

"Well, I know that he was trying to…"

"Was this investigated back in '34?"

"No. I mean, after we killed Jake Hickey we had no need to because he was the prime suspect in the case. But that is only because it was what Hallett wanted us to think."

"Did you depose the councilman prior to his death?"

"Like I said, there were just some general conversations."

"At the police station?"

"No," I responded, sounding defeated. "Just in his office."

Freeland's smile was supposed to be warm and gracious but came across looking like a parent who caught his kid in a lie.

"We have a solid case against Jimmy O'Donnell. State Attorney General Harold Fatzer has instructed me through my superiors to bring a charge of murder against this man for the heinous killing of his own mother. The state will seek the death penalty for it. Now, if we muddy the waters with a possible crime from fifteen years ago with only hearsay and no evidence, the jury might believe a defense case for voluntary manslaughter is valid. No, we have got to stay focused on this case and this case alone. Mr. O'Donnell has an appointment in Lansing."

That put an end to it. Jimmy O'Donnell had killed Heather Devore in cold blood. He was the last of a group of vicious gangsters and corrupt politicians and businessmen from a time when I worked hard to keep Ark City safe. He deserved punishment and Heather

Devore deserved justice.

Even though I stared straight ahead on the ride back, I caught Sally looking at me out of the corner of my eye. I was certain she was ready to lecture me in some fashion about what obviously became an obsession, but I just wasn't in the mood to hear it. Nevertheless, she spoke.

"I've been thinking that if Frank had only been able to catch this kid and lock him away, Regina O'Donnell might still be alive."

I shook my head at her comment.

"That's like saying if I helped Heather Devore when I had the chance, she would still be alive."

"Exactly."

I finally looked over at her as I drove. She made her point without lecturing me. When it was all over, the state would likely execute Jimmy O'Donnell for the killing of his mother and I would be one of the only people left to remember Heather Devore.

Sally and I chatted for a bit at La Bella Vita, discussing when we would drive up for the trial, the hotel we would be staying at, my phone calls back to the *Traveler* office to file my report, and how there were likely no decent Italian restaurants in Winfield. She looked at me strange as I looked around the property.

"I never asked but where do you live?"

We took a few steps away from the restaurant down a path that led to a cottage. It seemed no bigger than a garage.

"Bedroom, kitchen, bathroom. Everything I need."

"That's all?" It almost seemed like the same set up Pat McArdle had.

"I've got a radio. I like to listen to Baby Snooks and Edgar Bergen and Charlie McCarthy. Anything to make me laugh after a long day. Did you want to come in and see the place?"

It was a gracious and heart-warming offer, but I needed to decline. Just as the assistant district attorney didn't want to confuse the jury with a long forgotten case, I needed to focus on my two jobs as both witness and journalist. Nevertheless, Sally Harper started to weave a path into my heart whether she knew it or not.

I went back home to the Elmo, took a long hot bath, and then sat in my favorite chair by the radio. Earlier in the month, I heard news reports a famous colored surgeon died because they wouldn't take him at a white hospital and a famous historian and literary critic committed suicide by jumping to his death from a hotel window. After everything that had gone on, I needed something to shine some light into the darkness. I turned the dial until I came across a man and a wooden dummy.

Edgar Bergen: This is a story that everyone should know.

Charlie McCarthy: Yes, but not everyone should tell it, and you know who.

Edgar Bergen: I'm going to tell it anyway. Now, many, many years ago.

Charlie McCarthy: I think I'll go out and wind the sundial.

For the first time in a long time I laughed.

Chapter Twenty-Nine

The Municipal Building in Ark City was a drab rectangular edifice that contained the offices of the local government and what passed for a courtroom. There weren't too many cases tried there, only minor offenses heard before a judge. Most of them were like automobiles being put together on Henry Ford's assembly line.

I had sat before a few judges and knew my way around a court case. For the most part, my instructions were to provide direct answers to direct questions. If it wasn't asked, it wasn't to be answered. Anything I said could then be countered or jumped upon by a defense lawyer like a cat pouncing on a mouse. We had our facts, and they were supposed to find theirs.

The Cowley County Courthouse, on the other hand, reminded me of castles I came across in France during the Great War. Not even a punk kid from the North Side of Chicago had seen such opulent structures before. While this was not quite as large as those structures, the magnificent gold dome sitting atop all that native limestone impressed me, nonetheless. I hadn't been here since 1935 when I explored the basement records rooms with the assistance of an Officer Elmore who I determined had finally retired. This time, I roamed around in what many considered a hallowed sanctuary as equally lost as before.

171

Polished wood and brass, marble floors, crystal chandeliers all gave the place the look of something regal. Either that or a fancy cathouse. It was awkward wearing my best suit for a second time in as many weeks but only Assistant District Attorney Gregory Freeland would know that, and I didn't think he much cared.

Sally and I were in the row immediately behind the district attorney's table. On the other side of the courtroom sat Jimmy O'Donnell with his attorney. I hadn't really looked at O'Donnell all that much and considered him even less. Now that he wasn't going anywhere for the foreseeable future, I could see he wasn't really a kid. In his early thirties by my calculation, he looked somewhat older, like a tired middle-aged man who'd worked hard all his life and had nothing to show for it. I thought I noticed a few gray hairs on the side of his head and lines around his eyes and mouth. While he didn't have any facial scarring, he still looked like he had run a hard race and lost.

His attorney, on the other hand, had all the makings of a character I saw in a couple of tough guy films from years ago. The man must have been my age or older. He slicked back whatever hair he had and dyed it jet black. He wore spit polished shoes with spats, a watch chain on the vest of his three-piece pinstriped suit, pants with a crease so sharp you could shave with it. There were a couple of gold rings on fat fingers, none of which looked like they came from a church or a pawnbroker.

It was a contrast in styles. If I didn't know better, I would have sworn we were in the Cook County

Courthouse some time around the late 1920s. O'Donnell, of the bootlegging family, would have someone like Easy Eddie O'Hare for a mouthpiece if O'Hare hadn't already been in Capone's back pocket. The judge, the jury, everyone who counted would have all been on the take, and this would be a sideshow for the boys in the press to sell more copies. The justice system as a kind of vaudeville show.

Instead, it was over twenty years later, the facts were overwhelming, and someone little more than a killer of his own mother was on course to go over Niagara Falls in a barrel.

The first witness for the prosecution was Dr. Louis Brenz. The questioning started with the facts of the death of Regina O'Donnell. Brenz explained how the bullet in her back pierced her lung and nicked her heart. The cause of death was internal bleeding. The clear indication was nothing I could have done would have saved her.

Then Freeland took his inquiry in the direction of Jimmy actually shooting his mother and how it could be determined if it was intentional or accidental. On an easel facing the jury was an enlarged photo of the main room of the house taken from above with cartoon like drawings representing Jimmy, Mrs. O'Donnell, and myself. I had not been around Doctie before when he testified in other cases, but his exactness and certainty were impressive.

"Given the angle at which Mr. O'Donnell was firing," Brenz stated, pointing to the photo, "it is clear he was aiming for his mother, likely to cause her to become an obstruction against Mr. Witherspoon, the only individual who could have any reasonable possibility of stopping him."

"Why is that?" Freeland asked, fully knowing the answer.

"Because Mr. Witherspoon had a gun and could fire back. Mrs. O'Donnell had none of those advantages."

"Well, why do you suppose Mr. O'Donnell simply didn't shoot at Mr. Witherspoon?"

As though appearing agitated or annoyed, Dr. Brenz stood up and got in front of the photo. He had his back to us but faced the jury.

"Mr. O'Donnell did not have a clear shot at Mr. Witherspoon. His only recourse was to shoot his mother and thereby impede Mr. Witherspoon's movements."

The defense attorney, one William J. O'Brien, postured a bit before approaching the witness stand in a blustery manner.

"Dr. Brenz, you maintain a private practice in Arkansas City, Kansas?"

"Yes."

"And you have performed autopsies at the city's request?"

"Yes."

"However, do you have any formal training as a medical examiner?"

"Formal? No." O'Brien was about to make a point but Doctie continued. "Nevertheless, I have acted in that capacity for nearly thirty years, and my reports have never been challenged in any court as inaccurate."

O'Brien ran into a brick wall in his attempt to disparage the findings of intent. The judge seemed perturbed by the effort.

Sally came up to the witness stand next. A strong

sense of pride surged through me as I watched her take the oath. I had no doubt of her strength and ability to get through any situation.

"Mrs. Harper, why were you at the O'Donnell residence that evening?" Freeland questioned.

"Mr. Witherspoon had asked for any recollections I may have had regarding my late husband's encounters with the defendant."

"Your husband was a sheriff?"

"Yes, in Jackson County, based out of Maquoketa, Iowa. He stood up against a bank robbery in which he believed Mr. O'Donnell was a participant."

"Objection," O'Brien blurted out. "Hearsay."

"Sustained," the judge responded.

"Did Mr. Witherspoon ask you to accompany him to the O'Donnell home during this investigation?"

"No. He actually told me to stay away."

"But you didn't."

"Yes."

"Why?"

"I thought I had seen Mr. O'Donnell somewhere in town and knew Mrs. O'Donnell and Mr. Witherspoon might be in danger. As she did not have a telephone, I went out there on my own. I had just gotten there when I heard a gunshot and then the defendant came out of the house brandishing a weapon. I shot him in self-defense."

"Thank you, Mrs. Harper." Freeland started walking back to the table then turned suddenly. "Oh, one more thing. Where did you learn to shoot?"

"My late husband," she said proudly.

O'Brien chose not to cross-examine her.

I was the last witness for the state. For a brief

moment, it felt like it was my debut on Broadway, butterflies stirring in my stomach and rapidly repeating my lines in my head. When it came down to it, I was nothing more than an actor in a play. The state of Kansas had dictated a course of action; I was simply there to do my part.

"State your name for the record," Freeland began.

"Baron Witherspoon."

"Where are you employed?"

"I am a columnist for the *Ark City Traveler*."

"And prior to that?"

"I was a patrol officer on the Arkansas City police force for nearly thirty years."

"Your honor," O'Brien bleated in a bored manner, "is the witness's résumé necessary?"

"The state is merely trying to establish the credentials of the witness for the purposes of declaring him an expert in this matter." Freeland did his best to make me appear important.

"Proceed." The judge sounded equally bored.

"Please tell us how you came to wind up in the home of Regina O'Donnell."

I recounted my first meeting with Regina O'Donnell and determining to assist her after learning her son may have been involved with Jake Hickey, someone I knew from my days in law enforcement. In tracking down known associates of Hickey, I hoped to narrow in on a location for Jimmy O'Donnell but found limited information beyond what Sally Harper presented me. While I had not been successful, Mrs. O'Donnell received strange communications from a man purportedly claiming to be her son and requesting money.

"What if it turned out this attempt at extortion…?" Freeland began before an interjection from O'Brien.

"Objection. It is presumptuous to declare a request for financial support from a son to his mother to be extortion."

"Had Mr. O'Brien allowed me to finish, I was going to ask the witness as to his thoughts on the matter if it turned out this so-called request was not from Mrs. O'Donnell's son," Freeland retorted.

The judge allowed the question and disallowed the objection.

"The fact of the matter was Regina O'Donnell was scared. She felt as though she were in danger. Whether the communications were coming from a long estranged son or a complete stranger, she considered her life to be in jeopardy. The matter of whether a crime was being committed was inconsequential compared to her safety." I liked the way I sounded. Could have given Dave Morton a run for his money.

When the questioning turned to the actual killing, I admitted to doubts about my ability to shoot Jimmy in order to disable him without accidentally hitting Mrs. O'Donnell. I had no other option when his hand moved in an aggressive manner.

"Unfortunately, my shot missed," I said, a slight quiver in my throat. "He appeared to have pushed Mrs. O'Donnell, and then he shot her. That forced her forward upon me." I indicated it was only after he ran out I heard the shot and found Sally standing over him. Going back inside, there were a few brief moments before Regina O'Donnell expired before me. My sense of grief apparently moved the jury. The prosecution rested.

Chapter Thirty

That afternoon I called Verna Sharer at the *Traveler* to file my column. I felt surprisingly good about the case and didn't allow the nagging feeling of justice for Heather Devore to creep up in my mind. My reporting was straightforward, at first, but I detected myself getting a bit melodramatic, leaning just a little toward yellow journalism. Mrs. Sharer relished the details of the case. The *Traveler* had a stop-press order in place throughout the trial until I could call in my column. That day's edition ran within thirty minutes after transcribing and typesetting.

I took Sally to a restaurant called Luigi's that served Italian food. It wasn't intentional, simply the closest place to the hotel. If I had thought about it, I would have found a place serving fried chicken and mashed potatoes and gravy. A pleased look filled her face while savoring the linguine in white clam sauce.

"How is it?" I asked mischievously.

"Not bad—"and then looking up—"but not as good as mine."

The dishes removed from the table, we sat finishing our wine while the waiter brought the check.

"What do you think the defense's case will be?" she asked.

"Not sure. The only thing I can think of is throwing himself on the mercy of the court."

"Did he really push Regina in your direction?"

"That is the way I saw it," I responded stone-faced.

The next morning wearing the same suit, I sat in court while O'Brien called the only witness—Jimmy O'Donnell.

"Was it your intention to kill your mother, Jimmy?" O'Brien started.

"No, sir." Jimmy O'Donnell was as quiet and gentle as a boy scout. I guess we were all acting.

"Why were you there?"

"I needed money. I needed to get as far away as possible."

"Did you think your mother had that kind of money?"

"I honestly didn't know. But I had no other options. You see, I got hooked up with some bad people a long time ago."

I leaned forward in my seat, hoping maybe he would fess up to all of his indiscretions.

"I met this kid named Tommy Price up in Topeka in '34. He convinced me we could hit a couple of banks and make some easy dough."

At that point, Jimmy O'Donnell fully focused his gaze on me. It was as though the judge, jury, and his own lawyer were not there. He talked out loud but spoke directly to me. For a moment, this was no longer a trial but a personal challenge, a showdown like bandits in the Old West.

"And it was easy. First National Bank in Topeka. Citizens Bank in Lecompton. Of course, we tried our best to stay away from Kansas City after the massacre up there. So we skirted around to Nebraska and Iowa and eventually up into Indiana. You know, Dillinger country." He had a boastful smile as he rattled off several more banks. I wrote them down in my note pad and wondered why he admitted to prior armed robberies.

"What became of Tommy Price?" O'Brien asked. Jimmy O'Donnell shrugged his shoulders as though the man he spoke of fondly didn't even exist. "Where did you go from there?"

"I've been doing everything I could to get by these last fourteen years. Holding up gas stations and liquor stores once they repealed prohibition. Worked on the railroad and in a brick making plant. Hoboed quite a bit."

"Why did you come back to Arkansas City?"

"I was working in a stockyard in Nebraska when one of the guys I worked with told me a private dick came by asking about me. They said there was a warrant out for a job I supposedly pulled in Iowa. I skedaddled out as fast as I could but figured they weren't going to give up the chase any time soon. Look, I was desperate. I knew my ma didn't think much of me, but she was still my ma. You know?"

It was apparent the defense wanted to show Jimmy was at his wit's end and only attempting a last ditch effort, as he would not have intentionally killed his mother since there was no reason for it. If they could keep him away from the gallows, anything else might be possible.

O'Brien, while addressing O'Donnell, went on a long speech about poverty, hard times, and desperation in an attempt to elicit sympathy from the jury. Freeland objected and the judge cautioned O'Brien while reminding him to ask a question or have a seat. O'Brien threw out his hands in defeat and sat down. Freeland buttoned his jacket upon standing up for his cross-examination.

"You heard the testimony of Baron Witherspoon indicating you shoved your mother toward him and then shot her?"

"I heard it." He still looked directly at me. "Maybe that's what he thought he saw but that weren't what happened."

"What did happen?"

"Like I said, I went to her house, got her a little upset on account of I was yelling to convince her I needed the money. Then that fella—"pointing directly at me—"comes racing in. I panicked and grabbed my ma. He shot at me, which scared the bejesus out of me. My ma kind of struggled and broke free from me, and I shot back at him just as she was running toward him. I just wanted the money, and I would have left. For good. I had no reason to kill her."

He hung his head, face covering up what I figured were crocodile tears. Mr. Freeland had no more questions, and Mr. O'Brien rested his case. The judge gave instructions to the jury, and all we could do now was wait for a verdict.

Something was annoying me like a mosquito buzzing my ears. That afternoon, I made two phone calls. The first was to Verna Sharer to file my column. My blood raced through me as I dictated, telling the story of a young man's pathetic attempt to make himself look like a victim in a trial for the murder of his own mother. Verna suggested I insert a reference to the Fifth Commandment for our church-going readers. It sounded reasonable to me. I was all ready to find him guilty even before the jury came back with their verdict. Sure, this was about selling newspapers, but I also got out a bit of my own frustration.

The fact he looked intently at me the entire time he wove his fable got under my skin. He wanted me to be a part of his deception by willingly letting me know, simply by looking at me with eyes that said "And here's a fairy-tale for you. Sleep well."

The second call I made was to Dave Morton. Reading off my note pad, I gave him names and places Jimmy O'Donnell claimed he had been, robbing banks with a character named Tommy Price. If it were true, he couldn't possibly have been part of Jake Hickey's gang hiding stolen goods in the tunnels beneath Ark City. I knew it was all a lie. Pat McArdle told me as much. The question was why did he lie.

Sally and I had dinner that night at a steak house called Lou's. I chewed the meat like a ravenous bull and swilled wine. I was angry, thrilled, and excited all at the same time. She reached across the table and touched my hand gently.

"Slow down and enjoy the meal. It's a good steak."

I took her advice on the second night we ate there. Just as we were leaving, a bailiff found us and indicated the jury had reached a verdict. They would deliver it the following morning.

Gregory Freeland, the young assistant district attorney of Cowley County, sat in an upright and professional manner. A conviction would put a feather in his cap. William O'Brien looked impatient, as though he were eager to step outside and smoke a cigar. Jimmy O'Donnell sat back in his chair practically slouching. This was a trial for his life, but he didn't seem to care.

Maybe he realized he died a long time ago.

The jury filed in solemnly and took their seats. The foreman handed the small folded piece of paper to the bailiff who delivered it to the judge. He read the writing without the slightest bit of emotion before handing it back to the bailiff.

"Mr. Foreman, has the jury reached a verdict?"

"We have your honor."

"What say you to the count of first degree murder?"

"We, the jury, find the defendant, James Kieran O'Donnell, guilty."

"Is this unanimous?"

"Yes, your honor."

"What is the jury's recommendation for sentence?"

"We recommend the defendant be executed by hanging in the manner prescribed by our laws."

After three days in Winfield, Sally and I drove back to Arkansas City. The matter of the State of Kansas versus James Kieran O'Donnell was not quite over.

Chapter Thirty-One

We got back just before noon. Sally asked me to take her to lunch at Daisy Mae's. I wasn't sure whether she wanted me to be relaxed in a comfortable place or if she wanted to steal some menu ideas.

After Tabatha took our order, we sat in silence staring at each other. I guess we were trying to figure out if this whole thing changed us much and if there were still a chance to find some peace in our lives, either together or apart. It struck me right then I really didn't want to be without her.

Dixie brought our sandwiches and placed them softly on the table. She had a solemn look about her, one I had never seen in all the years I knew her.

"How'd it go up there?" she asked quietly.

"Guilty."

"They gonna hang him?"

"Eventually."

"I kinda wish things were still like they were back in the land rush days."

She walked off with her head hung. I knew what she meant, the sense of swift justice they had in the Old West. Once they convicted a man of a crime, he served his sentence no matter what it was. All the appeals did was give lawyers an extra job to do and put more cash in their overstuffed pockets. However, I had known from the very start this was a long road to walk, and I'd have to be on it every step of the way. Maybe it wasn't so bad knowing I had someone alongside me.

I drove Sally back to her shack. She would have a couple of hours of rest before needing to get everything in the restaurant ready for that night's patrons. I decided she didn't need an accompaniment back to her bungalow. However, she did look back at me.

"You gonna be all right?" she asked.

"Eventually," I said with a smile. She smiled back, knowing a thing or two about that long road as well.

It was early afternoon, and I was tired but didn't want to go back to the Elmo and just go to bed. Junior's wouldn't be open for a while. Besides, the notion of just drinking away the night wasn't very comforting. I finally realized I needed to write a column based on today's verdict, so I headed over to the office.

Mrs. Lindstrom finished her filing and was ready to leave when I walked in. She smiled at me and touched my shoulder as a way to recognize my commitment to what I needed to do, both in the courtroom, for the newspaper, and for myself. I figured I could get in the final installment for the Friday afternoon edition and give the good folks of Arkansas City something to carry them through their weekend.

My opening paragraph admittedly was a bit melodramatic but it was in keeping with the others that had come before it.

Today puts to rest the case of Jimmy O'Donnell, a hoodlum from the old days whose time has long since passed. This wasn't a dream or a B-picture shown at the Burford. This was a wayward punk who was found guilty of the heinous crime of killing his mother. Today Justice was served.

Part of me wanted to philosophize on those days from long ago but it started to become too painful to do so. I lived it once when Jake Hickey unexpectedly appeared. I relived it further by venturing to Chicago and walking the streets of my old neighborhood and talking with a relic from those days who was slowly slipping away into oblivion. At times, I felt that way as well. Perhaps I reached a thoughtful note on the closing paragraph.

When the sentence is finally carried out, it will not mean an end of the gangsters or murderers in general. But it will mean the forces of Law and Order still work in this state. No matter how long it may take, our Judicial system prevails and the good men and women of this city can once again walk with their heads held high.

A little more than a week later, Dave Morton invited me to lunch. I suggested he let me take him to La Bella Vita for dinner. He agreed. A kind of sly smile simply appeared on his face after Sally sat at the table with us, and he kept noticing the way I looked at her, glued to every word she spoke.

"Well, everything the kid said was true."

"How do you mean?" The surprise in my voice was noticeable.

"I tracked down a bank robber and sneak thief named Tommy Price and looked up those bank robberies. Of the six you passed on to me, Price was involved in three of them."

"What about O'Donnell?"

"That's where it gets interesting. There is no mention of him in any of the reports."

"I don't get it," Sally interjected. "O'Donnell

claimed to have been in on those robberies with Price who was part of three of them?"

"Yeah, that's what has got me confused, too." Dave sat back in his chair, an empty plate and a full glass of wine before him. I stared off at nothing, my brain clicking like a teletype machine.

"You remember me telling you he was practically staring at me during his testimony?" Dave nodded. "All that stuff about Tommy Price and those bank jobs is a lot of malarkey. Pat McArdle placed him in Ark City in '34. He was sure of it. There was no way he was in Topeka, except maybe after October of that year."

"Then why the tall tale?"

I was lost in thought again. After a lot of time spent together, Sally looked at me as though she understood how I thought.

"Baron, didn't you say his appeal would be based on the state's claim of O'Donnell's intention to kill his mother?"

"That is all they've got to go on. I was there. You were there. His guilt is obvious."

"Yes, but if it winds up he can prove it wasn't intentional, couldn't they find him guilty of second-degree murder instead and—"

"And either send it back to the lower court," Dave continued, picking up the thread, "for a retrial or the defense attorney gets the district attorney's office to take a plea for a life sentence."

"But if there is a possibility of another murder having been committed," I went on, as though it were a game of tag, "the state would have plenty of opportunity while Jimmy is whiling away his time in prison to put together a case for the contract murder of

Heather Devore."

"Exactly." Dave was proud of himself.

"And that means the state can't lose the appeal." I heard myself sounding disappointed and doubtful. "They need Pat McArdle."

"Baron, the evidence against Jimmy O'Donnell for the murder of Heather Devore is circumstantial. Even McArdle won't be able to prove it. And everyone else is dead." Dave finally returned to his proper and logical self, the desk sergeant in the Arkansas City Police Department. That way of thinking was the only way he would wind up as chief of police. Nevertheless, I knew we didn't need to prove anything about Heather's murder, just that there was a possibility Jimmy could have done it.

The next morning I contacted Gregory Freeland who was preparing for the appeal in Wichita in the 18th Judicial Court of Appeals in four days. I explained our lengthy discussion and how Jimmy was just looking for the long prison sentence without the possibility something evil from his past could come to light. I recommended someone in Chicago needed to depose Pat McArdle to verify Jimmy was indeed in Ark City for most of 1934 and couldn't possibly have been with Tommy Price.

"What good does that do, Baron?"

"I assure you, sir, once that is presented in court, his lawyer will know Jimmy is bound for a death sentence. It'll either be sooner or later. And if he does win the appeal and gets a life sentence for second-degree murder, I will do everything I can for the rest of my life to prove he killed Heather Devore. Whatever it takes."

"So you aim to be a thorn in my side for many years, Mr. Witherspoon?"

"No, sir. You'll be long gone by then. Of course, I suppose you'll pass on some stories about me to the next assistant district attorney."

Gregory Freeland laughed a bit and agreed to have the Cook County district attorney's office track down Pat McArdle and depose him. Mr. Stauffer called me at the office to remind me my presence as a journalist would be required in Wichita. Unlike ten years ago, I had the law on my side this time. I was eager to go.

Chapter Thirty-Two

The last time I was in Wichita, I did everything possible to track down a vicious murderer who turned out to be some demented young police officer with an obsession with his mother. They scuttled Ronald Roché away to an insane asylum for his own protection as well as the reputations of the Wichita Police Department, City Council, and Mayor. It didn't occur to me to inquire as to his well-being as I was certain they all wanted to forget him.

Mr. Freeland stood outside of the courtroom with a folder in his hand. Despite the smile on his face, he acted concerned and not as pleased as I thought he would be.

"The Chicago Police Department was able to track down Pat McArdle and depose him. This," he announced, holding up the folder, "is his sworn testimony."

"Why did they need to track him down? I told you where he lived and worked."

"He wasn't there. They determined he had been stricken with pneumonia and was in Cook County Hospital." He hung his head solemnly and then looked up at me. "He died a few hours after he gave his statement."

Pieces of my past were falling off a cliff, fading away, or just dying. At times, it all seemed like perhaps it was just a dream. Was there ever an Eric Kimble? What really happened to Baron Witherspoon in the forests of France in 1918? When the lights come up in a theater after a movie is over, you return to your real life. What if the world on the screen was more real?

I grabbed the folder and walked down the corridor seeking out Mr. William O'Brien. He stood smugly near a window looking out over the same city streets where I chased a killer, the smoke from his foul cigar as toxic as the gasses used by the Hun. Unlike my encounters with the late Councilman Hallett, I wasn't going to let it nauseate me. I strode violently to him, stopping within inches.

"We need to talk," I demanded.

"I'm certain the court frowns upon *ex parte* communications." He turned away. My hand on his arm prevented that.

"I believe it would be in the best interests of your client to give me a scant two minutes of your time."

He waved in the direction of an empty antechamber.

"Please understand," he continued, "I have nothing to say…"

"You don't have to. I'll do all the talking." I gathered in a deep breath intent upon staying true to the time limit I set for myself. "If you are successful today, the judges may direct a retrial or you may, with all your bluster, negotiate a deal to secure a life sentence for Mr. O'Donnell. In this state, that means he would be eligible for parole in about seven years. However, during that time, I will use every resource at my disposal, including the state's attorney general, the Kansas Bureau of Investigation, my many acquaintances in newspapers all of the country, as well as the numerous former co-workers of mine at the Arkansas City Police Department, to prove beyond a reasonable doubt Jimmy O'Donnell killed Heather Devore in cold blood. That, sir, will be first degree murder and an appointment with the gallows in Lansing."

"There's no proof…"

"There will be. You're giving me seven years, counselor. And it starts with this deposition by Pat McArdle, an admitted associate of Jimmy O'Donnell who places him in Ark City as late as October of 1934. That malarkey about him and Tommy Price in Topeka won't hold up." I stared at him, but he kept looking away. "Your client is going to swing. It is either sooner or later." I turned and walked out, letting the door slam behind me, a few seconds short of two minutes.

Gregory Freeland responded to the three judges on the appeals court with clarity and conviction of the evidence presented during the trial. He answered each question with definitive comments, never wavering or being uncertain. When William O'Brien stood before them, the first question asked was whether he had anything he wished to add to his brief. He looked over at me, a face that appeared queasy after a drunken revelry, and then declined further comment. One judge closed his eyes. Another shook his head lightly. They were confused as to why an attorney would not make a stronger case for his client in a murder trial appeal. They finally indicated their opinion would be set down by the end of the week.

"What did you say to him?" Freeland asked outside of the courtroom.

"We discussed the law."

"What law?"

"The Law of Inevitability."

The following day, the panel of judges delivered its summation indicating the appellant, James Kieran O'Donnell, as represented by William O'Brien of Kansas City, Kansas, had failed to cite authorities supporting his position the state's determination of willful homicide was unjustified nor provided any substantive evidence to the contrary indicating a possible outcome of second-degree murder. Prison officials brought the defendant immediately to the Kansas State Penitentiary in Lansing for the carrying out of his sentence.

Appeals on death row can typically take a year or more. However, I received a call from Mr. O'Brien a little more than a month after O'Donnell's transfer that there would be no appeals. Jimmy O'Donnell determined his only remaining course of action was to wait for death. As much as it might be pleasurable for a convicted man to force the state to expend resources and time, the blank emptiness of a prison cell is more like a living death.

Next, came a phone call from Warden Charles Edmonson indicating my publisher, Mr. Oscar Stauffer, personally requested my invitation as a witness to the execution. I remembered watching old Westerns where they referred to it as a necktie party and wondered if there was a proper wardrobe. The date scheduled was Thursday, January 25, 1951. That was to be Jimmy O'Donnell's last day on this earth.

Time had rolled along without my even knowing it. It was just between Christmas and New Year's Eve, a popular and busy time for La Bella Vita. Part of me didn't want to impose upon Sally, but I knew I owed it to her to provide this information. It was on Thursday, the 28th of December. I sat in my car, the old jalopy gifted to me by my best friend Dave Morton. I watched merry revelers come and go, enjoying what I knew to be a delicious meal in an inviting and romantic atmosphere. Surprisingly, my face didn't bother me. No twitching or feeling of droopiness. Perhaps it was the cold weather, the frosty Kansas evening. I didn't know. At that moment, all seemed right.

At the end of the night, when the last car left, I walked to the front door and knocked. As though expecting me, Sally opened up and said, "When?"

I advised her of the date.

"Well, at least it's after the holidays, huh?"

I appreciated the effort of putting on a smile to soothe my fears.

"Is your boss springing for hotel rooms again?"

"If I ask him."

"You plan on asking him?"

"Should I?"

She nodded and then abruptly reached forward and hugged me, close and tight, as though I were a Mae West and we were both trying desperately not to drown in a sea of emotions. After what felt like a lifetime, she broke the embrace.

"I got to clean up. You go get some rest. You look awful." That smile emerged again from out of nowhere.

On the drive back to the Elmo, my mind wandered to the past. Not all the way back to the North Side or even the war. Just back to 1934 when everything was easy and smooth. Jake Hickey had brought more than trouble to Ark City. He carried a reminder of the violence in the world I no longer wanted a part of. He brought people like Jimmy O'Donnell.

Since then there had been killings in my town, sinister murders in Wichita, and a foreign threat in the form of a German POW right on our doorstep. Jimmy O'Donnell's execution would only put an end to a chapter. There was still the rest of the story to tell.

Chapter Thirty-Three

The New Year came and went as silent as a grave.
There was no celebrating, carousing, or revelry for me.
It was one day to the next without the scant recognition
it was now 1951. It felt like we spent all of 1950 in
courthouses. It was over breakfast on New Year's Day
Sally told me she had a packed restaurant all evening
and didn't get to go to bed until well after one in the
morning.

"So?" I looked at her wondering what she was
getting at. "What is your plan?"

"It is a pretty long drive. I figure on heading up on
the 23rd. That'll give me time to rest."

"You need to be well rested to watch a hanging?"

"I don't want to look defeated."

She understood. What little I knew of her late
husband revolved around his passion for the job and the
pride of being a sheriff. He would have wanted to stand
upright and square-jawed and watched the lousy cur
swing like a banshee in a storm. That same feeling
overcame me as well, but I tried hard to suppress it. It
wasn't Vengeance I was interested in. It was Justice.

Heather Devore was a good time girl who hooked
up with the wrong guy and found herself caught in a
struggle of men more powerful than she could ever
realize. Jake Hickey played a hand with nothing in it
and lost his life. Martin Childers died in a mysterious

car accident, likely betrayed by the same forces that offered him a share of power and glory. Councilman Hallett overdosed on insulin, smirking at me as he went, carrying his secrets with him to the grave. He might never have been accused, caught, or tried for his crimes on this earth. I had no doubt he was burning in hell.

Now, all that was left of this sad affair was a pathetic man who as a kid wanted to be tough and prove himself. All he got out of it was a life on the run and a date with a noose. It was certainly not what he planned.

"So what swank joint has your boss got us in?" I could tell Sally enjoyed these side excursions and the feeling of importance it conferred upon her. Sadly, I had to disappoint her this time.

"There are no swank joints in Lansing. Lady by the name of Olsen runs a boarding house. Two rooms with breakfast. For as long as we are there." I realized it was a silly thing to say.

We would arrive late on the 23rd, meet with the warden on the 24th, be witnesses on the 25th, and come back the next day. This was not a vacation or a joy ride. It was more like a pilgrimage. Only there was no baptism or salvation at the end.

My car wasn't anything worthy of a racetrack so I figured it would take a bit over six hours not including any necessary stops. We left on a Tuesday a little after eight in the morning. No rain or snow impeded us but a winter chill settled in the air. Sally just looked out the windows, her head swiveled like a windmill as she watched all the countryside through the Flint Hills. I got the impression she stuck mostly to herself, her cousins, and the restaurant since she moved here after her husband died. We didn't talk much. I was rather grateful for that because I did not want the time filled with empty words. What we needed was to give each of us space.

It had certainly been a long time since I drove anywhere of great length. I completely miscalculated the trip and was surprised it took us all of eight hours to get where we were going which included thirty minutes of asking for directions to the Olsen household once we got into town.

Mrs. Louise Olsen related she was a widow who made ends meet by renting out rooms in her spacious old home. She had a young girl who did the laundry and cleaned and Mrs. Olsen herself did all the cooking. Our rooms were on the second floor across from each other. There was a bathroom with a tub down the hall.

"Are you here for the prison?" she asked solemnly.

"Yes, ma'am."

"I get a lot of them for that reason. I do not know much about that sort of thing. I just hope it is God's will."

"I'm sure it is."

The next day, Wednesday, I drove up to the prison to meet with Warden Edmonson. Sally decided to remain in the room. She was here to support me and to be one of the State's witnesses. The business side of this event did not interest her.

Charles A. Edmonson came across as a bureaucrat whose job was to add humanity and humility to a gruesome task but wound up standing in front of a runaway train. Rehabilitation was not in this part of his job, just a straightforward and ritualistic set of proceedings that would result in the death of a man who the state declared would not add anything further to our society and was required to pay the ultimate price. He was simply a man who held a pocket watch and marked the course of time.

He shook my hand firmly and explained the process: At the proscribed time, the warden and two guards would go to the cell located on the second floor of the S&I, or Security and Isolation building where they maintained death row. Only one other prisoner, Preston McBride, was there. He was a young man convicted of the cold-blooded murder of a sixty-two-year-old cab driver at the urging of narcotics dealers. According to the warden, McBride spent a lot of time with the prison chaplain, Patrick Delahunty, to be received into the Catholic faith. Jimmy O'Donnell repeatedly rejected the chaplain's services, saying he was only waiting to give his confession to one person.

That, it turned out, was me.

I knew I was there for more than just being a witness. Not more than two words had passed between us since that night in his mother's house. My bitterness and anger would not allow me to visit him in Winfield or Wichita. Now, however, at the very end, I needed to see him as much as he wanted to speak with me. Now was the time.

The metal steps of the stairs leading up to the second floor clanged like a church bell high in a steeple. O'Donnell was in the first cell while McBride was at the end. Jimmy looked tired as though the fight he put up all his life finally ground him down to ash. A strong wind would blow away any memory of him.

"You ever been here before?" he asked.

"First time."

"Heck of a place. You would love it. Shower once a week but only one of us at a time. The guard locks my safety razor the two times a week I actually get to shave. No mirrors, no bottles, no glasses. No knives and no forks. They don't want us to off ourselves and take away the state's right to kill us." He smirked. I was unimpressed.

"Makes sense."

"Really?" I saw him grit his teeth, grind them as though he were maybe trying to choke to death on the enamel. "There's no radio, movies, no TV. No cards or games. Not even exercise." There was the sting of vinegar now in his voice.

"What do you do?"

"Eat. Sleep. Write. Think. Sometimes I even dream."

"Do you pray?"

"For what?" he spat.

I was tired of hearing his plea for pity. I had none for him. Neither that nor any compassion or consideration. This was turning into a boxing match where one fighter kept swinging and missing. It was only a matter of time before he fell down.

"Why did you want me here?" I asked bitterly.

"It wasn't supposed to be like this."

"Yes, it was. The moment you did the bidding of a crooked politician and a corrupt refinery owner. The devil didn't put a straight razor in your hand, Jimmy. You did. You reached for it and embraced it."

"This make you feel all powerful being here, watching me swing?"

"No." My voice was almost a whisper, the kind of

way you talk in a library. I knew that response disappointed him. If I was there simply to watch a man die, he could walk up those steps without batting an eye and show who was stronger.

"Then why are you here?"

"For me. For your mother. But mostly for Heather Devore. She deserved more."

"Yeah? Well, so did I." He pointed his chin at me in defiance.

"But you saw to it that neither of you came out ahead."

I stared at him. He did not back down. Yet somewhere in the back of his eyes he realized the past seventeen years had been a complete and utter waste. One misguided action in a hotel room in Ark City had begun the process of emptying his life of any significant meaning. All I could think about was what remained for me.

Chapter Thirty-Four

That night, Sally and I found a joint offering fried chicken with mashed potatoes and gravy and fresh hot buttermilk biscuits. For the briefest moment, I was taken back in time to just after the war, when "Baron Witherspoon" came back from Europe a broken young man tended to by his father and mother in the clean living town of Arkansas City, Kansas. Life was good and simple and pure. Except Eric Kimble didn't know anything about living and working on a farm or how to exist in such an environment. There were several dinners just like the one I feasted on now. It would take many years to truly fit in. As for being comfortable, I wasn't sure exactly when that happened.

I sensed Sally was eager to find out how my visit with Jimmy O'Donnell turned out, but she was respectful enough not to show her eagerness. After sopping up the last spot of gravy, I put my fork down on the plate.

"I don't think he has any notion of what he's done," I started. "Either now or in the past. Always someone else's fault. Always someone else's problem. He'll go to his maker thinking someone else made a mistake."

"Any confession?"

I smiled broadly, which certainly caught her off guard.

"Not in so many words. But I heard what I needed to hear."

We spoke quietly about the following day. We would stay in our rooms or perhaps one room and just read the newspaper or listen to the radio. Maybe take a nap in the afternoon. These events took place late in the evening, after midnight. Outside of patrols, I wasn't all that used to being up late anymore. Now that I was getting older, it was even more of a challenge.

The plan was to drive up to the prison around eleven p.m. She would be able to wait in the old warehouse while I accompanied the warden on his official duties. After it was over, I would call in what would be my final column on this case. I knew Verna Sharer would not enjoy the notion of me calling her up close to one in the morning. But seeing as how we had a chance to put out an exclusive for the morning edition, she allowed her professionalism to cover her personal disappointment. I am certain she was eager to get back to writing about young debutantes.

Mrs. Olsen's breakfast was a sumptuous as before. This time, however, sensing this was the day in question, she did not say anything outside of grace over the meal.

I was surprisingly energetic and alive, a contrast to what I was about to witness. Certainly, I saw Jake Hickey shot to death, watched Natalie Dixon end her life, marveled at FBI Agent Alex Gordon's sharpshooting, and somehow put a bullet through a panel truck to kill a German conspirator. This was something different. It wasn't the lawlessness of the Old West or a lynching. This was a state sanctioned execution, done with all elements in order from top to bottom. It was a solemn proceeding with no room for anything beyond the circle in which it took place.

It was just after three in the afternoon. I listened to a CBS national news broadcast while Sally looked over a two day old copy of the *Leavenworth Times,* commenting the writing was not as good as mine. A sudden knock at the door broke my smile.

Standing before me was a young girl, a teenager, maybe barely twenty. She had dark hair and dimples with deep brown eyes that had a touch of emerald. While she was physically mature, something completely innocent about her face reminded me of a far off time.

"Are you Baron Witherspoon?" I nodded with a certain degree of uncertainty. "My name is Meghan Devore."

Like a rocket going off emitting showers of sparks and bright lights, I saw her and recognized the face, almost like a reincarnation from so many years ago. I was so surprised to see her I hadn't considered how she managed to locate me. I waved her into the room. Sally offered her the chair where she was sitting.

Either I was mute or had lost any ability in the English language because words failed to come out of my mouth. Here was a previously unknown daughter of a good time B-girl who hooked up with the wrong gangster and willfully slaughtered by powerful men who wouldn't have given her the time of day. To them she was nothing more than a pawn in a power play. Yet she was some child's mother.

"My grandmother raised me. Always told me my mom died of influenza right after I was born."

"You didn't believe that?" Sally asked, exhibiting a

maternal side I never realized she had.

"Well, I did at first. But I kept having these memories of her when I was real little. About the time I went into parochial school, I started to have these dreams. The nuns told me I was just sad I didn't have Mother anymore. I continued to press my grandmother until she finally gave in and told me the truth. It was right after I turned fifteen."

"I'm so sorry." I heard myself say the words, but I didn't recall speaking them. It was as though I wanted to say them for years. "But how did you know to find me here?"

"My grandmother has a cousin on your police department. Well, old police department."

"Who?"

"Clifford Smiley."

I nodded my head. The quiet unassuming desk sergeant who never raised a ruckus or caused the department any embarrassment likely followed everything I had done on this case by talking with Dave Morton and reading my articles in the *Traveler*. "I called your newspaper to find out where you'd be."

This young girl's gumption and determination truly impressed me. She mentioned she held off going to the secretarial school her grandmother saved up for in order to find me and get answers. She mentioned nothing about this case or the execution to take place in less than nine hours. For my part, I offered a portrait of a young woman who recognized the mistakes of her past and wanted to break free and start anew. I didn't hold back by referring to her late mother as smart, savvy, and seductive. I recalled the shock of finding her brutally murdered and wondering why it had to come to that. I wound up admitting Heather Devore's death haunted me for so many years.

Meghan was not interested in the police case or the legal case. In the end, she was just looking for someone who remembered her mother and could say something nice about her. It was gratifying I managed to accomplish just that.

Based on Mrs. Olsen's suggestion, I scurried around the block to find a small grocery store where I had sandwiches made and bought three bottles of Royal Crown Cola. We ate in the room in silence. It was getting close to six o'clock.

"Do you want to go with us tonight, Meghan?"

"Oh, no, Mr. Witherspoon. I couldn't stand to watch. I know you'll be there representing my mom."

"And, Baron," Sally chimed in, "I think I'm going to just stay here with Meghan." She turned toward the girl. "If that'll be all right with you." Meghan smiled and nodded. This would be an experience I would have to go through on my own.

I felt no need to put on a fresh shirt or wear a jacket and tie. There wasn't any kind of formality to stand on. I was there to witness a ritual of the state. My job was to tell the story to the interested parties in my community.

I still wondered. About after. When all remnants of this event were gone like dust in the wind, becoming fading memories. The better part of the last two years, shortly after my forced retirement from the police force, had been practically dedicated to finding this man. With him gone, what endured for me?

Chapter Thirty-Five

10:57 p.m.

Sally and Meghan chatted away about some such thing. It had all the looks of a mother and daughter gossiping. It was like watching a silent movie, lips moved but I did not fully understand what they were saying. Even without the title cards I could guess at the conversation. I figured Sally had a maternal instinct. I saw it in little bits and pieces in the way she showed concern about my well-being. Would Pete still be alive if they had kids, perhaps giving up his job as a sheriff for something less dangerous and maybe not enlisting when the war broke out?

Their minds, as far as I could see, were as far away as possible from the forthcoming events. Perhaps my eyes could not see the truth. This might have been their way of dealing with all of it. I had to find my own way.

There was no need to say "Goodbye" or "I'll be back when it is over" because all of that was a given. I walked to the door and closed it softly behind me. For the first time I could remember, my face started to twitch. I hoped this would stop. I didn't want Jimmy to see it as a sign of weakness.

****

11:13 p.m.

No traffic was around this time of night. With the prison being a few minutes away, I arrived earlier than I anticipated. A cold silence hung in the air. Nothing moved or stirred. I sat in the car for a moment, screwing up my courage. Using techniques offered to me by Dr. Brenz, I lightly massaged my face hoping blood would flow through the scarring and make me feel more relaxed.

The thought returned to me of how I never witnessed such a thing as this. Was it a blessing or a curse?

It was certain the guards were used to this rigmarole. They had just gone through it with George Miller, a sixty-year-old colored man, back in May of last year. I wasn't sure about Edmonson. Being a staunch administrator, he would appear firm and upright. He may not have had the typical hours of a banker but this was to be business as usual.

The gate guards recognized me from earlier in the day, checked to make sure I wasn't carrying any weapons, and then led me casually to the warden's office. Edmonson wore a freshly pressed suit as though he were about to attend a baptism. I hoped I had dressed properly. He explained everything in detail and assured me I could use his office in private afterward to file my newspaper report. He made sure I wrote his name down correctly. The brevity of fame requires correct spelling and punctuation.

****

11:53 p.m.

I spent the better part of thirty minutes merely looking around the warden's office, taking in details, trying to get my mind to focus on something other than the scheduled activity. I looked out the window, seeing nothing I could identify, perhaps not being aware of anything in my field of vision. It was as though I struggled in a maze of barbed wire, felt pain but did not comprehend where it came from.

Warden Edmonson, two guards, O'Malley and Johnson, and I walked from the warden's office to the S&I building. Edmonson looked back at me for a brief moment. Perhaps he wanted to be sure I wasn't turning green and approaching nausea. He had his job to do. While he was extending every courtesy, he could not stop for me or anyone else. This was the road to Calvary.

I looked into the cell. Jimmy had his back to the entrance while he stood in the middle of the room, presumably staring out the window. I wondered what he saw that was different from what I couldn't see. The jailers fitted him into a leather harness that prevented his arms from moving. I speculated they likely handcuffed him in front. Leg shackles did not allow for anything more than a gait similar to a penguin.

Surprisingly absent was any kind of clergyman. I knew he was raised Christian but likely dispensed with any religion from the moment he took to being a gangster. There were others who discovered the notion of Repentance and wanted their afterlife to be different from what transpired here on Earth. My guess was Jimmy had no use for the salvation of his soul.

Two other guards were in the cell, leaning on walls on opposite sides. Their job was simply to keep everything in order, talk to Jimmy to calm him if he got too upset, or prevent him from violently thrashing his head against the wall. The state would have their pound of flesh. O'Malley told me on the way over Jimmy ate his final meal completely, as though he were going on a long journey. He ordered a steak, rare, mashed potatoes with brown gravy, cornbread, and for dessert a large piece of pecan pie a la mode. They turned down his request for a whiskey high ball. Maybe he ate that well back in the day with a bankroll in his pockets and bravado puffing out his chest. Of late, he was lucky to get beans and biscuits.

****

12:00 a.m.

Warden Edmonson cleared his throat to get Jimmy's attention. Jimmy turned slowly, his face blank and cold, and stared directly at the warden

"Jimmy, I've got a warrant here I need to read."

"Go ahead." O'Donnell spoke as though he gave the warden permission.

"WHEREAS, JAMES KIERAN O'DONNELL, having been found guilty of the first degree murder of one Regina O'Donnell by a jury of his peers in the 19th Judicial Court of Cowley County; and

WHEREAS, the 18th Judicial Court of Appeals of Sedgwick County affirmed the trial court order denying JAMES KIERAN O'DONNELL'S Motion for Postconviction Relief as well as affirming the trial court's order denying his Motions for Collateral Relief; and

WHEREAS, further postconviction motions and petitions filed by JAMES KIERAN O'DONNELL have been denied and affirmed on appeal,

NOW, THEREFORE, I, FRANK CARLSON, as Governor of the State of Kansas and pursuant to the authority and responsibility vested in me by the Constitution and Laws of Kansas, do hereby issue this warrant, directing the Warden of the Kansas State

Penitentiary to cause the sentence of death to be executed upon JAMES KIERAN O'DONNELL in accord with the provisions of the Laws of the State of Kansas."

Edmonson looked up at Jimmy after he had read from the paper. Jimmy acted as though he were waiting to get going, expecting the next train at the station to be rolling along at any moment. He had no response. Johnny Law had spoken.

The two guards in the cell came from behind and guided Jimmy out of the cell. O'Malley and Johnson stood alongside him, rifles in their hands. Edmonson and I fell in behind.

"You got a date with The Corner there, Jimmy?" Preston McBride squawked from his cell at the end. A brief smile crossed O'Donnell's lips. Jailhouse humor is thick with black clouds; only the inmates are able to smile.

"I'll be seeing you later, Pres." Like two best buddies.

From the S&I building, we took a long walk across the baseball field. A raw wind blew and made it feel like the North Pole. I hadn't brought gloves or a hat, not having given any thought to the Kansas winter. A shiver spilled through me that I convinced myself was due to the weather. I knew better.

No one played any games on this field. No one exercised or passed the time. It was empty and bleak. The lone face of Preston McBride watched us as we strode. He awaited his turn and likely contemplated how he would react not too far from now.

****

12:11 a.m.

We arrived at the old brick warehouse. By my count, there were about fifteen people already waiting. I recognized a few court officials from both Cowley County and Sedgwick County. I assumed the others were prison officials. The closest thing the victim had to a next of kin was me.

There were only three overhead lights in the whole building. One was at the entrance. Another was high up in the middle, hardly illuminating anything. The last one was directly over the gallows. They were located in the corner of the warehouse, hence the nickname used by McBride. I counted thirteen steps to the top. Just below the trapdoor, where the body would drop, stood a man in a suit with a stethoscope around his neck. No one made any reference to his name. He was just another man doing his job.

Sliding quietly through the crowd was a man whose face I could not see. He wore a gray wool suit and a large black hat pulled down closely over his eyes. He walked past Jimmy, the warden, and the guards, and quietly climbed the steps. He must have worn crepe-soled shoes because he did not make a sound. It was as though he hovered but never stood on the ground. I never knew what the Angel of Death looked like until that moment.

"Jimmy, do you have anything to say?" Warden Edmonson asked.

"What's the point?"

If those were to be his last words, they exhibited a kind of callousness I saw in him all along but hoped would fade as this time approached. He turned out to be tougher and meaner than Jake Hickey.

Just before he turned to walk those thirteen steps,

our eyes met. I thought I saw a brief nod of his head, an acknowledgement of something unstated. Maybe those last words were a question to no one in particular as to how his life turned the way it did. He had plenty of opportunities to explain or make excuses but never turned any of his thoughts into words that I could print and save forever. Like Hallett, I would have to make my own assumptions or live with the not knowing.

Johnson escorted him up the steps. The leg shackles encumbered his walking but he did not falter. Johnson guided him to the center and placed his feet appropriately, one on either side of the trapdoors. I could see him tie a leather strap around his ankles. Jimmy was now completely immobile.

A man somewhere in the crowd who coughed suddenly broke the silence.

The rustling of impatient feet sounded as annoying as crickets chirping.

It was cold in the warehouse, but the wind could not attack us in here.

The man in the gray wool suit unfastened a screw on the trapdoor lever. He looked down at the warden who nodded his head in affirmation.

O'Donnell fell through the trapdoor at 12:17 a.m. While it appeared to have snapped his neck, his body bounced twice before swinging slightly and then spun back and forth.

The man with the stethoscope waited until there was no further movement. O'Malley and Johnson held the body still. The man with the stethoscope placed it against Jimmy's chest. We waited. The pronouncement of death for one James Kieran O'Donnell came at 12:26 a.m., Friday, January 26, 1951.

Chapter Thirty-Six

There were others to clean up behind us. These were men I never met, tasked with removing the tools of death and leave behind the gallows as a kind of monument to the power of the State of Kansas. Warden Edmonson and I went back to his office. He turned on all the lights, which immediately blinded me. To that point everything occurred in the subdued lighting of a cold winter evening. He motioned me toward his desk and told me to take my time.

Verna Shearer started out with a yawn when she finally answered the phone as it was later than she was used to being awake. While I felt bad for the circumstances, I didn't have the patience to be concerned with her lack of sleep. I wanted to submit this article. I wanted all of this done and behind me. For good.

It started out as a simple news article.

"James Kieran O'Donnell was executed tonight for the murder of his mother, Regina O'Donnell. This was the only crime for which he was convicted of, but we can assume his long history included other such offenses. May those unknown victims rest in peace knowing Justice has been served."

That was for Heather Devore and young Meaghan. But something else had to be said to the people of the city that took me in when I had no place else to go.

"It is sad to consider this young man chose the path he did when so many others opted to change. Perhaps it is because following the true path of Good requires too much effort. I have witnessed it nearly every day since I came back from the Great War. For over thirty years, I've watched the people of Ark City work hard for the simple pleasures in their lives. Their struggles are real, but for the citizens of my fair city, the rewards are sweet.

"In Proverbs 4:18 it is written: But the path of the Righteous is like the light of dawn, which shines brighter and brighter until full day. *That light shines on you today, dear friends and readers, and you are all the richer for it."*

I waited until Mrs. Shearer read back every word to me. When I heard it, I honestly couldn't believe I wrote it. She assured me this would be our morning extra. Despite her sleepiness, she recognized I composed something special that transcended the occasion.

I thanked the warden for his courtesy and consideration, shook his hand firmly, and walked out of his office. As I proceeded through the grounds toward the gate, I did not look back once. It was just after one in the morning. I wanted the light of dawn to shine on me.

There were so many things I could have done at that moment: sat in my car in the parking lot and cried; driven around until my head finally cleared of the madness; find a cheap juke joint somewhere that served some mean hooch. Too much time passed in my life for any of those things. I simply drove back to the rooming house.

I found Sally and Meghan curled up on my bed.

The opening of the door stirred them. Meghan stood up first, stretched like a sleepy cat, and then stood stock-still. She hardly even blinked.

"Is it over?"

"Yes." I could barely hear my own voice. She went to the side of the bed and grabbed her satchel.

"There's a bus leaving Leavenworth at 2:55 this morning. Could you take me there?"

I looked over her shoulder to Sally. She raised her eyebrows.

"Yes. Certainly."

Meghan turned back.

"If it's okay..." Sally didn't need to hear her request it be just us two. She got up and came over to Meghan. The hug was deep and personal. It was to be a long goodbye.

We drove a scant three miles up the road to the station on a frontage road. The building was no bigger than someone's living room, had two wooden benches, and a booth where a man sold tickets. Meghan and I sat patiently.

"You came all this way. You didn't attend the execution. And now you're heading back to Chicago. I don't get it?"

"Mr. Smiley told my grandmother everything that happened back when my mom was killed. He said you were the one who tried hardest to help her. All I could think of was how hard this must have been for you."

It took everything I had to keep a tear from trickling down my worn and scarred face. The last several years allowed me to see the true nature of all my emotions.

We sat for quite a while in silence. Shortly before

the bus arrived, I needed to be sure she would be all right.

"What will you do in Chicago?"

"Well, my grandmother has saved up for me to go to secretarial school. I'll wind up getting a job, meeting a nice guy, getting married, and have a family. I'm sure it is what my mother would have wanted."

The simplicity of it was nothing to make fun of. It was a good life filled with positive things, nothing dark or mean or evil included in it. There shouldn't be, not for her. She would have what her mother would have wanted for her, what Heather Devore herself could never achieve.

She gave me a hug before she got on the bus. I watched it drive toward Topeka where she would connect and go on to Chicago. That city belonged to people like her now. I was glad.

Sally read the same newspaper she read earlier the day before. She looked up at me and smiled.

"You hungry?" I asked.

"Famished."

We found an all-night diner, shoveled fried eggs and bacon into our mouths, and drank close to two pots of coffee. It never occurred to me before how stressful situations could make you hungry.

"Let's go home."

We were on the road just after four thirty. I dropped her off at the restaurant just after one in the afternoon and assured her I would be by later in the evening. My next stop was to the office of the *Traveler*. The morning edition sold out. A call from Mr. Stauffer indicated several wire services picked up my last column. He light-heartedly commented he might lose me as a columnist if the article spread like wildfire. I doubted that would be the case. Besides, my worldly adventures had worn me out to a point where staying put seemed like a more promising idea.

I was exhausted and needed to shut my eyes. Dave Morton caught up with me just outside the Elmo.

"You know, I never told you this before," he said, "but I am really proud of you."

"I don't understand. Why?"

"All the things you've been through your entire life. You've made it past all of that. You're much more than the Baron Witherspoon I knew." He smiled, tapped me on the shoulder, and walked away. I couldn't tell if he was referencing recent events or Eric Kimble. I no longer needed to be concerned.

I slept later than I intended but it was still earlier than when the restaurant closed. I put on a fresh clean shirt and pair of pressed pants and my best shoes. It occurred to me I needed a reason to dress up like a gentleman. Sally was the reason.

As I had done before, I waited until the last car left La Bella Vita. I knocked softly on the door. It seemed Sally had the same idea. She wore a silk blouse, wool skirt, with her hair pulled up, and a coat of fresh lipstick applied.

We sat opposite each other near a window. It had been an unbelievably warm day, making the drive home feel like a vacation. Just the day before it was frigid and today felt like spring. Perhaps it was a time of renewal.

Her cousins had left for the evening, dirty dishes still in the kitchen. Sally stopped me from trying to help her clean up. She just wanted to sit in the silent darkness and drink wine.

"Isn't it time we both put the past behind us?" she asked softly.

"What else is there?"

She reached across the table, her soft hand holding mine in hers.

"The future."

I looked up and into her eyes. It was time to wake up from the dream.

Part Two:
Return from the Land of Nod

To me belongeth vengeance and recompence;
their foot shall slide in due time: for the day
of their calamity is at hand, and the things
that shall come upon them make haste.
~Deuteronomy 32:35 KJV

Chapter One

Sally Harper and I got married on March 6, 1951 at the Cowley County Courthouse in Winfield, Kansas. It was a Tuesday, an unseasonably warm day in the upper sixties, almost like spring. Sally wore a simple white skirt and pale yellow silk blouse, her hair pulled up revealing a face both stoic and loving. I wore the only suit I owned but made sure to have it dry-cleaned before this day. Her cousins, Rosa DeFrancesco and Anna Pascuale, acting as maids of honor, had tears in their eyes. According to Sally, Italian women get emotional on such occasions and many others as well. Standing up for me was my longtime friend, Dave Morton, now a Captain in the Arkansas City police department. He opted to wear a suit rather than his dress uniform. I couldn't recall ever seeing him so formally attired.

I had spent some time researching in the basement files of the courthouse in 1935 for a series of murders when I was still a police officer. It was an austere set of rooms, my shoes echoing ominously on the marbled floors. Of course, Sally and I were last here together less than a year ago, testifying at the murder trial of Jimmy O'Donnell, who was executed at the Kansas State Penitentiary back in January. Those were times of apprehension and uncertainty. It was good to be here for something far more worthwhile.

La Bella Vita, the Italian restaurant Sally ran with her cousins, rivaled Daisy Mae's, the longstanding diner, for the taste buds of the community. My appearances at Daisy Mae's were less frequent due to my wife's business. The small cottage Sally previously used as a residence became a storage facility for the restaurant after Sally and I bought a house on South C Street in between Washington and Adams. It was just behind Sacred Heart Catholic Church, which gave Sally some comfort.

She started attending church more regularly presumably as a way to find more balance in her life. She invited me to join her but I declined. Those places never provided me with the same kind of peace that others often found. I had encountered too much in my life to allow a scant bit of doubt to remain. However, I was happy to see her with a smile on her face more often.

Julia Lindstrom, the librarian who came out of retirement to become my research assistant at the *Traveler*, retired again, this time to a small farm in Rochester, New Hampshire. Her replacement was Miguel Cristales, a young Mexican who took classes at the Arkansas City Junior College. He was bright and eager, willing to help me in many assignments as I continued to write my daily column. I was certain he would make something of himself given his forthright attitude. After the murder of Regina O'Donnell and the ensuing trial of her son, things calmed down quite a bit. Nothing of stunning importance occurred, so my columns took on a decidedly "homey" feel to them. The bump in circulation fell back to normal. I was just another journalist with very little talk of a Pulitzer Prize swirling around. The publisher, Oscar Stauffer, was not overly concerned. He was grateful enough for my efforts that I felt as though I would have this job for the rest of my life if I so decided.

The primary thing that changed was the condition of my face. Falling into a span of barbed wire during the First World War, having primitive reconstruction surgery, and dealing with a series of traumas related to being a police officer for nearly thirty years had definitely taken their toll. Dr. Louis Brenz, my long-time physician, retired from regular practice but continued to see me as a special patient. He was the only one in a fifty-mile radius who had any grasp of my condition.

The flesh sagged in part because the surgery was not ideal but also because I was older. My facial muscles were not as strong as they had been in my youth. While there was not as much stress in my life, the dreams of the past returned as well as the occasional headaches brought on by extreme sunshine and bright lights. Doctie never said anything directly but implied there was nothing further to do medically at this point in my life. We didn't discuss what would or could happen in the next months or years. I never brought any of this up with Sally, perhaps not wanting her to worry or take time away from all the things she enjoyed and could finally do in peace. Perhaps it was selfish of me, but then I had never been married before and couldn't be sure if my efforts were in vain. To see her smile meant everything to me.

With a true love in my life and my heart, I could say I achieved more than I ever thought possible. If my time were soon approaching an end, I would have no complaints.

Three years passed. I woke up each of those mornings, went to the office to write my column, headed on to La Bella Vita to help my wife in any way I could, and went to a home that was a place of comfort. It was as though life had begun anew. For both of us. The thought of an eventual end faded from my mind. Each day was a precious gift.

It was just after our third anniversary, and a week before my birthday Garrison Reed, the toothless mail carrier who plowed the streets of Ark City since the days of prohibition, dropped by the house late in the afternoon.

"How's married life treating you?" he chided.

"I could be doing a lot worse." A warm smile on my face let me know I could actually feel something. Garrison handed me a postcard. "What is this?"

"Well, that's what I've wondered. It went to your old address at the Elmo, same apartment number and everything. But it's not your name. I talked with Carl Pearson, and he said they ain't got no one by that name there now. Or ever for that matter, as far back as he can remember."

Carl had been the night clerk at the Elmo back when it was the Gladstone. He had a droopy face and looked like he was always tired. However, he was sharp as a tack with a memory to boot. Probably could have been successful on one of those television game shows they started showing more frequently.

I had no idea what I was supposed to do with a postcard that wasn't even addressed to me. Maybe Garrison figured I could dredge up my old police skills even though I had been retired, so to speak, for six years now.

It was when I read the card I felt a rolling sea of nausea and a cold sweat hit me from top to bottom. All the joy of the present blew away like a tornado carving a path through a cornfield. The past stared me in the face on a four by six postcard.

Chapter Two

Sure enough, the street address and apartment number were for the Elmo, my former residence. The problem was I hadn't lived there in three years. It was shortly after Sally and I got married that we bought our house and moved out. However, the confusion of the address was nothing compared to the text.

Eric Kimble, We know where you live.

For so many years, I struggled with the fact that I, Eric Kimble, a North Side Irish tough, had taken over the life of Baron Witherspoon, a dear friend who saved my life during the First World War. Eventually I became Baron, or at least a new version of him, and had put aside my past. That is, until Jake Hickey showed up in Arkansas City in 1934. And a sweet old lady named Regina O'Donnell asked me to locate her wayward son who was involved with Hickey. A ghostly arm reached out from the grave presumably to draw me down into it.

Someone out there identified me as my former self with a direct message to a place I used to live. As late as 1951, an unknown person or persons physically saw me while living in the Elmo and knew who I had been once a lifetime ago. I had no earthly notion who they were, where they were now, or if they followed Sally and me to our new home. There was a sudden breathlessness as though a gust of wind blew through my lungs.

I had to presume they hadn't; otherwise, I would have received something more directly. Then, why the postcard to the old residence? And was there really a "we" or just a single person intent on terrorizing me?

My head started to throb. The blood left my face making it feel cold.

A hazy sparkle in front of my eyes turned into a kind of dizziness. I was no longer able to determine if this was the shock of the postcard or a deterioration of my condition. I sat with my face in my hands clutching the postcard when Sally came home in the afternoon. She sat beside me quietly. I simply handed her the postcard.

"What does it mean?" she asked.

I sat up stock-still, took a deep breath, and gained a measure of control. For the next forty-five minutes, I recounted every detail of my life to the woman I married. From the beginnings in the Market Street Gang to a recommendation by Dion O'Banion to go off and fight the Hun. From my friendship with a Kansas farm boy to hiding behind a scarred face and starting a new life. From a transition into a respected lawman, going up against a boyhood acquaintance, discovering a woman I might have loved was a brutal killer, and having to remain quiet about a madman in the Wichita police department. Revealing the truth about the near tragedy in our town during the Second World War. Every story I could think of that I had tucked away for so many years. All the secrets, others' and mine. I was not going to hold anything back from Sally even if it meant she could no longer love me or respect me.

She touched my arm lightly after my dissertation. I thought I noticed a smirk on her face. At first, I wondered if she even believed me.

"Have you ever heard of Paul Ricca?" she asked.

"Name rings a bell. Italian?"

"Oh, yeah," she said, her eyes lighting up. "You know of Frank Nitti, right?" I nodded. "Yeah, well, Frank, because of his age, was the guy everyone said took over after Capone went to jail for his tax issues. Paul was really in charge. He was far more brutal than Nitti was. Nitti should have been an accountant with his attitude."

"How do you know all this?" I was having trouble with my facial muscles, but I could sense my eyebrows squeezing together.

"Ricca had a bodyguard named Pascuale Galliardi. And just like Jake Hickey and "Bugs" Moran, Ricca sent Galliardi away. There was a weapons charge on him and Ricca didn't want to be associated with someone who could bring him down. Only thing is Galliardi thought he was leaving town for a short spell, just like Hickey. He and his wife, Silvana Galliardi, first went to Wisconsin and then Indiana before winding up in Iowa. He got a job as sheriff."

My eyes opened wide, and my mouth became dry.

"Pascuale Galliardi became Pete Harper. You see, Baron, we all have secrets."

So much about Sally became clearer to me as I assumed she fully understood my struggles. We had both trudged through the fire to come out what we thought was renewed on the other side. The problem was this postcard was like a shovel digging up graves. It would have been considered a sacrilege if it didn't scare me so much.

"Baron," she said, emphasizing my name, "our

pasts are long behind us. We've started a new life."

"Not when this is staring us in the face." I shook the postcard like it was stuck to my fingers. She took it from me and studied it closely.

"It's signed." I reexamined it. I hadn't noticed anything other than the block text before. Underneath it was AZ 1096. I shook my head.

"Whatever this is, whoever it's from," she continued, "we need to find out what it's about. My guess is it is certainly no prank."

"It was so long ago. Who would even care?"

"Oh, believe me, if someone thinks you did them wrong, they will hold a grudge until one of you is dead."

In retrospect, the comment didn't shock me knowing full well how true it was. Jake held a grudge of unimagined proportions.

"Why don't you visit Dave and finally clear the air?"

Dave Morton had been a co-worker on the police department and a friend for twenty years. He helped me stop Jake Hickey from turning our town into an Old West shootout, find a brutal killer, and stop a German POW and his cohorts who were intent upon an act of sabotage. Dave was smart and had a strong character. While I never doubted our friendship, I felt this sort of thing would be a burden to him and perhaps undermine my ability to live life peacefully. Additionally, I didn't want to damage Dave's reputation on the force by the public finding out he was friends with someone of my background. Besides, I felt the sender of the postcard had different intentions.

This was not going to be like the group efforts of

the past when a collective of men had a singular mission. For the time being, it was to be Sally and me, alone, trying to unravel a puzzle. It would mean our lives and certainly our futures.

Chapter Three

Miguel Cristales stayed on with the paper as an office boy after his graduation in 1952. While it was not the best paying job, for him it was better than being a worker in a packing plant or trudging through his days in a refinery. He may have only had an associate's degree, but he was the first in his family to have any kind of schooling. He reveled in his ability to assist me in tasks beyond mere manual labor. As time went on, he took over the role of the late Sandy Clevenger, and the now retired Julia Lindstrom.

I positioned the signature inquiry to him as a challenge without actually showing him the postcard. These kind of mental challenges made him feel included in the newspaper process. What could AZ 1096 mean? I made sure to let him know this was not a priority but merely an opportunity to show off his skills. He took to it like a fish to water.

Meanwhile, I considered what the letters might mean. To that end, I went through the dictionary to look up all words starting with AZ.

Azimuth: an arc of the horizon measured between a fixed point and the vertical circle passing through the center of an object, usually in astronomy and navigation clockwise from the north point through three hundred sixty degrees. *Was the sender some kind of fanatic who felt divinely guided?*

Azoic: of or relating to the part of geologic time that antedates life. *A reference to the old neighborhood and a time before I became who I was?*

Aztec: a member of a Nahuatlan people that founded the Mexican empire conquered by Cortes in 1519. *A local Mexican who I arrested or perhaps a relative of the same? Certainly not Miguel.*

Azure: the blue color of the clear sky. *The color of the sender's eyes?*

Not a lot of options and certainly none that made any sense to a man who investigated many serious crimes. Nevertheless, as I was finished with my columns for the week, I reviewed these words for any possible meaning. I approached it as I had all my previous police investigations, asking myself deeper questions and keeping all options open.

If it had to do with navigation, the "1096" would be something directional in nature. A quick phone call to a professor at Miguel's old school clarified that more numbers would be required. While the geologic definition referred to a time past and made some degree of sense, the number had no additional bearing. The Mexican angle and the color reference did not connect to me at all, at least anything I had any recollection of immediately.

There were other technical terms starting with the two letters, but I couldn't see where the writer of the postcard sounded like a scientist. While sorting through mail at the office, I came across a response from an inquiry one of our reporters made to *The Arizona Republic*. Based on the letters, it occurred to me that this postcard might have come from there as well. It was just a hunch. Perhaps the numbers were even some sort of postal code.

Keeping in mind the time difference, I placed a call to an acquaintance of mine, Derek Dykstra. He was a young reporter who contacted me after the war to tell my story on how we captured Eihann Hammerschmidt, the escaped German POW. I had reached out to him after my retirement from the force to advise I also joined the Fourth Estate. He was happy we were now in the same line of work, perhaps believing my correspondence with him inspired me to a new profession. I hated to let him know it was all due to a police chief who hated my guts.

I simply told him I had research to do on an old crime case as part of a series, and the expression "AZ 1096" appeared in the police files. He indicated he would gladly set his mind to it and call back in a couple of days. When he did, he had all the sadness in his voice of a hound dog that lost the scent of a rabbit. By the end of the week, Miguel advised that he, too, could find no reference to the phrase anywhere.

It was a frustrating endeavor largely because someone had taken the effort to shake up my confidence by revealing they knew a hidden truth. The phrase must have significance; otherwise, there would be a signature with a name. Unless, this was their name. Now, that line of thinking took me in a different direction. I would have to rack my brain to think of someone with the initials A.Z. I would have to think back to nearly forty years ago and try to recollect the young hoodlums I ran with and called friends. Even if I were successful in that regard, trying to track them down would prove even more difficult than locating Pat McArdle had been.

235

My appointments with Dr. Brenz became more frequent, seeing that he wanted to monitor my condition as it progressed with age. I had become his clinical specimen. Doctie immediately saw the stress in my eyes and my slumped posture. He said nothing during the examination but finally spoke with his back to me while making notes in my file.

"It is unfortunate when the past comes creeping into our lives. Often, we feel helpless to do anything about it, which is only natural." A lump formed in my throat. He had been skilled in osteopathy, but I always wondered if he were a psychic as well. He came and stood before me. "And to be perfectly honest, even I feel helpless in dealing with your facial muscles. They have atrophied to a certain extent. I am not sure any of the massages I have referred you to will have any further impact."

"What then?" My voice was as quiet as a young child.

"Inevitability, Baron."

"How long?"

"That is uncertain. Your case is rather unique in the annals of medical history. It is a privilege to be your guide on this journey, and I am encouraged by your efforts. However, there will come a time when nothing of this earth will salve your pain. You will have to face this demon alone."

I knew Brenz referred to the horrific injury during the First World War, the primitive facial reconstruction surgery, and the subsequent deterioration. Yet it felt so much as though it was about the personal struggles I had in my life since coming to Arkansas City. The two were like Siamese twins, connected forever. I wondered if the deterioration of the soul came before that of the body.

The Angel of Death might have sent the postcard, for all I knew, if I believed in such things. This was not, however, some kind of Biblical reckoning. Whoever sent it tried to instill fear before some final act of retribution. All my experience convinced me that much was certain.

There was one thing about which Doctie was wrong. At least for now, at this point in my life, I would not have to face my demons alone anymore.

Chapter Four

Sally took a night off from the restaurant. Her cousins encouraged her to do so wanting her to spend more time with me. It was perhaps imperative now. I could sense a dark solemnity, lacking energy, feeling as though thousand pound boulders crushed me into the earth. How ironic that Baron Witherspoon saved me by pushing me into a trench. Now, there were times I left work mid-afternoon and just slept until Sally got back. It was hard to believe one rectangular piece of paper could do all that. It was almost as though I could hear the pocket watch winding down.

I reclined on the love seat in the sitting room when my wife stormed in like a drill sergeant. There was not going to be a soft, sweet, and loving approach to my malaise. Her Italian nature came to the forefront.

"This has to stop," she said straight away. "We've either got to figure this out or let it go. This is not living, Baron. This is not you."

I sat up and she alongside me. You could have sworn I had just awoken after sleeping for days. She reached across me and grabbed the postcard, which was never too far away from me since it had arrived. I guess I kept it as close as many people held their bible.

"So?" I was willing to let her lead this parade.

"Let's look at this a different way. If this magical AZ 1096 is at the bottom of the text and not somewhere else, it might not mean a location."

"Like a signature?"

"Exactly."

"That's what I thought as well. But we've already gone through just about everyone I ever knew. Chicago. France during the war. Ark City. No one with those initials. So if it is not someone's name, it could be his or her identification. But I don't know what it means."

Sally grabbed the postcard from me, held it close to her face, and then blurted out "Alcatraz."

It was like Bert Parks had just asked a question on *Break the Bank* and Sally was now the grand prizewinner. I honestly didn't know where she was coming from with her answer. She held the postcard up, her finger pointing to the nearly faded postmark: San Francisco. How we had not noticed that before was beyond me.

"So AZ 1096 is a prisoner's identification."

She nodded.

"That is going to make it tougher." She looked at me confused. "I was in the police department from 1922 to 1948. There were arrests and various court proceedings and testimonies. I certainly don't remember everyone involved in those cases, and Chief Gray will ensure I can't get access to the files."

"But Dave…"

"No." It was all I had to say. I was not going to get Dave Morton involved in this now no matter how close our friendship was. It dawned on me I was less concerned about his efforts to be chief of police than mine in hiding the truth. "I will try to do this a different way and use my press credentials to get information. I'm going to be smart about this and not run around like a chicken with its head cut off."

Sally smiled, her pride in the confidence she knew I had shone brightly. I was back to myself.

This was not going to be a research assignment for Miguel. The next day at the office, I contacted the Federal Bureau of Prisons in Washington. It took me three different conversations to find out who oversaw Alcatraz in terms of prison records. At the risk of incarceration, I fabricated a story about working closely with the Arkansas City Police Department on a case involving a prior bank robbery. Part of it was true enough to dampen my feelings of lying as well as get myself out of any possible trouble.

After having a phone pressed against my ear for nearly thirty minutes, I finally got the prisoner's name—Neil McCauley. They were not, however, at liberty to provide any further information over the phone without a direct official request from the department. It was a small step closer but not enough to provide any peace of mind. After all of my efforts, the name had no meaning to me. I still needed to figure out how this inmate connected to my background.

I chatted up a few old timers at Junior's, the former juke joint and hangout of the small time gangsters back in the '20s and '30s. Whoever remained had little recollection of the name much less what they ate for breakfast that morning. The times were changing in Arkansas City.

My connection with Eliot Ness had long since faded. Alex Gordon was too important a figure in the FBI to bother with such preferential treatment. I started simply considering this inconsequential. After all, what could a prisoner halfway across the country do to carry out a threat? I hadn't considered his acquaintances, who they might be, and how far their scope could reach.

The routines of my life started up again but with less vigor. I tried my best to just drop this matter altogether and not let it weigh me down like a lead anchor. But Sally saw it all as a mask, a sad effort on my part to relinquish concern after being frightened so horribly. I retreated into the shadows of today to avoid a blinding light from the past.

"You need to go," she said one evening over dinner at home. I stared at her blankly. "San Francisco."

"I don't know this man."

"He knows you."

"Does he? Look, this is a gag or a practical joke for all I know. Some guy with time on his hands looking for a cheap laugh halfway across the country."

"Baron, I would accept that if only for one thing," she said softly as though reciting a prayer.

"What's that?" I asked, trying to be as defiant as I could.

"Eric Kimble."

That one point woke me from a dream. This was no joke perpetrated by a bored prisoner. This was someone who somehow had an intimate knowledge of my past and was rattling me for some unknown reason. A hoodlum made an effort to take my life from me, perhaps not literally. By not acting upon it, I allowed it to happen. For so long, I fought against a painful medical condition, haunting dreams and memories, and a sadness I did not fully realize until Sally made it go away. Life was good now, and I meant it to stay that way.

In 1938, I journeyed to Cleveland to understand

how a madman's mind might work. In 1948, I returned "home" to Chicago to dig deep into the past and face old demons. Now it was 1954. One lone hand was reaching out from the grave to hold onto me, perhaps draw me in as well.

There were only two scant choices. I could either sit and do nothing and wait for a meeting with Fate. On the other hand, I could take yet another journey and proudly fight the dragon once again. In that light, sitting before my wife, the decision came easily.

Chapter Five

We poured through railroad timetables and our finances to determine how we could get this done. Sally was prepared with what appeared to be chicken scratch notes on various pieces of scrap paper. She kept pushing my hands away as I tried grabbing at them to take a look. Time was of the essence, and she wasn't about to let my impatience interfere with her well laid plans. The uncertainties of a cross-country train trip were overwhelming. However, there was never going to be a moment when we determined it was too costly or just not feasible. With her directing traffic, no doubts would be allowed in the matter.

The Atchison, Topeka and Santa Fe Railway had just inaugurated the *San Francisco Chief* on June 6. How fitting it was ten years after the anniversary of D-Day there would be another new bold adventure. Based on what we understood of the schedule, all told it would take a day and a half to get from Wellington, Kansas to Oakland, California with a bus connecting to San Francisco. As I read it, there was a possibility the car connecting in Ash Fork, Arizona could be the one to go all the way to Frisco. We had much to plan: cost of tickets and other travel expenses. lodging while in San Francisco, access to the prison. As far as I was concerned, this was a lot of time and expense to determine it was nothing more than a joke. Sally felt in her blood this was a search for the truth. If that were true, I could not dismiss this journey.

According to the timetable, a scant twenty-minute stopover was allotted in Clovis, New Mexico. Other than that, the train barreled on through. The dining car may or may not have run out of food or be closed during any stretch of this trip. There were just too many variables. Being a cook and a restaurant owner, Sally determined she was going to pack sandwiches for me just in case.

"The roundtrip coach fare is seventy-three dollars and fifteen cents, but that doesn't include the fifteen percent Federal tax," I commented

"Why don't you spring for the ninety-eight dollar and twenty-five cents first class fare? You'd be a whole lot more comfortable," she responded.

I smiled at her and declined. This kind of journey would not be more comfortable by a better seat. Just maybe the struggle was part of it, the idea of the Truth being something pried from those who possess it. Perhaps I listened too much to Sally talk about the sermons in church. Ultimately, I had no concern about my appearance before a man incarcerated for an undetermined cause in a prison of such magnitude.

I reflected back on my encounter with Jimmy O'Donnell shortly before his execution. My only concern was not showing fear, not appearing to be overly concerned with his well-being or fate. It was going to be the same for Neil McCauley. Whatever the reason for the postcard, I needed to stand on higher ground.

"Strange how this quest begins on a Sunday, the Lord's Day," Sally noted quizzically. It had some meaning she couldn't quite pinpoint. To me, it was just another day of the week. Despite the fact she and her late husband were Catholic, she had never much attended church. There was something about their former lives still imbedded in their minds. Of course, there were those old time gangsters, like Dion O'Banion, who saw no conflict between their religion and their vocation. The only conflict she experienced now was waking up extremely early to drive me to Wellington on Sunday, June 20 to make the 4:50 a.m. departure.

A light breeze gave way to a steadily warming day. I could tell it would be a typical summer day in Kansas. Sally handed me a large brown paper bag and seemed so much like a mother sending her child off on the first day of school. The assurance in her voice was an attempt to muffle the extreme concern.

"There are two marinated beef sandwiches on rye with that mustard you like," she said eagerly. "I figured they would hold up better than the Italian meat sandwiches. You know how messy they can get. Oh, and Rosa made some chocolate chip cookies that you always ask for."

"I'll be okay," I stated quietly. She nodded with tears in her eyes as the earnest smile started to fade.

"Yeah, I know."

The front part of the engine was red with yellow markings that made it look like it grinned. Perhaps it was a friend to accompany me on this journey or a sinister guide. I kissed my wife and stepped aboard the train. I didn't look back, but I knew she was crying. I guess most people are fearful at the start of things not knowing for certain how they will end.

Despite the large breakfast Sally prepared, I needed to dig into the paper bag when the train took on a connecting car in Amarillo. I could only imagine what other passengers might have felt as I savored a sandwich whose aroma wafted through the car. My eyes stayed focused on my meal. My mind roamed elsewhere.

The landscape outside my window was vastly different from any other trip I had taken previously. When I went to see Eliot Ness in Cleveland, I found the Missouri and Illinois countryside to be primarily farmland. When I went back in time, so to speak, visiting Chicago, it was largely the same outside of a stop in Kansas City. Now, the panhandles of Oklahoma and Texas looked sparse. Perhaps farmers worked the land, but I couldn't imagine what they would bring in. The elongated Santa Fe depot in Amarillo had a red Spanish tile roof. It was a kind of elegance I didn't expect for Texas.

For the next hour and a half, I saw nothing but sand and brush, an oil well here and there off in the distance, a lonesome diner in Hereford, Texas that I saw only in passing. A sandy gray emptiness that passed for life in these parts replaced the abundance of greenery from prior trips. Yet folks worked hard, lived and died here. It was always hard to imagine life beyond your own small world until you came face to face with it.

Sally and I read the train schedule wrong and didn't take into account the time zone change for New Mexico. In Clovis, I would have an additional hour while the train took on more cars including a sleeper and meal car that rode in from New Orleans. Despite chowing down on one of Sally's sandwiches, I decided to take the opportunity to stretch my legs. I felt shoved into a small parcel sent out in the mail.

The town was a lot like Arkansas City, a sleepy little burg but a tad bit hotter with a lot of railroad activity. The buildings looked considerably different, though, and it was a style I had not seen before. While the *San Francisco Chief* was a luxurious and elegant train with a high dome lounge for the big timers, I felt more at home walking down these streets. The warmth felt good on my face, and I didn't experience a single twitch in spite of the stress of this journey. While Ark City had been my home for thirty-five years, I realized there were other places I could feel comfortable if I gave it half a thought.

Sandy's Country Junction served up a mean plate of biscuits and gravy. Their coffee was hot and had a kick like a mule. I smiled so much. It was like a betrayal of Dixie and Daisy Mae's. I strolled down the street and settled back in on the train. It would be a little over twenty-four hours before we got into Oakland. There was a whole new world out there before I arrived at my destination and then another world once I got there.

Chapter Six

It had been a long time since I experienced a time zone change. What had been an hour and a half stopover in Clovis was a mere twenty minutes by the time the train continued on its way. I stared out the window simply watching the sunset and reveling in the oranges and reds and yellows of the sky. I found a beauty to it I could not recall seeing before that gave a certain sense of hope. I wished Sally could be here with me before I reminded myself of the reason for this journey.

Right after the stop for Williams, Arizona and the signs directing toward the Grand Canyon, I fell into a soft and peaceful sleep. When I finally awoke, we were approaching Fresno, California. Making my way down to the dining car, I had to shake out the pleasant thoughts from my head. This truly felt like a vacation thus far. In reality, it was an attempt to face a man who threatened my future by bringing forward my past, all of this from a prison halfway across the country. Never had something sinister been clouded in a beautiful landscape.

After a plate of scrambled eggs and bacon and a couple of cups of coffee, I retreated to my seat for the last three plus hours waiting for the conductor to call out my destination. This train was indeed moving on to Frisco with the towns called out by the conductor as though they were the Twelve Tribes of Israel.

Stockton.

Pinole.

Richmond.

Berkeley.

Oakland.

Finally, San Francisco. The station was located at Pier 39. The boat to Alcatraz was at Pier 33. Sally found the Hotel Zephyr on Stockton Street within walking distance from the train station. The owner was a man named Halim, a refugee from Algeria who left before war broke out there.

He had dark hair and shiny olive skin. His handshake was strong and certain. Facing each other was as a mirror image as he, too, had scars on his face, though not as extensive as mine. He was soft-spoken and very welcoming, ready to provide whatever I needed to make my stay as pleasant as possible. I referenced my journey by train, the reason for my being there, and casually mentioned I was so relaxed I was too tired to do anything else. He recommended a place I could go for dinner and shyly admitted a fellow Algerian ran it who appreciated Halim sending him business. I smiled, knowing I would have sent anyone visiting Ark City who asked to La Bella Vita if not Daisy Mae's.

After dropping my valise off, I was both too tired and too restless to do anything else. I walked back up Stockton Street and all the way to the end of the pier. Off in the distance, I could see the place referred to as The Rock, a former fort and military prison, now a maximum-security federal prison. There, a man named Neil McCauley, who I had never met, sent me a postcard referencing my former self. While it was only implied, that knowledge and that revelation were a threat to my current way of life. I was determined to face him. The Truth would be mine.

I took Halim's suggestion and visited his friend's restaurant. Accepting a recommendation from the gracious owner, I tried the lamb kabob and rice pilaf with a fattoush salad. They were like nothing I ever experienced either in Kansas or in France. I doubted, however, Sally would have enjoyed the experience.

By the time I left after dinner, the sun started to set. I had a clear view to the bay and beyond it the Pacific Ocean. It was as though eternity lay before me, although I knew there was always a finale somewhere just around the corner. My hope was I could settle unfinished business before that end appeared.

As had happened so many times in the past, I woke up disoriented in a strange place. A light breeze blew in through the open window carrying with it the salty flavor of the ocean. It was almost intoxicating. I had no watch and there was no clock in the room. I got up to shower and find a place to get breakfast. As it turned out, I was just in time for lunch.

I came across a little place on Beach Street that looked inviting. It was strange eating crab cakes and French fries as the first meal of the day, but I knew I needed something. By the time I was done, it was just before one in the afternoon. I kept walking along The Embarcadero heading toward Pier 33. Perhaps I thought it was a shorter distance but I wound up wasting time that I could have saved by hailing a hack. However, after my misgivings, I was on a ferry heading for Alcatraz by two-thirty. It was Tuesday, June 22.

The last time I was on any boat of any sort was a steamer transporting troops to England for training and then a smaller one bringing us to France. Then, of course, we were fortunate enough to come home, in my case after an extensive stay in a hospital. This vessel was decidedly smaller and the waters considerably rougher. My face grew colder and pale. While that stopped any twitching, it also made me uncomfortable. I had the sensation of late fall or early winter and we were only in June. The last thing I wanted to do was vomit overboard or, worse yet, after I got to the island.

There were young women with children, who I later determined were the wives of employees who actually lived there. I found it hard to imagine such a thing—waking up every morning and taking your meals while two or three hundred dangerous men lived just behind the walls of this fort. I was only too happy to conduct my business and leave.

After a considerable walk to the administration building, I presented myself before a guard who processed those arriving. There were pangs of uncertainty as I had done no thorough research prior to my arrival to determine the protocols.

"Prisoner name?" the guard asked while viewing a clipboard.

"Neil McCauley."

"Your name."

"Baron Witherspoon," I blurted out. The guard looked on several papers twice, and then shook his head.

"Your name's not on the Accepted List."

I could say I feigned ignorance, but it was more likely than not it wasn't an act.

"I'm sorry. I'm a newspaperman. That is my byline. I'm probably down by my given name. Eric Kimble." It was the first time in nearly forty years that I admitted to who I really was. Surprisingly, the words did not stick in my throat. I spoke them as though I sang an opera aria. The guard found that name on the list. He looked over at the clock on the wall. It was 3:45 p.m.

"Looks like your visit would be real short. Visiting hours end at four. You might want to come back earlier on Thursday."

"Thursday?" My voice rose to a higher pitch, a tone of disappointment in it.

"Next visiting day." The guard looked at me blankly. He was simply doing his job. There needn't be any emotion accompanying it.

I walked back down to the dock. There were fewer people returning to the mainland. The long train ride and the late waking threw me off. For someone who meticulously investigated heinous crimes, I was grossly unprepared. I stared out into the waters of the bay feeling defeated before I had even begun.

Chapter Seven

The waters were choppy and the wind blew colder against my face than it had when I came out. A slight twitch below my left eye reminded me of the past. I felt the unmistakable presence of time hovering over me, taunting me. The day and a half to get to San Francisco. The ferry ride to the prison. The denial of entry. The further wait. How much more time would pass? How much time remained?

I practically fell into a hack at the pier and was oblivious to the driver's inquiry as to where to go. A painful hunger snapped me out of my doldrums. I had a hankering for some Italian food. While it might have seemed like a betrayal, having some good pasta would remind me of the comfort of home, where the feeling of being welcomed was natural.

Luigi's was on Turk Street just north of the Civic Center. All told, it had five tables with two seats each, a mahogany bar with brass foot rail, and a curtain that covered the kitchen area. A man claiming to be the namesake was my waiter, spoke in an exaggerated accent, and offered the daily special of linguine and meatballs. I graciously accepted. It was close enough to Sally's cooking to allow me a bit of peace of mind. I likely would have been comfortable behind the curtain watching the meal being prepared as I witnessed my wife do so many times.

The sun was still out by the time I finished my dinner. A warm orange glow was like a baptism reminding me of the light at the end of the tunnel. I meandered around aimlessly, turning south on Taylor until I ran into Market Street, right in the middle of the theater district. I came across the Fox Theater, a former grand dame among movie houses. The sheet in the glass box outside advertised *Death Does Not Come Easy*, a brash cops and gangsters flick. Starring as the main detective was Sheppard Breckman, the one time crooner who put on a few pounds while losing some of the slick black hair. A cigar stuck in his mouth was supposed to give the idea of toughness. This was his last role as the poor fool died of alcoholism shortly before the film's release.

It was on Market and 6th that I stood in front of the Ross Emporium with an apparently endless array of lights flashing and twinkling, a beacon of gaiety and entertainment. After having just had my memory backpedal sixteen years, I couldn't help but wonder if this was the same Jeanette Ross, the one I used as a decoy and came to grow quite fond of after the melee subsided. I entered the lobby and stood on the elegance of a red velvet carpet feeling as though I was at the gates of temptation. The Burford in Arkansas City was nothing like this. I don't think there was anything in Kansas that could match this opulence.

As I stood there dumbfounded, a voice behind me spoke with a kind of assurance I wasn't expecting.

"I didn't think you ever left Kansas."

I turned and there she was. From my recollection, she would be in her early or mid-forties but her face was as smooth as silk, her eyes as sparkling as champagne, and as alive as I remembered. She was not dressed as a performer but neither as an uptight conservative businesswoman. The chiffon dress showed off her ample and buxom figure, one that I had been very close to sometime in the past. A long black cigarette holder added to her elegant demeanor.

"Well, you're still sassy." She shrugged in agreement and beckoned me to follow. We were in her office with a desk large enough to serve as a bed, wood filing cabinets, and photos on the wall of her as a performer with many famous people throughout the years. Except for a lone green glass globed lamp on her desk, the room had a tranquil mood, something between the Garden of Eden and a bordello. I could hear nothing of the outside in this sanctuary.

"My friend Charlotte took me in and gave me a job. Before long, we were partners, but still performing. And then it happened."

"What?" I asked in great anticipation.

"She met a man." I smiled. "She sold me her share, ran off, and married a guy named George. They moved back to Boston and had babies, and I owned an emporium. Got tired of performing so I just do paperwork, stroll through and glad-handle my patrons, and keep the cops off my back."

None of this would have happened had she stayed with me in Ark City or Wichita for that matter. What would my life have been like if I followed her? I guess it didn't matter since I found love with Sally. The questions persisted and would remain unanswered.

At her request, I recounted the time that had passed.

"Well, we had an escaped German POW during the

war try to assassinate an Air Force general. I left the department and became a columnist for the *Traveler.* And I witnessed an execution of a kid who wanted to be a gangster but failed miserably."

"I know all of that." The look of surprise on my dilapidated face must have been palpable. "I've read your column. What about your love life?"

As I described my life with Sally, she seemed genuinely happy for me, perhaps realizing we both came to the best places in our lives independently of each other. Nevertheless, I couldn't help but feel a kind of melancholy.

The place was rather busy for a Tuesday night. She invited me to lunch the next day and told me of a place on Fisherman's Wharf. She held my hand and kissed me on the cheek as I left. There was something magnificently gracious about the gesture.

On the taxi ride back to my hotel, it dawned on me it was sixteen years since I had seen her. By that time, I had been in Arkansas City, Kansas for nineteen years. Suddenly, a funny feeling emerged in the pit of my stomach like indigestion that made me gasp. I realized it was the anxiousness of age. Time rolled into itself, a massive ball barreling down a hill like a runaway train. I finally had in my life some peace and quiet, a love to put me at ease. I could only wonder how long that might last.

Chapter Eight

It was a pleasant enough morning, and I needed to push the cobwebs out of my head. I walked from the hotel to the address Jeanette told me about the previous night. I experienced a little tightness in my leg, and a breathlessness, which I thought came from walking these remarkably steep streets. Yet this area was relatively flat. I had to chalk it up to just getting old. It was a painfully stunning admission.

The twenty-minute stroll brought about a fantastic appetite. For a brief moment, I forgot about the actual reason for my visit to this city and all that waited for me when I was done. The restaurant was fancier than anything I experienced before, even though Jeanette referred to it as "this old place" a number of times. Our lives apparently had diverged greatly since those relatively brief moments together in Wichita in 1938. There were wide windows all around, offering a view of the boats and seagulls and the infinite possibilities of the bay. The pace and mood inside was casual and relaxed, not the harried rush that most restaurants exuded. It was such I would have been able to take a nap after my meal.

I never had Dungeness crab before largely because such creatures do not exist in the waters of Kansas. Jeanette laughed at my attempts to break the shell with a hammer and pick at the pieces inside. When I was able to get a hearty forkful in my mouth dipped in rich and savory butter, I imagined what Heaven might be like. This world was unlike any I encountered in the past. It was both strange and fascinating. Was Jeanette really the serpent in this Garden of Eden?

We talked as old friends, never rehashing the attempts to apprehend Ronnie Roché, the trauma of her nearly getting killed, or our one solemn night together, even though I assumed that was all floating around in our respective minds. Instead, the discussion was about her business efforts and her love for the city.

I was embarrassed when she grabbed the check, but she laughed it off as a business expense. We stood at the entrance and looked into each other's eyes. She had been a very special lady in my life even though it was for a brief time. "What might have been" was a story for a fairy-tale. She kissed me softly on the lips, turned, and left without a word to intrude upon the moment. My heart swelled, and then my mind came back to earth.

I headed back to my hotel, thinking I would just pass the time until the next day for my visit to the prison. Instead, my wandering mind carried my feet along. A beacon stood out in the distance, and I soon saw signs for Coit Tower. I headed in that direction.

As I approached Washington Square, I came across a building that passed itself off as a church but was nothing at all like the magnificent structures I had seen thus far. While it was a material similar to limestone, its design was basic and very nearly bland. The roughly painted sign indicated it was the Church of the Wayward Redemption, an odd name for sure. The doors were open while a woman preached on a pulpit inside to a group of what appeared to be indigent men. The white robes she wore were like old sheets, and an elaborate cross dangled dramatically around her neck. Unfortunately, I did not sense the aroma of frankincense and myrrh but one of mildew and decay.

I stood in the doorway while the midday sun bled into the vestibule. What I saw when I walked several steps forward took me aback. It was Sister Celeste, although I had no idea how she referred to herself now. She was as passionate as she had been at Lawrence Stadium in Wichita so many years ago. This time, however, the gathering was lackluster and barely paying attention. Nevertheless, the fire and passion in her voice remained.

She stopped in the middle of her sermon, such that it was, and beckoned me to enter further. Doing so made me more visible. Her eyes grew wide in recognition. I wasn't sure if it was a smile or a smirk that passed across her lips.

"Is it time now to share your secrets, brother?" she bellowed.

"They have been already, sister." It was awkward referring to her in that fashion.

"And have you been redeemed?"

"I have been."

"Then go in peace." I wasn't sure if those instructions were those of faith or a desire to keep me from revealing her secrets. Perhaps she fully accepted Isaiah 55:7.

The signs for Coit Tower no longer mattered. I could see it like a beckoning angel ahead of me. Though it appeared to be close, the steep hills made me feel as though I walked backward even as I continued to approach it. Perhaps that was how it been for most of my adult life. When I arrived, I walked around the lobby and marveled at the murals depicting the plight of the worker in modern society. What I really wanted was an unfettered view of the city where I made this pilgrimage.

From high above, I could see the unbelievable curves of Lombard Street. At one point, I thought I saw my hotel. I then turned toward the bay. There, off in the distance was Alcatraz, that fortress which held prisoners apart from the rest of us while still allowing them to have impact on our lives. I found it hard to believe this island away from all civilization could reach a withered hand out to me so far away in Kansas and cause a tremor in my heart.

As I emerged from the tower, I was overcome by exhaustion. It was not only all the walking I had done but also the instances of coming face to face with so much of the past, so much left behind. I had moved on, intentionally, not wishing to do anything but survive. Until recently with my marriage to Sally, all I wanted was to get to the next day. Now, the newspaper column, the restaurant, and a true sense of family were my life. Yet I knew it could all come unwound.

A taxi roamed around the parking lot like a gull looking for fish. I gladly accepted his ride. Arriving at the hotel late in the afternoon, I realized how truly tired I was. If I were to face Neil McCauley, I would need my complete wits about me. My lunch did enough to hold me over for the evening such that I really didn't feel like going out for dinner. I undressed, took a hot bath, and changed into pajamas, simply lying on the bed.

While up in the tower, the strong winds numbed my face. Now, in the warmer room, I felt little throbs, as Dr. Brenz referred to them like worms under my skin. I tried my best to ignore them. I focused, revisiting in my mind the postcard and its disruption to my life. The discovery of the name behind AZ 1096. The discussions with Sally. The long train ride. I was a Crusader and this city was the Holy Land. And rather than a horde, there was but one infidel to face.

Chapter Nine

From having gone to bed early, I awoke at six a.m. It wasn't as early as a typical Kansas farmer, but it was like I was back on track in my daily routine. I bathed, shaved, and dressed for the day, looking like a man going on a job interview, ready to take on whatever the world threw at me. I had a certain air of respectability. My face felt smooth and untouched. I was renewed.

I walked a block to a small diner for breakfast and ate a meal that would choke a horse. While morning commuters ate dainty pastries and sipped coffee in a hurried attempt to get to the office on time, I gobbled a mountain of scrambled eggs, bacon, biscuits with butter and jelly, and then asked for an order of flapjacks with more butter and syrup. I couldn't have cared less what the embattled businessmen thought.

I caught the first ferry of the day at 8:30 a.m. It was a little chilly but I did my best to ignore the weather. My passion warmed me and drove me onward. By the time I landed at the dock and walked up to the administration building, it was just past nine.

"I'm here for AZ 1096," I stated. "Neil McCauley."

"Name?" the new guard said solemnly.

"Eric Kimble."

The guard reviewed the clipboard and nodded.

"You've been approved." He looked over his

shoulder at the clock on the wall. "Rest period is at 9:30. We'll have him brought to the visiting room." He explained to me I would be in a small cubicle separated by a thick glass. Communication would be solely via intercom. The discussions were not to include anything relating to the routines of prison life or current events as inmates were to have no knowledge of the world beyond these walls. Guards monitored all discussions. Any violations of these rules would result in the end of the visit. He affirmed my acceptance of these protocols.

I fidgeted in the chair staring at an empty glass, stained with fingerprints and smudges. The entire room, from the walls to the partition where I sat, was a pale tan, almost lifeless. It was a far cry from the elegance of Jeannette's theater or the magnificent restaurant where we dined. From my view, there did not appear to be any other convicts receiving visitors at the time.

The far door suddenly opened and a guard motioned a man toward my cubicle. He wore standard issue light blue denim buttoned down shirt, white undershirt, dark blue denim pants without a belt, and a pair of scuffed black work shoes. As he sat, I observed him carefully. His head was egg shaped, his watery gray eyes looked bored, and his ears were rather large. His complexion was pale, and his mouth was down turned. He had a high forehead, receding hairline, and a bit of a cowlick sticking up in front. This was Neil McCauley. If I hadn't known any better, I would have taken him for a delivery truck driver or itinerant farmer back in Ark City, someone you wouldn't think about twice.

We picked up the phones on our respective sides at the same time. He looked at me with a kind of puzzlement.

"Who are you?" he asked nonchalantly.

"Eric Kimble."

"Never seen you before," he said nodding negatively. "And with that face I would have remembered." It was a matter-of-fact comment more than any attempt at insult. "Do I know you?"

"You sent me this," I replied, pressing the postcard up against the glass. He smiled as though in response to the punch line of a joke.

"Oh, yeah. That." He spoke in an offhand manner, as though I should have been more aware of his meaning.

"Care to enlighten me?"

He looked up over his shoulder, not necessarily at the guard near the door, but more just away from me.

"Maybe," he finally responded.

"You playing games with me, McCauley?" My face grew tense. I waited for what I knew would be those worms.

"What else have I got to do for the next seven to ten years, seeing as how you came all the way out from Kansas?"

Time is a precious commodity, as much for the rest of us as for prisoners. However, as a free man, I felt as though I wasted the last four days of my life on a wild goose chase just to come face to face with a flippant convict. There was no use in wasting any more time. I stood up to go.

"Wait. It was just a joke," he shot back a muffled sound of desperation in his voice. I sat down but with a stern look on my face. For the moment, I was the parent castigating a rebellious teenager.

"Well?"

"I was on the inside in Atlanta before I got sent here. I met a guy who asked for a favor."

"The postcard?"

"Yeah. But seeing as how I didn't know you, I couldn't put you on a list for correspondence once I got here. And I wasn't going to waste a name on my limited mail. After all, I've got a shyster hard at work on an appeal."

A voice clicked in on our phones.

"Do not discuss prison procedures." It was some official monitoring the call.

"Anyway, I gave it to my lawyer to mail once they transferred me."

"What was the point of the card?" I squinted my eyes and shook my head, feeling quite perplexed. He shrugged his shoulders.

"No idea. I thought it was a gag."

"The guy. Who was the guy?"

"Name of Tom Hickey."

My eyes went wide, like a Halloween stick figure, almost popping out of my head. I had only known one Hickey in my life and he was bad news from the start in the North Side of Chicago to the end of his days in Arkansas City, Kansas.

"What did he look like?" The words stuck in my throat.

"Shorter guy. At least shorter than me. Mostly dark hair although starting to show some gray. Mean dark eyes. Never smiled. About forty maybe."

"Where was he sent up?"

"Nowhere. He caught the chain," he said shrugging again. "His mouthpiece had gotten him parole. He flat out told me once he was out he wasn't going back. Ever. Had bigger fish to fry."

"What did he mean?"

"You tell me." McCauley was aloof. He told me everything he knew and was now tired of talking about something that meant nothing to him.

This was turning into a macabre carnival with me riding a Tilt-A-Whirl, spinning backward and forward, up and down, unable to see or think straight. Someone was playing me for a sucker on the midway. I traveled halfway across the country to find my past reaching out to me.

"When did you get here?" I blurted out.

"Couple of months ago."

Thoughts started running through my head quickly. I needed a quiet place to settle down and put it all back together. I stood up feeling dizzy and looked down at Neil McCauley. He was just a convict in the middle of a sick game. I couldn't be mad at him, nor was I in the mood to feel grateful for his information. As with all inmates at Alcatraz, he had given up certain rights and privileges of society. I simply nodded at him and walked away. He was likely disappointed at the brevity of our meeting.

Once I was outside of the main building, I paced up and down the pathway to get a clearer picture of what I just discovered. Unless this was some ruse, Jake Hickey's younger brother had somehow located me and decided to taunt me, for what purpose I was currently unaware. He encountered McCauley on his way west to Alcatraz and requested an intimidating postcard sent to me. That was likely to throw me off the track. In order for him to know where I used to live, he would have had to be in Ark City at some point within the last few years, certainly prior to 1951. Had I actually encountered him in some fashion? If McCauley was to have sent the postcard after arriving to Alcatraz, it was likely to allow Hickey more time. But for what? I could only assume Hickey made his way toward Ark City, toward my home. Or possibly could be there right now.

It was a domino effect. The ferry got me back to the pier. A hack took me to a Western Union station where I sent a frantic telegraph to Sally.

AM TAKING THE 11AM OUT OF FRISCO. STOP. SET TO ARRIVE WELLINGTON 1055P 26TH. STOP. BE CAREFUL UNTIL I ARRIVE. STOP.

I realized the last line sounded desperate and uncertain but only after I sent it. I knew I needed to say something but couldn't think of anything better. It wasn't as though I had the luxury of time as I did writing my column.

When I arrived at the hotel, I made my arrangements with Halim to check out the following morning, Friday the 25th. It occurred to me it was a scant six months before Christmas. There was nothing celebratory about it.

I was surprised to find him in the parlor the next morning with strong coffee and pastries. He invited me to sit for a spell, perhaps noticing how frantic I had been. When he spoke, his tone was calm and soothing.

"You are a most excellent guest, and I have been honored by your presence." His head bowed slightly in acknowledgement. "However, I am concerned about you and your journey."

"Well, the train has been a rather pleasant

experience. I'm sure I'll do well."

"I do not refer to the train but your journey beyond." Like Doctie, this Algerian had a sixth sense of some kind, an awareness of "things" he had not been privy to. I did not know how this was possible. "It is important to remember to always move forward."

Without a complete understanding, I shook his hand warmly, appreciating the sentiment. There would come a time when the meaning of his words became clearer.

Chapter Ten

I remembered a spring day in 1917, hanging out in the kitchen of McGovern's Liberty Inn in Chicago, as my friend Deanie, Dion O'Banion, gave a rousing rendition of "Danny Boy" right in the middle of the dining room. Jake Hickey, not yet having acquired his nickname, slapped me on the arm, reminding me to continue going through the overcoat and jacket pockets of the patrons, just as our older friend taught us.

Later that evening, while splitting up the take, Deanie looked at me more like a father than a big brother. He was twenty-five, I was nineteen, but his brief stint for safecracking and assault matured him quickly. He relished the role. He could see the world ahead and had big plans. He also recognized I probably would not be part of them.

"Boy-o, you seem more interested in my singing than skinning the flints." His thick Irish accent lulled anyone who heard it, except the Italians.

"I don't know," I mumbled.

"I do. You might be better suited to fighting the Hun. After all, you are a patriotic American, aren't you?"

The sense of pride he raised allowed me to stand upright and puff out my chest, more than I ever had as a member of the Market Street gang. Eric Kimble ran off to fight in the war in Europe and returned to the states as Baron Witherspoon. Dion O'Banion ran the North Side Gang and Schofield's flower shop before his merciless death. An awful lot of water flowed under that bridge.

The meandering journey west became the impatient and anxious voyage home. I felt as though I stayed awake the entire time, even though I knew I dozed off periodically, waking up at various moments and wondering where I was again and again. The stress of trying to determine what the brother of an old rival was up to tired me. The possibilities were infinite.

The one thing I could be certain of was that Tom Hickey had been in Arkansas City some time prior to 1951 as Sally and I moved into our house shortly after we got married. The thought occurred to me Hickey might even have attended the trial of Jimmy O'Donnell or followed the case, trying to determine if any information about his late brother had come out. There was no use attempting to remember all the little details as they floated away in a tidal wave of events.

In my head, I calculated the young Hickey might have been in his early twenties, perhaps still in Chicago, not necessarily part of the Moran gang but a hanger-on like so many others. I certainly didn't recall a young child among Jake's group. Likely, he told his mother to keep the kid out from under his feet. The Irish, like the Italians, typically had large families.

Then I wondered how Tom had known about his brother's whereabouts as Moran initially sent guys south on the Q.T. Knowing Jake, however, I could picture him sending telegrams to trusted friends and family while in Kansas bragging about his exploits in an inflated fashion, claiming he finally achieved a measure of status. Once the young brother knew what was going on, he could follow the rest from there.

So much time had passed. Jake died in 1934; Tom was old enough, I supposed, to figure out a way to take revenge then. Unless, that is, he didn't cotton to the notion of being executed for the murder of a policeman. At this point, the "whys" were not as important as the "hows" and "whens."

It was around Bakersfield I realized how all the excitement and heavy dose of thinking created a powerful hunger. I drank some strong coffee and ate a couple of pastries seven hours earlier and knew it wouldn't be enough to get me through the remainder of this ride.

I ventured forth to the dining car, not remembering my earlier concerns about extended conversations. That proved unavoidable when the only seat remaining was with an elderly couple. I nodded politely as I sat and lowered my head while looking at the menu, hoping my mealtime would pass quickly. It was not my intention to be rude so I looked up and nodded once or twice. I ordered a hamburger and a cup of coffee and then looked impatiently out of the window.

"Good evening, sir. Allow me to introduce myself." The gentleman's voice was dripping with the kind of courtesy from a bygone era, one where Baron Witherspoon's father felt comfortable. "My name is Herbert Beacham, and this is my wife, Sally."

"Baron Witherspoon," I replied as I shook his hand and smiled. He looked at me curiously. "My wife's name is Sally as well." With an engaging smile on my face, that kind of broke the ice right there.

"Are you a veteran of the war, Mr. Witherspoon?"

Mrs. Beacham inquired in a quiet manner.

"The first one, ma'am. The scars are a permanent reminder."

"We honor your service, Mr. Witherspoon." Mr. Beacham sat upright, his shoulders thrown back, and was as proud of me as he would have been of his own son.

"Where you folks headed?" I was not feeling as put upon as I thought I might, and they were so friendly the words seemed to just pour out of me.

"Ft. Madison, Iowa. Our son and daughter are farmers there."

"We have three grandchildren," Mrs. Beacham added lovingly.

The rest of the meal passed in amiable chitchat. I noticed Mr. Beacham place his hand sweetly on his wife's hand. I hadn't asked their age or inquired as to how long they had been married. The numbers didn't really matter all that much. The gesture alone was an indication of a lifetime spent building something together.

I sat more comfortably in my seat warmed by the love and commitment I witnessed between the Beachams. My thoughts drifted to my wife. Though we had come together later in life, I hoped we could still turn out like this sweet couple, with a degree of affection that comes through a renewed purpose. Time would tell.

This train was taking me home. The word echoed in my head. Not the North Side of Chicago or the fields of France but Arkansas City, Kansas. It was not important how I started out but who I had become. My transgressions had been atoned for by the way in which

I lived my life, my good deeds, my friends, and my reputation. "Home" felt warm and comfortable.

I drifted off to a peaceful sleep, awakened only by the conductor's call for Gallup, New Mexico. It didn't take me long to bring my thoughts back to Tom Hickey.

Chapter Eleven

There were many times in my role as a beat cop that I walked the streets of Arkansas City well past midnight. I knew all the subtle nuances of sights and sounds within the town at night, what demons lurked in the darkness. This time was eerily different. When the *San Francisco Chief* rolled out of Wellington, it was as though I were in the pits of hell. Fortunately, Sally was there to draw me back into the light.

"Are you tired?" she asked.

"I slept on the train."

"Hungry?"

"Famished."

We sat in the kitchen of our house, me eating an Italian beef sandwich with giardiniera on the side while she drank a cup of tea. I went over the details of my brief conversation with Neil McCauley, repeating every word as I remembered it, describing the look on his face, and the desperation in his eyes. The meeting with Jeanette Ross was not a part of the discussion.

For the first time I could remember, Sally looked worried. Her eyes squinted, her mouth was tight, and her hands held the teacup a lot tighter than it needed to be. That troubled me just a bit.

"He has no idea where you are now," she proclaimed, a somewhat triumphant tone in her voice.

"How can you say that?"

"If he sent a postcard to the Elmo, well, that was 1951."

I nodded my head lightly in agreement.

"My guess is Tom Hickey read about the Jimmy O'Donnell case, made his way down to Kansas, and followed me around the city while I focused on both my testimony and my column." It was logical to think Hickey blew out of town after the trial and the execution. He probably figured I still lived in the apartment when he met up with McCauley who was on his way to the west coast.

Everything I thought of, the entire timeline of what might have happened and the speculation of what could happen were all ordered and logical. The one thing I didn't have was an answer, a solution. If this were the kid brother of Jake Hickey, he would have been roughly fifteen years younger than I. At this point in my life, my face was in more pain than ever, I had lost a great deal of my reflexes, and I no longer had the full force of the Arkansas City Police Department to back me up as a fellow officer. I was just another John Q. Public, the guy the cops were supposed to protect and serve.

Once again, Sally recommended I consult with Dave Morton. While it made more sense now than when I first received the postcard, something made me continue to be hesitant. I had the image of a large ball of twine unraveling with a mess at my feet and feeling frustrated at having to clean it all up. Perhaps I had grown too comfortable with my life, surviving nearly thirty years as a police officer without so much as taking a bullet. The good fortune of Sally in my life and disregarding how long I might have her made me complacent. I thought I might pass peacefully in my own bed with my devoted wife looking down upon me as some kind of angel. Now, I had to consider it might come in the form of an Old West shootout in the middle of Ark City.

Captain Dave Morton agreed to meet me at Junior's. By wearing civilian clothes, his only affiliation was as my longstanding friend. We caught each other looking around in fond remembrance of years past. We each saw in our own way what the place was and what it had become, and recalled who passed in and out of these doors. Nothing looked the same anymore. Somehow, it was much cleaner, the darkness warded off by lighting to give it an upbeat appearance. No one there was guilty of anything more than excessive drinking.

I went over everything that transpired from the moment I got the postcard. We discussed my independent research, my trip to the west coast, even referencing the encounters with Jeanette and Sister Celeste. He smiled fondly in remembrance.

I was as specific as possible regarding the conversation with McCauley. There was nothing about Eric Kimble or the North Side other than Jake Hickey himself. It probably wouldn't have mattered if it did, but I wasn't ready to open that door just yet.

"For the life of me, I could never figure why "Crazy" Jake had it in for you," Dave commented casually. "I mean, what's a tough Mick got against a beat cop from Kansas? You didn't happen to meet any of his mates in the war, did you?"

I reminded him of several discussions we had regarding Eric Kimble. It was awkward referring to my former self as another person. Dave nodded as I retold those stories. I couldn't be sure if he remembered them, doubted them, or was still coming to a decision about them.

"Look, I'm not going to insult your intelligence or your experience." Dave's voice now sounded like the senior officer he was, deep and resonant with an official tone that had a kind of finality to it. "While everything you told me makes sense, this guy doesn't appear to be in town, at least that you know of. And even if he were, until he does something directly, he hasn't committed any crime."

"I know that, but—"

"Wait." He held his hand up like a traffic cop. "I know you. I know the resources you have. Now, it's one thing to go out, research, and investigate. However, if this guy does come to town and you do anything, you might be the one arrested for assault. Or even murder." He reached across the table to touch my shoulder, like a friend. "Look, you've got yourself a good life, one I'd always hoped you would have. Nothing from the past matters. Not now anyway. I don't see any sense in looking back. Do you?"

Like so many others, I couldn't be sure of what Dave did or didn't know. His friendship meant more than anything else. Yet his words also rang true. To continue to worry about the past meant I would always be running. Sally had found a kind of peace in our marriage. Her late husband's difficulties were a lesson from the history books and not a guidebook for her current life. Between the restaurant, her cousins, and our marriage, she was able to see all the good in life now.

I resolved to try to do the same. Just being grateful

for my current blessings might be the thing to allow me to live in the sunshine and step out of the shadows.

Another envelope to my current address brought the darkness back again.

Chapter Twelve

It was a plain white envelope addressed to E KIMBLE, this time with my current home address. The postmark was from Wichita three days prior. Inside was a yellowed article from the *Chicago Daily News* with the headline MASSACRE 7 OF MORAN GANG. Fortunately, the infamous photo was not included.

There was no need to second-guess or rethink anything. To me, this was a threatening taunt, a reminder of past times even though I had been on the Arkansas City Police Department and lived in Kansas for five years by the time of this horrific event. This was a clear indication the sender, presumably Tom Hickey, knew my current location. The local postmark meant he was nearby.

It was amazing to consider how simple it was to instill fear. Never any direct threat of any sort. The first communication merely stated someone knew who I had been and knew where I lived. This second correspondence referenced a piece of history no longer relevant to anyone but the sender and his long-deceased brother.

However, I did not allow this to influence me quite as greatly. I did not hide it from Sally or shy away from needing to be resolute. I caught Garrison Reed on his regular route and told him it was okay to bring me anything with my current or former address on it, and he needn't worry about the addressee. I contacted Dave Morton to advise him of the recent letter. He merely reiterated what we discussed at Junior's. As we both realized, no crime had been committed. Therefore, all I could legally do was be vigilant. Nevertheless, I cleaned and oiled my Smith & Wesson revolver, my personal gun that I hadn't fired in years.

In some small fashion, I could relate to Jimmy O'Donnell after the trial. All he could do was wait after the pronouncement of the death sentence. There was to be no changing of course, no alterations in plans. The State of Kansas determined Jimmy O'Donnell would die. In his case, however, the manner and time of death was stated. I dealt with infinite possibilities and likely uncertainties.

I wasn't willing to allow whatever it was to just happen. For a long time, I had hidden behind a mask, literally and figuratively, fearful of discovery. It took time before I felt comfortable with whom I became. I took over my own life and made my own happiness. This time I needed to come out swinging.

It had been a while since I communicated with Alex Gordon. He sent a telegram when Sally and I got married. I had to have someone look up what "Mazel Tov!" meant. Prior to that, I consulted with him regarding Jimmy O'Donnell. I allowed Miguel Cristales to make the inquiries to track him down. It took several phone calls just to leave a message. Eventually, Alex reached me at the *Traveler* office about three days after Miguel started his inquiry.

While Alex spoke more effusively than ever before, he did not state anything specific about what department he worked in or the nature of his job. The execution of Julius and Ethel Rosenberg for espionage occurred the previous year. The other convicted members of the spy ring, David Greenglass and Morton Sobell, were Jewish. I could only wonder if a renewal of anti-Semitism, whether stated or implied, would temper Alex's ascendancy in the FBI hierarchy.

I outlined the correspondences, my trip to Alcatraz, and my own personal speculations expediently but efficiently. In referencing Jake Hickey and his brother, Alex led me to believe he was well acquainted with the North Side Gang and their leadership and members. His comments were similar to those he made when we captured Eihann Hammerschmidt, the escaped German POW.

"Things are a little…hot around here," he said, his voice soft and not as gregarious as in the past. "But I may be able to dig up some info from the archives. I have to tell you, Baron. I agree with your friend Dave. This could easily turn against you. A generally law-abiding citizen making secretive threats or sinister comments against a former police officer is not a crime. You taking revenge before he does anything is one."

So there it was. My oldest friend, a high-ranking officer in the Arkansas City Police Department, and a well-respected member of the Federal Bureau of Investigation, both more concerned about my committing a vigilante act than the possible harm bestowed on me by a man who sought some kind of unfounded revenge. The world truly turned upside down.

Of course, I had no doubt Dave and Alex would perform their due diligence as both friends and professionals. Dave would instruct beat officers to be on the lookout for suspicious individuals who were newer to town, perhaps suggesting mob affiliation or Russian operatives, something not directly connected to me. Alex would certainly reach out to the Chicago SAC requesting any information regarding one Thomas Hickey, a probable younger brother to the late "Crazy" Jake Hickey.

All of that was to put me at ease for a relatively short time. The resulting reports would have a "not yet" quality to them in terms of substantial information or viable alternatives. Eventually, they hoped, I would allow my deeply rooted fears to subside and simply carry on with my life. I felt this way not because I thought less of Dave and Alex, but because it is what I would have done as well. Things were tougher when you had been on the other side of the fence and knew the course of action that was standard operating procedure.

By my accounting, it was just Sally and me. I certainly wasn't going to put her in harm's way any more than I considered risking my life. At the very least, I needed to look into all the possibilities and prepare myself for whatever might come at me.

Given the most recent letter had a postmark of Wichita, it figured to be a good place to start. It would be a lot easier to be invisible in the bigger city than the small town. But where to start?

I considered all my possible acquaintances in the Peerless Princess of the Plains. I hadn't been there since Jimmy O'Donnell's appeal back in 1949. Gregory Freeland, the assistant district attorney in Cowley County used the case as a springboard for an appointment in Topeka. In contemplating further, I determined there were a cop, a private investigator, and a criminal who might be able to provide some guidance. If nothing else, I would make myself feel as though I were making an effort.

Too many old men sleep in their beds simply waiting for Death to walk in the room and invite them on a journey. I would make that old cuss look for me.

Chapter Thirteen

I first encountered John Rackler in 1938 when I went to Wichita to assist their police department in the Ripper case. At the time, Rackler was as blustery as a bull in a china shop. After his recent promotion to detective, he acted as though he had all the talent to be the next Dick Tracy. As far as I was concerned, he didn't have enough talent to be the next Gorgeous George.

There was no sense in making an appointment to see him and further massage his bloated ego. It was better to just walk in and ask for him. If I got lucky, maybe he would have something worthwhile to pass on to me. I knew it was a lot to hope for from someone who wanted only adulation for his limited talents. As it turned out, that was not to be.

Upon first seeing him, I was definitely surprised. He was in his late thirties but looked more like his beefier partner Charlie Sells who passed away several years ago. He walked slower because of his size and acted far more tired than a typical man his age. This, it turned out, was due to the fact he was now a father of three with a wife who was desperate for him to buy a house. He was a far cry from the confident braggart I first encountered. He appeared out of breath, and the fire in his eyes waned. Nevertheless, his dismissive attitude was still crystal clear.

"So you've got a stalker?" he said casually in response to my predicament. He was a hair's breadth away from a sly smirk. "Well, I can't say it surprises me."

"Why is that?" I asked, as though I was the college professor he never had.

"Just look at all the bad guys you've dealt with. Heck, I wouldn't be surprised if some Nazis marched right through your town looking for you."

"The postmark on the letter was from here. It was dated just a week ago," I continued, trying to keep him on the point of my inquiry and as professional as it was feasible to be. "Might there be a way of tracking him down?"

"Son, we've got nearly two hundred thousand people living here. We don't have a file on everyone, especially not upstanding citizens." It was all I could do to hold back from punching him straight in the nose.

"Could you check to see if there have been any arrest reports in the past month or so?"

He looked as though I asked him to build the pyramids in Egypt. He picked up the phone and called another department, using his name as though it were scripture. He developed the unfounded expectation fellow officers would jump if he snapped his finger. I got the impression they felt he was over the hill a long time ago. It was a little more than a minute before I got an answer.

"Sorry, buddy, but we've got nothing on a Tom or Thomas Hickey. I even checked back to the first of the year." He made it sound as though he exerted a great effort on my behalf. I hoped this was simply his attitude toward me and not the way he conducted police business with everyone. He threw me a cartoonish "Good luck" as I left his office. I hoped this would be the last time I would ever set eyes on him.

If the police could not be of any help, perhaps a criminal could. It took a bit of searching before I was able to locate Carson Stankey, the pimp who ran a few more unknown illegal operations when I encountered him in 1938. His private club in Delano was now a diner, very different from the seedy establishment desperate men frequented. After asking around, I found he ran a joint north of town in the building that used to be Tangerine Smith's bar-b-que restaurant. The irony was thick.

It wasn't quite a smile on his face when I entered. Standing behind the bar, it was two old warriors stepping onto the field of battle once again. He still wore a thick goatee and moustache tinged with far more gray. I walked directly up to the bar.

"Ah, the policeman," he uttered for the benefit of the few malcontents sitting at their tables.

"And the altar boy," I responded. I looked around, especially toward the curtain covering the back area. "And Montisse?"

He shook his head in disappointment.

"He was shot by the police. Resisting arrest. Or so they say." For some strange reason, we both smiled. It was perhaps the realization that Montisse got off easy, and the two of us were still living relics while time passed by, watching us pitifully.

"This is a far cry from the club in Delano," I mentioned casually.

"It was attracting the wrong kind of clientele."

"Oh. Who?"

"The police. Being out of the city limits affords me, shall we say, other opportunities." He still had his hand in some shady dealings. Knowing him, he always would.

While he poured me a cheaper version of Old Grand Dad, I sat down and leaned in to speak. It wasn't out of concern for others listening as the three reprobates in the place were hunched over in oblivion. I wanted him to know I sought his trust. Once again.

Without going into too many details, I outlined my situation. In essence, I was seeking a man who was reminiscent of the gangsters of the thirties, figuring Thomas Hickey had not adapted or changed with the years, too caught up in the way things used to be. Just like Stankey. He would never have been able to fit in with the Mob as it existed now. If his efforts of the past several years were any indication, he had but one thing on his mind. He wouldn't associate with those who would divert him from his goals.

Stankey, unlike Detective Rackler, was genuinely concerned. It was the epitome of irony when I thought about it. Just by having shown Stankey a little respect, I was able to meet him on his terms. He always recognized me as a policeman, a natural adversary, but one who was willing to allow some space between us. Rackler always viewed his position as some sort of a game, always needing to have the upper hand, even though we were both seeking the same resolution.

The thing Stankey pointed out was someone like Hickey would likely want to stay within the city limits and mingle in with others. Coming to a distant roadhouse would single him out and identify him more quickly. I agreed with the perceptive assessment. He offered to contact me at the newspaper office if he found anything out.

As I started to leave, he reached out his hand. I shook it firmly. We looked at each other plainly. While there was not warm and cordial friendship, a recognition existed we were no longer adversaries. I marveled at how the times had changed.

One option remained for me in Wichita.

Chapter Fourteen

When I first went to Wichita in 1938 to assist in the investigation of a series of brutal murders, the young officer who served as my liaison turned out to be the killer. He was a troubled young man with a personal history from which he could not escape. However, one or two other cops I met provided additional assistance.

Harold Bergman was the first Jewish person I encountered in my life. I understood Alex Gordon more clearly after dealing with this young man. This young patrolman was highly intelligent and aggressively seeking to become a detective. I felt at the time he would have greater success than Rackler and wished him well.

Over the course of years, especially since my days as a newspaperman, I discovered he fought in the war, came home with some kind of injury, and set out a shingle as a private investigator. I spoke with him only one time since then but had seen clippings indicating his involvement in several high profile cases. I hoped he would remember me.

He lived in an apartment on North Market that appeared austere. After entering the building, the first door on the right had a sign that read H BERGMAN, INVESTIGATOR. I knocked on the door. His look of recognition preceded a warm smile. We sat in his parlor where pocket doors hid the rest of the area and talked over strong coffee. I noticed the result of his war injury in the limp as he walked toward a settee.

"How is your father?" I asked, remembering how often he spoke about the gentleman.

"He still wants me to be a rabbi if you can believe it."

"It's not too late," I offered.

"And you are married."

"Yes, I am. It wasn't too late for me either."

Harold wasn't much for chitchat. I suppose some people might consider him cold but I was enthused by his directness, his sense of getting to the point of a matter. He listened intently, perhaps as a psychiatrist or even, dare I say it, a rabbi. He nodded at key points, squinted in contemplation, and waited for me to finish. I outlined the encounter with Jake Hickey in 1934 without elaborating on the past and detailed everything that transpired since receiving the postcard and now the letter.

"Well, I certainly agree with your assessment about the original postcard. But what makes you think he is here in Wichita now?"

"The postmark."

"Ah, but there is another possibility," he said, holding up a finger. "He might just as easily have driven up to Wichita, dropped that letter off in a post box, and driven back, all within the span of a single day. He could be in Arkansas City right now, awaiting your return." Apparently, my sagging scarred face gave the appearance of dismay. "Don't worry. There is nothing he intends to do behind your back."

"What do you mean?"

"Consider the effort he has expended. This revenge

plot is not the rash impulse of an Irish mug. It is concerted and specific, designed to inflict as much fear as possible before the ultimate retribution."

"Killing me," I stated the obvious.

"That would be my guess."

I shook my head in frustration, stood up, and found myself pacing. I recognized it was a sign of desperation so I sat back down again.

"I've got to find him."

Bergman placed his coffee cup down on a side table, and stood up, his hands in his pants pocket, now looking like a lawyer ready to deliver a summation.

"Yes. And no." He saw my perplexed response. "You might consider allowing him to find you."

"Harold, that's ridiculous. He already knows where I am."

He then proceeded to detail a few methods of drawing this character out into the open, forcing him to be where Sally, I, or anyone else could see him and notice him. A creature in the darkness, Bergman said, has more power. The light has a way of destroying them.

"Evil shall slay the wicked: and they that hate the righteous shall be desolate."

I looked at him with uncertainty.

"Psalm 34:21." He smiled. The former cop turned soldier, now private investigator sounded like a rabbi after all.

We were both veterans, albeit of different wars, as well as former cops. We both had war injuries that dramatically changed our lives. We were both seekers of the truth regardless of the outcome. At this point in my life, doing the right thing was of paramount importance. I took his words and suggestions to heart.

He shook my hand firmly and delivered the same warm smile as he had upon greeting me.

"*Zie ga zink.*" His smile remained upon seeing the blank look on my face. "It's a wish for good health."

"I'll need it."

The drive home to Ark City was intentionally slow. I wanted to be able to process everything I took in during my visit to Wichita. Detective Rackler's commentary I came to realize was not personal but a reflection of a policeman's mentality. An individual sending correspondences was not committing a crime, especially if the nature of the writing was not directly threatening. Until an overt act became apparent, the police could do nothing. Carson Stankey suggested this particular kind of criminal would not openly associate with others of his ilk. The goal was to blend in which may or may not have been possible in the smaller town of Arkansas City.

It was Harold Bergman who provided me a stronger sense of moral courage. This was a beast, a devil, a form of evil needing eradication. There was a challenge presented in the form of a declaration. There was an implied intent. Thus far, I had run all over the place, to the west and to the north, to find this creature. The goal now was to stand my ground and face the demon. It was a Goliath, and I was an old and infirmed David. It was time to find the stone that would bring it down.

Chapter Fifteen

It was over thirty-five years ago since a mortar shell exploded behind me in a dense forest in France. The force of the blast caused me to flail blindly before winding up entangled in a mass of barbed wire. The resulting injury to my face received treatment through a primitive form of surgery. There were grafts of bits of skin from other parts of my body onto the tears and rips on my face. All these years later, I experienced tremors and twitching, tingling sensations, as well as night visions of horrors trying to determine who I really was.

Since then, however, I devoted the better part of my adult life as a policeman, finding it an honor to serve the people of Arkansas City after it turned into my home. It had become my solemn duty. In essence, I became accustomed to fighting. I needed to continue to do so.

Sally wasn't around when I got home, having gone to La Bella Vita to prep food for the evening's crowd. I grabbed a glass of milk and a sandwich and sat down transcribing my thoughts from the afternoon in Wichita. Looking at everything without emotion, I considered what was going on. Thomas Hickey was intent upon revenge for the death of his brother, "Crazy" Jake Hickey, some twenty years prior for reasons known only to him. He was not showing himself, so to speak, except to me and only in a roundabout way. His plan was to create fear for my wife and me before presumably killing me.

The police could be of no assistance as there was no crime being committed. The local criminals would not aid someone and jeopardize their domain. This was to be a showdown perhaps played out like a Wild West shootout in the streets.

When Sally came home, I hugged her closely. She was the thing that grounded me the most, made me feel stronger than I actually was. I relayed to her in great detail the experiences of my trip. It appeared as though the sun snuck behind the clouds, turning what was a bright day rather gray. I had a thought that I would need to see the optometrist because Sally started to look a little fuzzy. Strange how I hadn't noticed that before. A tingle started in the right side of my face accompanied by a tightness, not quite a twitch. I breathed but did not take in any air. The last thing I remember was Sally's shriek.

When I opened my eyes, I was overwhelmed by a pervasive whiteness and an odor of antiseptic cleaner. My fuzzy vision started to clear and focused on Dr. Louis Brenz who stood above me, holding my wrist while he looked at his watch. He appeared far more serious than at any time I had seen him in the past. It suddenly dawned on me how much older he looked as well.

"Where?" I muttered.

"Arkansas City Memorial Hospital." The former Mercy Hospital, torn down and rebuilt with more beds and given a less soothing name. "The attending physician thinks you had a stroke. He doesn't know you like I do."

Doctie had been my personal physician since I returned from the war in 1919. He examined me on a regular basis since then, even after he unofficially retired. We had gone through so much together I often wondered if he doubted my identity as Baron Witherspoon. Then again he was one of those doctors that took his Hippocratic Oath seriously and was duty bound to treat the patient at all costs.

"What do you think?" I asked, my voice sounding like a small child.

"Sally filled me in on what has been going on lately. Sounds to me like you've been under a great deal of stress."

"Nothing I haven't dealt with in the past."

Dr. Brenz pulled up a chair and sat alongside the bed.

"Baron, when you were a cop, there was always the threat of imminent danger. You prepared for it and your body reacted accordingly. A married newspaperman doesn't have the same kind of worry. You're a lot older than you were as a policeman, and your prior injuries have taken a toll. You're just not equipped to handle this kind of excitement anymore."

Everything he said was medically correct. This time, however, there was a man aiming for me. Either he or the stress of a real stroke would do me in. When Doctie recommended complete rest, I smiled graciously and nodded. He gave his advice, and knew I would either take it or not. Sure, the thought of a vacation down in Hot Springs sounded pleasant. Or maybe take the train down to Corpus Christi to lie out on the beach. He and I both knew when I returned the same dilemma would exist.

The biggest problem with most men's lives was not knowing when your time was up. Back in the war, they said it was only the dead who didn't hear the shells and bullets meant for them. This had been mostly true for me, except that I lived. At this point, I had a second chance that lasted more years than I expected.

A physician's advice to rest was valid. I could not disagree with Doctie's medical recommendation. Perhaps it would prolong my life and provide me with more quality time with Sally. This, of course, assumed there was not a person out there in the world intent upon killing me as an act of retribution.

Staying still would make me an easier target for Tom Hickey. With defiance building up in me like water coming to a boil in a teakettle, I decided to take Harold Bergman's suggestions over those of my personal doctor. I would not live as a coward and die in bed. I would take the fight to the streets. This would be my last stand.

Chapter Sixteen

Demons lurk in the dark.

The plan was for Sally and me to spend a great deal of time out in the open but only during the day. She arranged with her cousins for them to run the restaurant at night while she did most of the prep work in the morning. I continued to go into the offices of the *Traveler* every day, writing columns or working with Miguel to help foster his potential career as a newspaperman. He catered to me, appearing deeply concerned over my health.

I went to Daisy Mae's for lunch more regularly, catching some guff from Dixie who claimed I was a traitor to my own wife. As her café was closer to downtown, I figured it might be a place where a stranger would come in for lunch to get a glimpse of the locals. La Bella Vita was too far out of town and much smaller. Someone like Tom Hickey would stand out even more.

As I had done several times throughout the years, I employed Larry Hammer's well-defined knowledge of everything in the city to keep a lookout for someone new, someone who was actually trying to stay anonymous. I didn't keep anything from him, explaining this was the now grown younger brother of the gangster who wreaked havoc in our town twenty years earlier.

"It just don't make sense to me," Larry commented while drinking his coffee.

"What doesn't?"

"Spending all those years holding on to that kind of anger."

At that point, I remembered my final encounter with Eihann Hammerschmidt, the escaped German POW who had a plan to cause a ruckus during World War II. The look on his face, even while wearing shackles and escorted by MPs, was one of pure hatred and defiance. Everything done for the Fatherland, a Third Reich supposed to last a thousand years but barely made it a dozen. I couldn't imagine such an anger subsiding. When I thought of it in those terms, I had more of an understanding of Tom Hickey.

Like a recurring character in one of those old movie serials, I saw a man in a light tan overcoat and gray hat on several occasions. It was mostly in passing but too often to be purely a coincidence. I could barely see his face or his hair. He never made eye contact or appeared as though he even looked at me. However, the occasions of encountering him were more frequent than I would have anticipated. This set the hair on the back of my neck to bristle.

It was then I realized I might have made a mountain out of a molehill. Given the fact the country's economy was doing well which trickled down to smaller towns like ours, I could guess there would be a lot more salesmen coming our way, representatives of companies looking to set up shop and use quality labor. If that were the case, figuring out who was who would be a lot more difficult. It wouldn't have been good to scare away a prospective business opportunity because of one edgy former cop.

Nevertheless, I did not see an abundance of new faces, different people ambling through town. This man alone kept popping up everywhere, same tan overcoat and gray hat pulled far enough down on his head to cover just enough of his face and eyes, as though by design. My imagination ran wild. It dawned on me this was the type of emotional distress such a stalker would intend to impose upon my life. Back in Chicago in the '20s and '30s it was as simple a task to fill a car with gangsters holding Tommy guns, race through the streets to find members of the opposing gangs, kill them, and drive off. I had not dealt with anything this sinister since the murders here in Ark City in '35 and the Wichita Ripper in '38.

At this time, there was no need to involve Dave Morton any further. I visited him once, got his feedback, and that was that. I could imagine him passing off this man who I felt was following me as pure coincidence. Dave would likely have indicated he wasn't even going to question the guy. Were I still on the force, it would have been my attitude as well. I hated the notion of being able to see both sides of the picture.

Sally and I passed our evenings listening to the radio or playing Parcheesi. We spent a great deal of time talking, mostly about ourselves and our feelings. We hardly had any discussion of who we were so long ago. That was a closed chapter in our lives. We stayed snuggled inside our house not concerning ourselves with whoever may have been on the outside.

After nearly two weeks of seeing this man, I walked into Daisy Mae's and greeted several friends and acquaintances. I had a brief chat with Billy Hipsher about a recent column concerning the history of Keefe and LeStourgeon where he pointed out an error in the timeline. I indicated a correction would be forthcoming.

As I sat down at a table in the middle of the room, a smartly dressed man in the next table asked unexpectedly, "Are you the mayor?"

"Beg your pardon."

"Well, I figured the way you were glad-handling all these folks you must be some kind of bigwig."

I smiled and thought back to Jeannette doing the same thing.

"No. Just a newspaperman."

"Even better."

I looked down at the menu, more to end the conversation than decide what I wanted. Out of the corner of my eye, I noticed the man wore a black pinstripe suit, black hat with maroon sash, pale pink shirt, and maroon tie. I thought he was on the young sound of forty or maybe just a tad older. He was a high roller eating a burger in a greasy spoon diner.

"You look like you're out of your element," I commented casually, hoping it didn't sound like an insult.

"For now, maybe."

"How so?" I continued, putting down my menu and turning toward him with my curiosity apparent. He leaned in my direction keeping the conversation between us.

"I've got it on good authority from a, shall we say, acquaintance in Washington, that the government has plans for a major highway expansion in the next couple of years. I got this idea to set up service stations all across the country, but not just filling stations, mind you. Chain restaurants where folks know what they're going to get. Like here. Gift shops to pick up knick knacks from their journeys. Rest areas to get out and stretch their legs. I got some investors to bankroll this, but I'm doing the research now by reaching out to the refineries to see if we can create a partnership."

"Pretty forward thinking," I responded, truly impressed with his ideas.

"I've had this idea for a long time." His face turned from amiable to dead-set serious, lips pursed and eyes aimed and focused like a gun. "Sometimes you get a notion, and you know nothing will come of it for a while but you've got to stay patient. You have to keep moving forward. Eventually, you'll hit your target. That is the only way to get what you want."

The comment could have been concerning just about any obsessive idea, business or personal. That sent a slight shudder down my spine. Suddenly, my eye caught the man in the tan overcoat, looking in my direction as he left the café. I decided I wasn't going to stay for lunch.

Chapter Seventeen

He headed east on Madison and turned north on Summit. He walked briskly, not exactly running away or trying to create distance between us. For all I knew, he might not have been aware I was hot on his heels. Then I second-guessed myself, realizing he had been following me for quite some time. He would have been aware of what I was doing now, perhaps even forcing me to do so.

Summit was the main street, too busy to hide from anyone. I tried figuring where he might head. The Leland Hotel was at 214 S Summit. Just beyond was the Osage Hotel at 100 N Summit. I was able to think quicker than I could move. His pace was faster than I was used to now as a desk jockey. That, of course, and being older.

As we crossed Jefferson, I snuck down the alley and doubled my steps. My lungs started to ache, and the soles of my feet were as heavy as concrete blocks. Surprisingly, I came out just north of the parking lot of W.B. Meats a few seconds before he caught up.

"Hey, buddy," I called out sharply. It wasn't exactly shouting but the stark suddenness of my nearly scratchy voice caught his attention. The genuine surprise on his face made him look weak. I walked quickly toward him.

"What do you want?" he said blandly.

"No. What do *you* want?" I returned, a sense of defiance as potent as the strong coffee from Daisy Mae's.

"Don't know what you're talking about, fella." With a bored look on his face, he turned to continue walking. I touched his arm, and he pulled it away harshly, pointing a finger at me as though it were a weapon but saying nothing in response to my assault.

"Look, I know you've been following me. For several days. If you want something, say it. If you want to make a move, go ahead." I didn't realize it but right then I was as prepared to die as ever.

His eyes grew wide, and he licked his lips. From beneath the hat pulled down to obscure his face, I noticed a trickle of sweat. He stood frozen in time, unwilling or perhaps unable to move. What took only several seconds felt like minutes passing, and yet somehow I could not see anyone else in the street.

His hand reached in his coat pocket. I sprung, faster than I imagined I could, grabbed his wrist, and wound up in a bear hug.

I pulled as firmly as I could on his hand, removing it from the pocket, and shook it to dislodge the revolver he held. I bent at the knees, picked it up, and pointed it at him, still in a position of prayer and supplication.

"Keep cool, friend," he said. His hand reached toward his inside jacket. I aimed the gun at him, my arms stiff. "Just getting my identification." His left hand held the lapel of his jacket, opening it wide. His right hand slithered inside, the fingers spread apart as his index and middle fingers latched onto a small leather wallet. He used the same fingers to open it up. A badge and an identification card were clearly visible.

Lawrence Caldwell. Federal Bureau of Investigation.

"Alex Gordon sent me."

My emotions ran between anger and relief. Part of me wanted to castigate the man for being such a lousy tail and thankful a friend thought enough to assist me. I felt myself starting to breathe normally again.

"Do you know where the guy is staying?" I asked.

"The Osage."

We started to move in that direction. Just as we got to the front of the building, a patrol car pulled up and two young officers stepped out. One stood at the passenger side with his gun drawn over the top of the car. The driver walked toward us, hand steady on his holstered weapon.

Caldwell and I looked at each other knowingly. We allowed the officers to handcuff us and bring us to the municipal building. It was apparent someone had witnessed the altercation and called it in. In one regard, I was proud of the citizens of Arkansas City. On the other hand, this was both an embarrassment and a problem.

We sat in chairs in front of the desk of Captain Dave Morton, still wearing those charming police bracelets. Dave entered with a folder and a key, unlocked the handcuffs, and threw them on his desk as he sat down. He looked at us with a sarcastic smirk on his face.

"Well?" A distressed parent couldn't have said it better.

"Captain Morton, I'm Special Agent Lawrence Caldwell of the FBI out of the Kansas City office. I'm here at the behest of—"

Dave held up his hand, this time like a traffic cop. Back during the war, we heard how eloquently the federal agents could speak while shoveling their load of manure. Twenty years on the force along with his elevated status meant he had the wherewithal to cut off a federal agent and get to the point.

"I had no idea the FBI would make personal concessions to ordinary citizens."

"In this particular case, Thomas Hickey is a known—"

Dave's interruption this time was a folder plopping down on his desk. He rifled through it with great drama, and then started reading, but it was more like intoning.

"Thomas Aloysius Hickey. Born August 26, 1915. This, coincidentally, is the Feast of Saint Adrian, patron saint of arms dealers and soldiers." Dave appeared bemused by the comment he made. "Two arrests for petty theft in Chicago, 1931 and 1933. Nothing further until a gun charge in Gary, Indiana in 1936 caught him six months in jail. Five arrests for gambling and pandering of prostitution, all between 1938 and 1941, all in Milwaukee. No convictions. Suspected in the murder of Terry McCoy of Madison, Wisconsin in 1943, Andrew Boyer in 1945, and Tad Morgan in 1946, both in Rockford, Illinois. No arrests, no convictions. Last known address was in St. Louis in 1948. Picked up for loitering." He closed the file and looked up at us, his head swiveling like viewing a tennis match. "Now, while I recognize Mr. Hickey is quite the troublemaker, he hasn't been convicted of anything in nearly twenty years and hasn't been closer than four hundred and fifty miles of our fair city. So tell me, Special Agent Caldwell, how he is of such interest to the FBI."

I saw Caldwell's shoulders slack. This was so much different from when Alex Gordon and his fake partner showed up back during the war, walking in as if they owned the city. Perhaps the national drama gave them more importance. I fully recognized this was a personal favor, and both Alex and Agent Caldwell had put themselves out.

"Okay. Alex Gordon, who I am aware you know, requested me to see if there was a viable threat to Mr. Witherspoon based on the correspondences he received."

"Correspondences? I thought there was just the postcard." I told Dave about the letter with the newspaper clipping and the postmark from Wichita on the envelope. I also fessed up to my visit to Wichita, and the information I received from the various sources.

"I thought I told you"—Dave started reprimanding me as though I were his teenage son.

"All I've done is the good research any newspaperman would do. You haven't picked me up for walking up and down Summit, waving pearl handled revolvers, and challenging Hickey to a shootout."

"No," Dave admitted, "you are not 'Two-Gun' Alterie."

Caldwell turned toward me.

"The guy you were talking to in Daisy Mae's earlier, did he say his name?"

"No."

"What were you talking about?"

"Said he was a businessman with investors trying to set up a chain of service stations across the country. He was meeting up with the management at the refineries."

"Did he say anything out of the ordinary?"

"Not really. Mentioned having an idea for a long time and sticking with it. Eventually he was going to hit his target."

Caldwell turned back toward Dave.

"Captain Morton, I've been following that man for several days. He's staying at the Osage Hotel. He's one of the newcomers to the city who just doesn't seem to fit in."

"Unlike you?" Dave said sarcastically.

Caldwell continued, ignoring Dave's comment. "I have seen nothing in his movements to suggest he's doing anything remotely to what Baron has indicated. He has been to none of the refineries and has spent most of his time walking around to various businesses."

"No car?" Dave asked.

"None that I am aware of."

"Let's go."

We drove in a patrol car back to Daisy Mae's, parking half a block away to avoid any confrontation. This was a long shot because it was a little over an hour after we had been there. Caldwell and I walked in from the east entrance; Dave entered from the front entrance on Madison. We looked around meticulously. He was gone.

Back outside, we huddled like the star quarterback, end, and tailback trying to figure out what play to run next. It felt like the fourth quarter with no timeouts and little time left on the clock.

Chapter Eighteen

"We'd better check the Osage," Dave said solemnly.

"He's long gone," Caldwell replied.

Dave simply strode toward the police car. Whether we followed or didn't, he was still doing his due diligence. I realized our best opportunities were slipping through our fingers.

Sure enough, in speaking with the desk clerk, Harry McWilliams, the gentleman who had given his name as Terry Hogan, checked out just that morning. He had a single valise, certainly not big enough to carry various dress suits or shirts for business meetings. As far as Harry knew, the man wasn't driving a car. Arriving to town became somewhat of a mystery. It either meant a vehicle stashed somewhere and hidden or traveling by train.

Based on his check in date of six days ago, we reviewed the train station for schedules. There are always a handful of hacks hanging around looking to pick up fares. Only one, a Mexican named Juan Morales, recalled a guy matching the description and dropping him off a block north of the Osage Hotel. No other drivers in town had him as a fare for those six days. No one had him as a fare that particular day.

It was easy to assume he got around by walking even though La Bella Vita was a good two miles away from this area on Summit Street. However, the bigger issue was where he was now. It would seem he simply disappeared as though he were never here. We returned to the Municipal Building and sat in Dave's office glumly.

"Is it possible he has some sort of confederate in town?" Caldwell questioned.

Dave and I looked at each other. Without saying anything, it was apparent we both thought about the flight of Eihann Hammerschmidt, the German POW who escaped from Camp Concordia. The FBI implied there was someone in town that lived here for a period of time, a plant to help foster sabotage and terrorism. Having to go through the trauma of figuring out which of the people in town you had known for so long could be an accomplice to a gangster was not something either of us wanted to go through again.

"Check your case files for 1943," Dave responded. "Talk to Alex Gordon."

"Don't even bother," I interjected. "Back then, it was about national security. The FBI isn't going to go through that again for little old me."

Suddenly, I felt a tingling on the right side of my face as though little ants crawled all over it. I wasn't going to let out a peep or show it in my eyes. I figured it was largely the stress. The realization occurred it was not my own safety I had any concern for but that of Sally. I would gladly have given my life if Tom Hickey made any move against her.

"If it's all right with you, Captain Morton, I'm going to continue my sweeps throughout town. I've made a list of locations where I spotted this guy. He may be using them to trail Witherspoon." Special Agent

Caldwell was the peak of efficiency even though I knew it to be a useless gesture. I voiced my opinion.

"What is the point?" My tone was on the border of blasé. "Whether he has a place to hide out or not, he's not going to make a move while you're following me like a puppy dog. And as Captain Morton will tell you, there are no outstanding warrants on this man and nothing to arrest him for, until he tries to kill me or my wife."

"Baron's right, Caldwell." Dave sat at his desk, his hands crossed firmly, looking somewhat like Chief Richardson with a fixed resilience about him. "There's a reason this mug doesn't have a conviction record. He's a lot more cool and collected than his older brother. Baron's not going to make a move knowing he has government protection. Even though we all know it's unofficial."

"And how long will it be until Alex calls you back to Kansas City on a real assignment?" I asked.

Special Agent Caldwell looked back and forth between Dave and me. He nodded his head lightly in agreement, understanding fully he could have no further impact on this situation. Dave indicated an officer would take him back to his hotel. He stood up and shook our hands and left. Like that, I was back on my own again.

Dave and I sat there for a bit in silence. We had a long history between us and dealt with many cases involving criminals of all sorts. This was an entirely different matter. It was personal and nothing to do with money or political intrigue. The amount of emotion flowing through this made it entirely unpredictable. Perhaps Thomas Hickey was simply trying to scare me to death, my health having placed me in a more precarious position. It was unlikely; however, he would employ something psychological. This was a gangster just like his older brother, a relic from a long lost era. These men fashioned themselves after Bogart and Cagney and Edward G. Robinson. They learned how to be tough guys from the pulp magazines. This one man kept all of that alive.

"What now?" When Dave asked that, I deflated. If this longstanding veteran of the police force, a man who was destined to become chief of police or greater, did not have an idea, I was alone. It occurred to me this was on Sally and me by ourselves. This threat was direct and profound. The law was unable to protect us until a crime was committed or attempted. By then it might be too late.

A man must stand guard over that which he loves and values. He must fight off all that would dare to take away his life and liberty. He must vanquish the malevolence that would manifest itself. This was not about law and order but simply right and wrong, good and evil. This was kill or be killed.

Chapter Nineteen

I recounted the day's activities to Sally over dinner that evening. Her response was levelheaded and methodical. To her this was a challenge, something to meet head on. Perhaps it was the notion of both of us getting a bit older and needing to know we were made of something better. Maybe it was just the roar of a lion and lioness in the face of the hunter's rifle.

It was my comment about the sensation on my face that got her attention the most. I tried dismissing it, but she kept pressing.

"Shouldn't you see Dr. Brenz?"

"What for? I know what he'll say."

"I'm not ready to lose you." Her tone was louder than ever before, and she resisted the urge to slam her hand down on the dining room table, the impulsive action of a feisty Italian woman. I heard a slight gurgling in her words, and saw her eyes glaze over, just short of tears. She was afraid, and even worse, allowing that fear to show. All her life, I imagined her strong for the man she loved. But now the stress of this wore on her as much as it was on me.

To be perfectly honest, I was at peace with everything. I had lived a long life beyond the time I should have died. I did some good in the person of Baron Witherspoon, both as a police officer and a well-respected newspaperman. Perhaps it would have been a joy to be a father with somewhat of a more traditional life, but overall, I could not complain. If a relic of the past would mean my death, I figured justice would come from somewhere for me as I had strived to do for Heather Devore.

I was neither hoping for death nor giving up in this matter. I knew it would come for one reason or another and knew I wouldn't have enough strength to keep the door shut when he knocked.

"We're going to maintain our routine." I spoke calmly and evenly as a way to get us back on track. "Daylight hours only. The *Traveler* and the restaurant are doing just fine without our presence at night."

"Where is he, Baron? Where has he gone?"

She had a valid point. I highly doubted the suggestion of a partner in town. This man worked quietly for twenty years, never seeming to involve himself in a gang for any period of time. He wouldn't be able to explain the single-minded obsession with the vengeance of his brother's death to any confederate, especially one whose objectives were monetary gain. We determined he was likely on foot. Other than the hotels in town, there were a few rooming houses. I knew of some, but it would take a great deal of time to search them all out. The question was—where else could a man hide in Arkansas City?

Miguel was up for another "research" project. I indicated I wanted to write somewhat of a travel article in the hopes it would be picked up on the news wires. Perhaps we could drive more tourism to our city. I asked him to determine all the places a tourist could stay in town and all the ways they could get around. For the most part, I hashed out as many of both as I could think of, but with his persistence, I hoped he'd figure out a few I missed.

Risking a tongue lashing, I checked in with a few of the younger cops at the station to pick their brains. While there I ran into Clifford Smiley. He was pushing sixty-seven but still sat behind the same desk, filing forms and assisting other officers. While he didn't look tired or worn down, in my opinion he was getting a little old to be doing what he was doing. After all, former Chief Gray thought I was over the hill at fifty.

"How come you've never written an article about me?" he jibed.

"One of these days, Cliff. Probably when you retire."

He leaned forward trying to keep his voice down.

"Scuttlebutt is you're walking on eggshells these days. What gives?"

I laid it out for him in a nutshell, also passing along my concerns for Sally's safety and mine. We talked as cops, guys who took an oath and not just a job, who realized there might be sacrifices in securing the lives of citizens. However, he had more empathy for me. I was no longer on the force, no longer walking a beat, and supposedly no longer a target. I was Joe Citizen, one of the many the cops were supposed to be protecting.

After finishing a column at the newspaper office, I headed home. It was late afternoon on a cool, crisp autumn day. The smell of the leaves refreshed my lungs. A lightness to my step was like walking on air. I stood in front of my house, the home I shared with Sally, where we truly felt safe. For the briefest of moments, I was imbued with a calm and serenity, as though nothing could go wrong.

It was right then my legs got weak, kind of rubbery as though they lost their ability to hold me upright. I went down to one knee just as a dizziness came over me like a flock of bees. A muffled roar rang in my ears like they were filled with cotton, and the sound of the wind became a dull moan. I could have sworn someone held on to my shoulders just as I fell into a deep black ocean, consumed by the emptiness. At that point, I was completely alone.

When I awoke, a man in white stood above me. This time it wasn't Dr. Brenz. My eyes finally adjusted, and I recognized Dr. Schaeffer. He was a younger guy, pleasant and likely very competent. He just wasn't as old as Brenz.

"Doctie will be here shortly. And one of the nurses notified your wife." I turned my head from side to side to get a view of my surroundings, and then looked back up at him. "Memorial Hospital," he replied to my assumed question.

"What happened?"

Dr. Brenz responded to my question as he walked into the room, Sally right behind him.

"Another one of those episodes." Schaeffer showed Doctie the chart, and they consulted silently. "Do you remember what you were doing or how you felt right before it happened?"

"I was standing in my front yard, breathing in the air, and feeling how good it was to be alive." On that last comment, I looked up at Sally. She smiled at me.

"Good. Let's keep you that way. Dr. Schaeffer is prescribing Hydralazine for hypertension and high blood pressure. We have a feeling that undue stress is causing many of these episodes."

"Many?"

"As you know, Baron, your medical history is filled with unique scenarios. There is really nothing we can do to treat those. However, as your wife has indicated that recent events have been weighing on you, it is our opinion these have been exacerbating your condition." He pulled a brown bottle out of his pocket. "Twice a day, morning and night. Come see me in a week, and we'll see how you're doing."

I heard Dr. Brenz, and I acknowledged what he said, but it hadn't sunk in. All I knew was I was getting out of that hospital bed and going home with my wife. I changed back into my clothes lickety-split, taking a final look in the mirror before leaving. My face looked like an ancient scroll, pale and withered, almost like Boris Karloff from *The Mummy*. Yet inside me was a renewed sense of purpose. I wanted to be victorious in this endeavor, whatever the cost may have been.

My eyes were still out of focus as I looked at a young woman walking down the hall toward us. I realized it was a memory from nearly twenty years prior coming into clarity. I had not seen Beth Handy Appleby since the death of her cousin, the murderer Natalie Dixon, back in 1935.

Chapter Twenty

I was too tired to feel surprised and not in any mood to hide it. She, on the other hand, was shocked at my appearance as Sally held on to me and guided me along.

"Baron? Are you all right?"

We were finally standing in front of each other. A whimsical and flirtatious young girl who had a crush on me for a long time was now a mature and upright woman. It was as though I had the pride of an uncle seeing his niece all grown up.

"Just getting old," I responded. "Beth Appleby, this is my wife, Sally." Then turning to Sally, I said, "Beth's father runs the millinery."

"Handy's," she replied. I knew she was familiar with the place having seen the receipts she brought home. The ladies shook hands graciously.

"And what are you doing here?" I inquired.

"It's dad. He's taken ill. The doctor doesn't think he should go back to work as it would put too much of a strain on his heart. We may have to sell the shop if we can't figure something else out."

I looked around behind her.

"Is Frank with you?"

"He'll be here in a few days. I really need him. He has a mind for these things."

"If there's anything we can do—"

"Thank you. And take care of yourself." She moved on down the hall. I looked back over my shoulder, but she did not. I couldn't help but wonder how she felt about my involvement with Natalie and whether or not she accepted the truth. Too much time had passed to make any difference in whatever her opinion was.

As we drove home, I recapped the story of Natalie Dixon to Sally. This was the only time I revealed the truth of those horrific murders in Wichita, how I was the only one who knew who committed them with any absolute certainty, and the sadness it brought me.

"It always hurts to lose someone you love." Even though I made no direct mention of my feelings for Natalie, Sally knew how I had felt back then.

Sally made coffee and served it with homemade biscotti, these sweet, tasty Italian biscuits I never ate before I met her. She allowed us a moment of silence before her face turned into that of a stern schoolteacher.

"I think this town holds too many bad memories for us. It might be time to leave."

I put my coffee and biscotti down carefully on the table, wiping my hands of the crumbs. I took in a deep breath and exhaled slowly.

"I went from Eric Kimble to Baron Witherspoon and was taken in by this town. I've had two very distinct and fulfilling careers here. And this is the place where I met you. I've lived longer than I ever expected. There have been troubling times, but I never expected paradise. If we run away, there is no guarantee Tom Hickey won't follow us. If we wind up in a brand new city with no friends or resources, it will be like a slaughter in a desert. I don't intend to leave our home under the threat of danger. When, and if we leave, it will be because we need a change in our lives."

Sally reached across the table and held my hands in hers warmly. I noticed a tear in her eye.

"Whither thou goest, I will go." I recognized it as a Bible passage. The funny thing, I started to be more familiar with these quotes.

That night after dinner, we went back to our personal investigation. The discussions were the same as before, trying to consider how a man with no car would get around and where he might be. The next morning Miguel presented to me a lengthy list of all the hotels, lodgings, and rooming houses in the city. I made phone calls. By lunch, I determined no man matching the description I provided was staying anywhere in town or had been there recently, outside of the Osage Hotel.

There was a hesitation to revisit the line of thinking. Back in the war, we desperately considered an ally to an escaped German POW who would assist in an act of sabotage. This was an entirely different situation. While it was possible to consider extreme political or cultural affiliations during a time of war, I could not conceive of anyone outside of Thomas Hickey who would hold such a grudge after twenty years.

Nevertheless, I quickly considered a half dozen possibilities, men and women I knew to be involved in the less-than-legal businesses still quietly operating in the area. None of them made sense, as I could not envision them sticking their neck out for something that would offer no benefit. As far as I was concerned, this was a lone man on a desperate final mission.

My weekly columns were uplifting travelogues,

highlighting the town, Cowley County, and the area. I knew I was losing the biting quality that made my articles something most folks wanted to read. Whereas I did not think our publisher, Oscar Stauffer, would fire me any time soon. I could not imagine continuing this career if it meant I became bland. I was fortunate to have this second career, to have created some meaningful memories for the readership, and to have been part of a significant trial that resulted in a delayed justice for a special woman.

My mind was too distracted. While I did not start to reconsider Sally's suggestion, I did imagine what life would be like somewhere else. I wanted it to be warm, with no snow to shovel or trudge through. I wanted the air to be clean so I could breathe easier. I wanted it to be a place where no one knew me or had heard of me. I wanted to be new again.

Regrettably, the old me still had a mission to complete. I just hoped I had the strength and wherewithal to complete it.

Chapter Twenty-One

Fortunately, I had written two weeks' worth of columns and was comfortable with Miguel getting them to press. I spent those two weeks resting. Another expression I could have used was "being bored," but I never admitted that to Sally. While it was true I slept a great deal and did not overexert myself, all I did was try to figure out where Thomas Hickey might be lying in wait and lurking. It was like reheating an old meal that never tasted too good the first time around.

My mind would then drift, mostly to the past but to random times. Some street scene on the North Side of Chicago and the clip-clopping of patent leather shoes on cobblestone streets. My first view of the forests in France, and the thick aroma of the pines. The ship returning to America, the Statue of Liberty with her welcoming arm. Arriving in Arkansas City, Kansas, and the sensation of being in the wilderness. Little snippets reminiscent of newsreels. My life became nothing more than a series of small events strung together on a wire. I dismantled all of the good things I had accomplished and discarded them like items for donation to a scrap drive. It no longer mattered we prevented a Chicago gangster from taking over our city and turning it into another Cicero. Stopping two crazed killers was meaningless. Averting a deadly act of sabotage and finding justice for a woman who deserved so much more were all simply newspaper articles designed to increase circulation.

How ironic this review of the meaning of my life had only come about because a gangster recommended I leave Chicago. Were it not for that friendly piece of advice, I might have found myself in a storage warehouse on a cold St. Valentine's Day morning. Like a cat, I had gone through a few lives and wondered how many remained.

Sally waited on me hand and foot. We would occasionally go out for a walk mid-day so I could get some fresh air and exercise. Fall was making its way into winter and the notion of staying cooped up worried me. My mind turned to Eliot Ness who I had not heard from in many years. I lost track of him and could only assume he fell on hard times. While I may not have known the complete truth of his Untouchables, to me he was a friend who showed nothing but warmth. I respected his diligence in fighting crime. I wondered if there was someone out there who thought of me in the same light.

On one of our walks, Sally and I passed the millinery. I nodded at Frank Appleby as he went in and out of the store with boxes of paperwork. He was well suited to this task. It was a shame to think of Handy's Millinery closing after so many years. Time has a way of blowing sand over the greatest monuments and turning all things to dust. I had seen many changes to this community in over thirty years and knew "progress" was inevitable.

I stopped suddenly a few steps just past the store. The strained look on my face likely made Sally wonder if another attack was imminent. A thought occurred to me, one that I hadn't considered in quite a while. We went immediately to the municipal building.

Captain Dave Morton agreed to meet with us privately in his office. He had the same look on his face I had just a bit earlier when I made the suggestion—the underground tunnels.

"If you recall, we closed them up during the war. Too easy for the enemy to use them against us. Only authorized police personnel can even access them."

"We only discovered the sections used by Jake Hickey and his gang," I responded. "There were a few sections that went off in different directions."

"What are you guys talking about?" Sally interjected. It was then Dave and I took turns explaining the situation with "Crazy" Jake Hickey's activities in more detail. The use of these tunnels, built sometime in the early part of the century, varied from safety and protection from tornadoes and Indian attacks to storing of contraband and other illegal items. Workers associated with the late Councilman Hallett likely used it before Hickey and his gang realized their full potential.

The flower shop, whose backroom served as one of the entrances, was still in business. The owners allowed access to those policemen who had a key to the padlocked entrance. A musty smell from the moment we opened the trapdoor made us aware very few people went down there on a regular basis. A feeling of nausea welled up inside me. Dave looked back from the first step.

"You don't have to do this."

"I need to." I looked back at Sally standing behind me. She was eager to see this small part of history but had more concern for my well-being.

Dave's flashlight was considerably brighter than what we had used twenty years prior. Yet the light showed only an eerie emptiness of unfulfilled promises and certain danger. Dust kicked up as we walked. Wooden doors appeared at regular intervals, as we got closer to a section that seemed wider and more open.

We came upon a room with small tracks on the far side where items moved in and out of the tunnels to an opening on the far end of the street. I remembered cases of whiskey, a table with four chairs, a clipboard with inventory and locations from here down to the Dallas suburbs, and oil lamps lighting the place up, as though it was more vibrant than anything was above.

For a brief moment, my head spun, not physically, more like images from somewhere in a dream running at full gallop in front of my eyes. So many years, so many memories, so many things forgotten. The notion of being where Jake Hickey hid out and made a concerted effort to run illegal operations within Ark City, the town I called home, the place where I vowed to protect and serve the citizens, now stood empty. The threat was gone.

However, out of the corner of my eye, I caught sight of a homemade bed frame around the corner in a cubby-like area. It was crammed with pillows and comforters to create a kind of mattress. By the side of it was a map of the city, various markings identifying Daisy Mae's, the Municipal Building, La Bella Vita, and my home. This was where Thomas Hickey had been after checking out of the hotel. It was history repeating itself.

"If that door was padlocked," I said aloud, "how

did he get down here?"

"Obviously, other entrances we weren't aware of."

I shook my head despondently. Dave looked at the area himself. We found no sign of a weapon or bullets but that alone didn't offer any relief. We looked at each other and understood what was at stake. Dave glanced down at the map. A circle drawn around Handy's Millinery. It all started coming back to me now.

Chapter Twenty-Two

That churning feeling in the pit of my stomach came back. I was breathless, almost dizzy. It was not, however, the time to bring this to Sally's attention. She likely would have preferred to get me to the hospital.

From the corner of my eye, I noticed her looking back and forth between Dave and me, the silence between us filled with unspoken words uttered so many times before.

"All right, boys," Sally said in that scolding tone she sometimes had. "What's going on here?"

In a measured voice, without turning to look at her, I detailed our final encounter with Jake Hickey. My tongue was covered with contempt as I spoke of a coward, a man who was so enraged with me he used a defenseless young woman as a shield in hopes of achieving my death. To what purpose we would never know. Chances are Dave or Ray Vernon would have killed him after my death. This, naturally, would have made our current predicament non-existent.

Dave was inclined to go to the municipal building and get a few more cops in on the action. I advised quite strongly we didn't have the time. In all likelihood, Thomas Hickey had left the tunnels for his final assault.

We drove around to the alley behind the block. A car was parked right behind the back door of the millinery. Dave approached slowly with his gun drawn while I followed, Sally tugging me back all the while.

Dave motioned for me forward when he came to the driver's side. It was Frank Appleby with a bruise and a small amount of blood on the left side of his forehead.

"He came out of nowhere, just smacked me on the head. I think it was a gun."

"Did you see him, Frank?" The tremor in my voice was entirely awkward.

"Just saw him grab Beth and drag her out of the car before I passed out."

Dave and I looked at each other. That feeling in my stomach churned even more. It was around the time of Arkalalah twenty years earlier that "Crazy" Jake Hickey made a final stand at this very location. I thought I had left all this behind. Instead, a cold skeletal hand reached out to pull me back.

I turned from Frank's car and started to walk down the alley. Sally stood in front of me while Dave ran up and grabbed me by the arm. I swung around violently, hate and anger filling my eyes with blood. There were so many times I faced Death and walked away. Maybe it was time to walk straight up to him and spit in his face.

"What do you think you're doing?" Dave asked through gritted teeth.

"It's history repeating itself, Dave. You remember how this went."

"Yeah. Me and Big Ray Vernon stood back here unaware what was going on, then breaking in, and I got shot in the shoulder. Which has hurt every time it's going to rain for the past twenty years. We do this my way, the police way."

I was too old and too tired for anything other than sarcasm and apathy.

"By the time you get a squad of men down here, Beth will be dead. And that lunatic will come out shooting and kill who knows how many others. No, it has got to be like before."

Dave stood there having released the grip on my arm, head hung in thought and concern. I could tell he was allowing many ideas to wash over him like water from a baptism. He had become the best cop I ever knew, combining strength of character with deductive reasoning. From the kid who had no other options for a job to whom I believed should be the next chief of police, Dave had experienced a lot and seen more criminal cases than even Cliff Smiley. As a citizen, I didn't have a say in the matter. He had every right to tell me to stand down or even arrest me for interfering with a police matter. But he knew what I knew, had been through this before. Time may have worn down our bodies but what we had in our heads was worth more than a squad of cops.

"Stay behind parked cars. Use your words to get into his mind. Do not, repeat, do not try to cross the street and confront him." Dave spoke to me as though he were my mother, something which I expected Sally to act like. "I'll give you five minutes to circle around to the front of the store and five minutes of talking. After that, I go in and blast that rascal."

"Keep in mind he has Beth. Frank wouldn't take too kindly to you shooting his wife."

His smile broke up the tension. For him and me.

I turned toward Sally. It occurred to me I might be looking into her eyes for the last time. I knew I wouldn't live forever and didn't have any sadness to that notion. My life had been more blessed than I could ever imagine. If someone wrote my story and I read it, I'd probably think it was a bunch of hooey. Beyond that were the scant few years I spent with this feisty and loving woman. A calmness came over me because of her. I was able to relax and care less about the past and just allow the day to happen, feel the sun or wind on my face and know it was all good.

She leaned into me for what I thought would be a kiss. Instead, she pulled a Smith & Wesson revolver out of her purse and placed it firmly in my hand.

"This was Pete's, the one he carried as a sheriff. I think it belongs in the hands of a cop."

At that very moment, Eric Kimble was no more, perhaps even only a memory and never a real person. Sally, who fully knew my background, had as much as told me I *was* Baron Witherspoon, the retired police officer from the Arkansas City police department who had spent the better portion of his life protecting and serving the people of this city.

The retired cop had one last case to close.

Chapter Twenty-Three

Even though this felt so much like October of 1934, it was very different. So many things had changed. I was no longer an official of the Arkansas City Police Department. I was twenty years older and endured the effects of a major trauma thirty-five years prior. The toll of time finally caught up to me. I had nothing to gain by doing this, no hero's reward or commendation from city officials. Dave and all of the other cops were fully capable of dealing with this situation. This guy was after me. Thomas Hickey, like his brother before him, had a personal vendetta, a score to settle. It was going to end right here and right now.

There were more people walking along Summit than I recall before. Waving my gun with a sweeping motion, I encouraged as many as I could to go in opposite directions from Handy's Millinery. Those who recognized me realized it was something of importance. The others just didn't want to be bothered. Fortunately, there were more cars parked along the street, including two directly in front of the store, which was on the opposite side of the street.

The sun shone brightly, bathing the area in a rich gold. It was almost too bright. The glare on the store's two large front windows prevented me from seeing anything inside. It was to be a shouting match yet again.

"Hickey! Let her go."

"Is that you, Kimble?"

Just like his brother, he saw this all as a game. He might have felt he had the upper hand, but what he didn't realize was I had nothing left to lose.

"Don't know who you're talking about."

"Eric Kimble. Sneak thief from the North Side of Chicago. Took the identity of a kid from Kansas. Don't you think those people would like to know?"

"They know who I am, who I've been to them for over thirty years." I paused for a moment wondering if anyone else heard me or even cared. "Let the girl go."

"I'm going to kill you even if that means using this pretty lady to do it."

"And then what? The cops will be here in droves. They'll shoot you down like a rabid dog. Just like your brother. He was a no-good two-timing cur that didn't have the brains to leave town while the getting was good. So are you as dumb as him?"

Part of me performed like a B-movie actor dishing out cheap dialogue that just didn't fit in with the times. Then again, I said what I meant, considering how fed up I was with all the Hickeys, and what I came to realize was the wasted lives of those gangsters.

A shot came toward the direction of my voice, followed by another. That second shot shattered one of the front windows of the millinery. I moved up and down the sidewalk across from the store, staying low behind the cars.

"So you want to kill me," I shouted, my voice starting to crack. "Are you going to do it like a coward? Like your brother?" The only way to get him to make a mistake was by taunting him into unbridled anger.

My head swiveled around in all directions as I

worked out a plan. I figured Dave was about three minutes away from storming in the back door. With Tom Hickey shooting wildly, this was about to get dangerous.

A man with a suitcase, probably some kind of traveling salesman, hunkered down behind a car nearly a block down. Smart guy, but I hoped he would just move on down the street farther. There was not much time to consider his situation.

"Come out. Show your face, Hickey," I yelled at the top of my lungs. At that moment, I was fully prepared to be shot to death in the middle of the street, as perhaps should have happened all those years ago, if it meant saving Beth.

The front door to Handy's Millinery suddenly ripped open. Thomas Hickey held Beth close to him, just the slightest bit of the side of his face peered out from the back of her head. His arm was around her waist, close to her chest, pulling her tightly to him, his gun stuck in her ribs. This was no wedding dance.

"You're going to die, Kimball."

Within seconds, I analyzed what I saw. A hostage held close to a captor. Hardly any room to shoot him. Uncertain skills for even doing so. Perhaps Dave coming in through the back could draw his attention. But what then? If I couldn't make the shot, it was likely both Beth and I would wind up dead and the people of Ark City would have a mess on their street to clean up.

It occurred to me in that one brief moment I had made a mistake. I should have let Dave get a squad of trained policemen to handle this situation. Too much time passed. I no longer was who I had been or thought I was.

From there, it all happened too fast.

I heard a crash, assumed it was Dave.

Hickey heard it behind him. He turned his head.

A shot came from inside the store. Hickey returned fire.

There was enough space for me to shoot at his arm.

I took the shot and missed.

Hickey turned toward my direction.

Beth squirmed from his grip and fell to the street.

Then, a crack rang out. It was almost deafening. The bullet hit Tom Hickey smack dab center on the forehead. He pitched forward, dead in the street.

Dave came out from the front of the store. Sally was behind him a moment later.

The clouds appeared to cover the sun. A swarm of bees flew around my head. The air was heavy. I took two steps away from the car I crouched behind. I swirled around and fell. I could hear footsteps running.

The traveling salesman stood over me. It was Alex Gordon.

Chapter Twenty-Four

It was an all-too-familiar scene—my eyes came into focus as I lay in a hospital bed. It is not something you can imagine when you are younger. However, as you get older and if you have a condition, it becomes a regularity.

Fortunately for me, the first sight was Sally. The only thought in my mind was to spend the rest of my life with her, just her and no one else. I saw a deserted island with one lone palm tree and white sand, the sun shining down on us like a heavenly light.

Standing over her shoulder was Alex Gordon. The smirk on his face passed for a smile.

"Nice shooting, Tex," I joked. The smile grew wider. "I didn't think the FBI was involved in this case."

"Oh, we weren't," he said as casually as Jack Benny did, his eyes rolling away in another direction. "I was on vacation. I heard there might be some good hunting here."

"Was that a .30 Springfield Sporter?"

"As a matter of fact it was." I smiled. Sally touched Alex on the arm.

"I'll leave you two while I visit with the doctor. We'll see when he's ready to let you out." My smile grew bigger.

"I have advised Captain Morton," Alex continued,

sounding official, "the FBI would file a report on this case and call it closed."

"I thought you were on vacation."

"Oh, I was. But that is just my last act as a Federal agent." I looked at him with caution, uncertain as to what he meant. "I realized a while back I'd never get Hoover's job so I went back to law school at night. Passed the bar last month. Got a job as assistant district attorney in Kings County. It's Brooklyn and not Manhattan, but it'll do for now. Plus, my dad's getting up there in years. Figured it was time to go home. What about you?"

"Home." I said the word out loud but with a slight question mark. In all honesty, I didn't know what the word meant. As a young man, the North Side of Chicago was my home, a place from which I practically escaped. For thirty-five years, Arkansas City, Kansas was the place I called home. At first, all I tried to do was fit in. Then I was more like Huck Finn, drifting along on a raft as it flowed from place to place. The only real home I had was when I found Sally. At that moment, she returned to my bedside.

"I don't know, Alex," I finally replied. "I guess it's all up to her." We all smiled.

"If you're ever up in New York City, look me up."

"We will."

He shook my hand with a firm grip, one of strength and commitment. I had every faith in his future success. He stopped and turned suddenly.

"So what was all that hooey about Eric Kimble?" he asked, an almost cartoonish smirk on his face.

"I haven't got a clue."

"Neither do I."

Alex Gordon left the hospital and moved on toward the bigger things in life.

"The doctor figured a spike in your blood pressure caused you to pass out. He wants you to continue taking your medication and…" I looked at her, my eyebrows raised in apprehension. "And eliminate any stress from your life." I lay there with a blank look on my face. While I was no longer a police officer, there had been a great deal of stress over the course of the last six years, first with Jimmy O'Donnell and now Thomas Hickey. This was nothing I asked for or brought upon myself. How was I supposed to manage the doctor's prescription? "I've got an idea," Sally said. Somehow, the lightness of her voice cheered me up.

****

They discharged me two days later. That evening, I sat at a corner table at La Bella Vita while Sally and her cousins served the dinner crowd. From all appearances, it was a busy evening. I ate a small plate of lasagna with garlic bread but limited myself to one glass of wine. To my surprise, several people came up to me and wished me well. They'd heard about the events of the previous day and treated me like a hero just as they had twenty years earlier. The funny thing was I had nothing to do with either event, unless you call the insanity of drawing fire from an enraged gangster an act of bravery. Nevertheless, I accepted these commendations graciously.

Before all of these crazy events with Hickey threatening us, Sally and I typically sat of an evening around the dinner table at home drinking wine and talking about our lives together. This time we moved the scene to the restaurant's corner table at the end of the evening after the restaurant closed.

Sally placed several photos and some papers before me. They appeared to be of a restaurant, somewhat like La Bella Vita, but far more glamorously decorated. The furnishings looked authentic to my untrained eye. I just looked up at her, my face as crazed as Spike Jones.

"This is in Los Angeles," she finally commented

"Okay."

"An Italian restaurant."

"Oh?"

"For sale." My face went from crazed to confused. I had no idea where she was going with this. "I've had several offers for this place. With that money plus a loan from the seller, we could move out there. I talked with the guy on the phone. Sweet old man named Salvatore Debella."

"So your idea of getting rid of stress is running a restaurant?"

She reached across the table, grabbed both of my hands with hers, and looked down at the table perhaps trying to form the words or say the speech she rehearsed.

"The past is what's stressful. We've both, you and I, been holding on to it for too long. And it's just always right there, over our shoulder. I want to go somewhere that people don't know us from Adam. Where it is just Baron and Sally, a couple of nice people who serve a good meal. I want to look out over the Pacific Ocean and see…" Her voice dropped off, choked up with emotion.

"What?"

"Tomorrow."

Her strength was what drew me to her and what

kept me glued to her now. It took a lot to suggest leaving a place that had been home for so long. Yet given the uncertainty of my health, I finally realized I wanted some happiness. I needed that. The future was beyond Ark City.

Chapter Twenty-Five

When you realize you will leave a place, you look at it with new eyes. It was early 1919 when I came to Arkansas City, passing myself off to Baron Witherspoon's father as his facially scarred son. Whether he fully believed it or not I would never know. I became a son and eventually a well-respected police officer.

People passed in and out of my life. I became a member of a community. All the time I was afraid the other shoe would drop and the mirror would break. It was thirty-five years later and none of that mattered any more.

Perhaps Dixie McGuire figured I was a food traitor having gone in the morning to Daisy Mae's Café for breakfast and staying through lunch and dinner. I sat and ate, drank coffee, and talked to anyone and everyone who stopped by. The ham steak and scrambled eggs started my day. In the early afternoon, it was a grilled cheese sandwich and tomato soup. The day ended with meatloaf and mashed potatoes.

Right around dinnertime, Larry Hammer came around and sat right across from me in the booth. As he had done so many times before, there was no need for an invitation.

"What's up, boss?" he asked casually. The man was in his mid-seventies but looked fit as a fiddle, ready to go back to work for anyone who might have asked but happy to stay "retired" if he had a mind to.

As I told him of the plans Sally and I had, he leaned forward with keen interest. Dixie finally joined us, picking up the threads of the conversation.

"Can't say as I blame you," Larry finally responded. "I've been looking for a way out for a long time."

"Says who?" Dixie chimed in, slapping Larry's shoulder. "Your backside is gonna wind up glued to one of these booths someday."

"Well, that just may be."

It was that kind of camaraderie I would miss. These two were the kindest to me of all the folks I ever met and made me feel like one of the family. I doubted there was any place in Los Angeles that served a better meatloaf.

The next morning I strolled into the Municipal Building, a place the Arkansas City Police Department called home. For nearly thirty years, the place had been my home. I could still hear the echoes of my footsteps from years past.

Captain Dave Morton sat behind his big desk with a large stack of files to his left, a smaller one to his right. The goal was to make the pile on the right bigger after reading and making memos. It was slow going. He looked up and waved, likely pleased at the opportunity to rest his eyes for a bit.

"How are you feeling?" he asked like a little brother.

"Like an old man. You?"

"I keep looking at these files thinking they're the key to my becoming chief of police."

"You'll make it someday. I'm just sorry I won't be around to see it."

He had a look of concern as though I was about to tell him what the doctor told me. Rather, I advised him of our plans to move to the West Coast. His shoulders eased, and a big smile appeared on his face.

"That's good, Baron. Real good." He looked down at his desk, his head hanging weary. When he looked up, there were tears starting to form in his eyes. "For twenty years, you've been the best friend I've had. You realize that, don't you?"

"I do."

"That is all I've ever thought of you as. It doesn't matter how a man starts out in life. All that counts is what he makes of himself. And you are one of the finest men I've ever known."

We stood up and shook hands across the desk. Then, he saluted me, as though I were his superior officer. It was something I never knew about or felt in all this time—respect.

I turned and left his office, not looking back. There were plenty of memories that would be fodder for stories later. It was time to move on down the road, hand in hand with my wife, the woman who had captured my heart.

It was time to head to Tomorrow.

A word about the author…

I studied film-making and creative writing at the University of Miami in the '80s, was involved in the Boston Poetry Scene in the '90s, and am a former president of the Kansas Writer's Association. My work has stretched from crime fiction to poetry, screen writing to experimental fiction.

I live in a one hundred-plus-year-old Victorian home in Wichita, KS with my wife, Shelia, and Sir Pounce Alot (the orange manx) and Lady Mittens (the tuxedo manx).

http://tikiman1962.wordpress.com

https://hbberlow.com/

Thank you for purchasing
this publication of The Wild Rose Press, Inc.

For questions or more information
contact us at
info@thewildrosepress.com.

The Wild Rose Press, Inc.
www.thewildrosepress.com

www.ingramcontent.com/pod-product-compliance
Lightning Source LLC
Chambersburg PA
CBHW051133030726
47504CB00004B/845